"We can't do this, Colin,"

Maggie pleaded.

"And if I don't agree?"

"Then you'll have to respect my decision."

"Or I could make you change your mind." He pressed his lips to hers, his mouth absorbing whatever protests she was about to utter. He didn't touch her, other than the soft, gentle caress of his lips, but still Maggie was ensnared, unable to pull away from him. The kiss continued forever, yet somehow it ended too soon.

He pulled back a fraction of an inch to whisper, "Do you want to give this up, Maggie?"

"Yes. I mean, no. I mean—"

"You're afraid that you're hurting me. But the way I see it, I'm feeling something again, feeling alive in a way I haven't felt in the past two-and-a-half years. Don't take that away from me. Please...."

Dear Reader,

Welcome to Silhouette **Special Edition**...welcome to romance. This month of May promises to be one of our best yet!

We begin with this month's THAT SPECIAL WOMAN! title, *A Man for Mom,* by Gina Ferris Wilkins. We're delighted that Gina will be writing under her real name, Gina Wilkins, from now on. And what a way to celebrate—with the first book in her new series, THE FAMILY WAY! Don't miss this emotional, poignant story of family connections and discovery of true love. Also coming your way in May is Andrea Edwards's third book of her series, **This Time Forever.** In *A Secret and a Bridal Pledge* two people afraid of taking chances risk it all for everlasting love.

An orphaned young woman discovers herself, and the love of a lifetime, in Tracy Sinclair's latest, *Does Anybody Know Who Allison Is?* For heart-pounding tension, look no further than Phyllis Halldorson's newest story about a husband and wife whose feelings show them they're still *Truly Married.* In *A Stranger in the Family* by Patricia McLinn, unexpected romance awaits a man who discovers that he's a single father. And rounding out the month is the debut title from new author Caroline Peak, *A Perfect Surprise.*

I hope you enjoy all these wonderful stories from Silhouette **Special Edition,** and have a wonderful month!

Sincerely,

Tara Gavin
Senior Editor

Please address questions and book requests to:
Silhouette Reader Service
U.S.: 3010 Walden Ave., P.O. Box 1325, Buffalo, NY 14269
Canadian: P.O. Box 609, Fort Erie, Ont. L2A 5X3

CAROLINE PEAK

A PERFECT SURPRISE

Silhouette®

SPECIAL EDITION®

Published by Silhouette Books
America's Publisher of Contemporary Romance

With thanks to Don Michael,
for introducing me to the Grosh brothers.

And with love to my husband,
Thane Tierney,
for always believing.

 SILHOUETTE BOOKS

ISBN 0-373-09960-6

A PERFECT SURPRISE

Copyright © 1995 by Carol Prescott

Printed in U.S.A.

CAROLINE PEAK

is a native Californian who has traveled extensively throughout the United States; and those journeys have provided this author with ample research opportunities. Her zeal for scholarly inquiry crystallized not long after her mother taught her what Caroline believes to be the three most important words in the English language: "Look it up." Not that she needs to take a special trip to do that—she works at a major university as a media librarian.

Caroline currently lives under the LAX flight path in Southern California with her two cats and one husband.

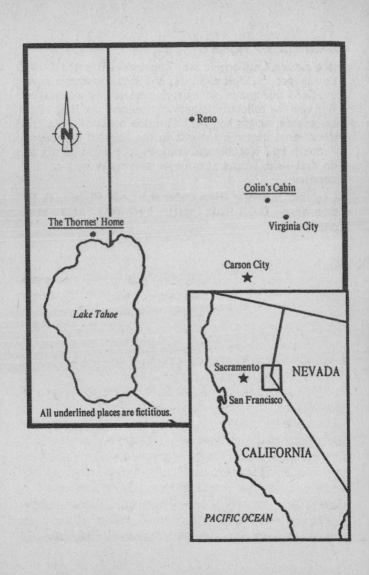

Reno

Colin's Cabin

Virginia City

The Thornes' Home

Carson City

Lake Tahoe

All underlined places are fictitious.

Sacramento

San Francisco

NEVADA

CALIFORNIA

PACIFIC OCEAN

Chapter One

Maggie jerked the wheel hard to the left, trying to counteract the skid. Her compact car fishtailed wildly across both lanes of the rain-slicked mountain road. Too afraid to pray, she concentrated instead on restraining the vehicle, staying on the road. Dimly she registered the salty tang of blood on her lower lip. The car hit the rough pavement of the shoulder, her tires gained traction and she finally brought the car to a halt inches from the edge, a heartbeat from tumbling down the steep mountainside.

For a few moments, Maggie sat motionless, clutching the steering wheel in a death grip. "Saints be praised," she whispered, her father's favorite prayer somehow comforting her, calming her. Gradually, she became aware of her trembling arms, her aching fingers. She concentrated on relaxing them, and forced herself to breathe deeply, slowly, to compose herself before she backed the car off the precipice and onto the firm shoulder of the road. Only then did she shut off the engine and allow her forehead to rest against the wheel. The driving rain pounded against the car, drowning out everything but the sound of her thudding heart and heaving breath.

The dog had come out of nowhere. When the large black shape had appeared in front of her car, Maggie had swerved reflexively, sending her car into its life-threatening skid. Calmer now, she looked back up the road, trying to determine whether she'd hit the animal. She couldn't be sure; everything had happened so fast....

A thump on the passenger window answered her question. A large, wet, black, shaggy beast rested its paws against the car door, its pink tongue lapping against the glass. Maggie almost laughed at the picture, then sobered as she thought of her near escape. But what to do about the dog? Was it dangerous? And what was it doing on this winding stretch of mountain road between Virginia City and Reno in the middle of a July thunderstorm?

For that matter, why was she there, instead of in her cozy, safe Boston apartment? Maybe her mother was right—maybe it wasn't smart for nice, single thirty-two-year-old college professors to go traipsing off to Nevada for a summer on their own.

The dog nuzzled the window again and let out a low woof. Maggie cautiously opened the door a crack.

The animal immediately shoved its muzzle into the gap, forcing the door open and bounding into the front seat. Eagerly, it licked at Maggie's face, dripping all over her.

"Whoa, boy!" Maggie laughed. The black Labrador's enthusiasm heartened her, but she was getting soaked. She shoved the dog away from her, and ordered, "Sit!" To her surprise, it obeyed instantly. Its tail pounded the seat in a steady rhythm as it watched her, waiting for her next command.

"Good boy." Maggie tentatively patted the dog's head and was rewarded with another slurp, this time across her outstretched hand.

"What are you doing out in a storm like this, huh? Don't you know it's dangerous to be out running around like that?" The dog hung on her every word, and for a disconcerting instant Maggie imagined it understood her.

"Do you have a name, fellah? Let's see this tag on your collar." Carefully, she reached over, alert for any movement, any threat. The animal's only reaction was to dip its dark head to be scratched.

"Come on, now, let's take care of business first, shall we?" she chided, reading the silver tag. "Seally." The dog's ears pricked up at its name. "Well, Seally, it's very nice to meet you. And your owner—" she paused to read the tag "—Lucy McCallum, I'm sure, will be very annoyed that you've been out wandering in the rain, instead of safe and warm at home. What should we do to find her?"

Maggie considered what little she knew about the area and weighed her options. The address listed on the tag could be anywhere off the winding road, and it was anyone's guess whether someone would be at home. The only sensible solution, she decided, was to drive down the grade until she found a phone, and have Ms. McCallum meet her there.

Still unnerved by her scare, Maggie eased cautiously onto the pavement. To her relief, the rain was easing up, and she found herself relaxing as she drove.

Seally relaxed, as well, lying across the seat with his head resting on Maggie's leg. A damp spot formed on her jeans. The musty odor of wet dog filled her subcompact, and she was only too happy to reach the gas station at the bottom of the grade.

She memorized the tag's phone number and chanted it while crossing the parking lot to the pay phone. The rain had stopped, leaving a fresh, pine smell in its wake, a welcome contrast to Seally's doggie odor.

She dialed quickly, willing Lucy McCallum to be home. A deep, resonant voice answered, "Good afternoon," after the third ring. It was so rich, so unexpected, that Maggie fumbled for a moment before answering.

"Yes, I'd like to speak to Lucy McCallum, please."

Silence greeted her request.

"Hello? Hello? Are you still there?" Her heart pounded again, and she didn't know why.

"Who is this?" The voice had changed, become ragged, hoarse. The contrast caused Maggie to fumble for words again.

"I—I'm sorry, but this number was on—"

"It doesn't matter. Listen, I don't know how you don't know, but Lucy's gone. She died two and a half years ago."

"Wait a minute," Maggie protested. "I didn't—"

Now the voice sounded calmer, deadpan, as if he'd made this speech before. "If you want to pay your respects, she's buried up at the Virginia City cemetery. I don't receive visitors, period."

Maggie gasped. "I'm sorr—"

But he had hung up.

Maggie stood for a moment, staring at the receiver, stunned. The man's pain had reached through the phone line, touching her, making her feel it, as well. Despite the late-afternoon sun breaking through the clouds, she shivered.

Slowly she walked back to the car, opening the door to let Seally out. "Well, boy, tell me what to do. Should I take you to Reno with me, try calling again, or do I drive you back up the mountain?''

Seally offered no help. He sniffed, pushing his muzzle against her hands, as if looking for something. Maggie belatedly realized that the dog might be hungry. No telling how long he'd been wandering down Geiger Grade.

Still pondering her dilemma, Maggie went into the nearby minimarket and bought a small box of dry dog food and a plastic bowl. Back at the car, she watched Seally inhale the kibble as if he hadn't eaten in weeks.

Glancing idly into the rearview mirror, Maggie belatedly realized why the store clerk had eyed her so suspiciously. The adrenaline surge from her wild ride had left her blue eyes wide and slightly glassy, her normally fair skin even more pallid, and somehow her wavy hair had come loose from its restraining combs, trailing dark strands across her face. The sum of these parts was the appearance of a madwoman.

She made a stab at repairing the damage, while Seally ate. They finished their missions simultaneously, and he licked his chops, settled down into the passenger seat and eyed Maggie expectantly.

''Okay, fellah. Where to now?''

Seally thumped his tail in response.

''You're no help, you know?'' A thought occurred to her. ''What if that man doesn't want you back?'' *No, no one who feels that deeply could be deliberately cruel to an animal.* The strength of the notion helped her make up her mind.

She hunted through the papers on the back seat for a map, no mean feat with Seally trying to ''help.'' After finding the street—no, an unpaved *trail*—on the map, she looked back up the mountain and sighed. The last thing she wanted to do was drive back up and down that twisting road, but if she didn't get moving, it would be completely dark by the time she reached Seally's home.

The sun had settled below the horizon by the time Maggie found the aptly named Stony Trail. At least the afternoon's rain hadn't made the dirt road impassable, she observed optimistically.

At last, a log cabin appeared. No mailbox indicated address or ownership, but a light shone in the window, and Seally's tail pounded the seat as he sat up expectantly, a high, frantic keening escaping his throat. Maggie knew she'd found the right place.

Grasping Seally's collar, she opened the car door, then hesitated, not eager to encounter the owner of that deep, resonant, aching voice. The cabin's front door opened, and the silhouette of a tall, broad-shouldered man emerged, outlined against the interior light. She couldn't make out his features against the shadowy porch, but Seally recognized him, and jerked against her restraining hand.

"Who's there?" It was the voice—sonorous, suspicious.

Maggie lost her courage. Releasing her grip on Seally's collar, she winced in pain as the dog went bounding over her, digging his claws into her lap on the way.

"Seally?" The voice changed, first disbelief, then delight. "Seally, it's you! Where have you been? I've been worried sick!"

Maggie watched as master and pet greeted each other joyously. A lump formed in her throat as the man embraced the dog, and she swallowed.

At last, the man looked up. "And who brought you home, girl?" He took a step toward the car.

Maggie knew suddenly that she did not want to face this man. At best there would be awkward apologies on both sides, and she could not endure that pain-laced voice again. Something about it reached too deeply inside her, touching places she didn't know existed, places she didn't want to acknowledge.

Pulling the car door shut, she shifted into gear and sped off, her tires sending a spurt of gravel into the air.

In the rearview mirror, she watched him, standing motionless on the porch, staring after her.

Colin McCallum paused, allowing his eyes to adjust to the dim light before he entered the shadowy restaurant. Good, Scotty was behind the bar—Colin could have a beer, look out at the river and make conversation or not. Scotty was a great bartender in that respect, steering people away if necessary, providing a friendly introduction if the situation warranted.

Tonight, Colin wasn't certain what he wanted, other than to be out of his cabin and among people. Solitude had its advantages, but for the past two weeks he'd been, well, restless, almost. An unusual state, to be sure—for the past two and a half years of his life he had arranged things to accommodate being alone.

It was the woman's fault. If he'd known she'd found Seally, he never would have been so rude, so curt. Hell, he hadn't realized that Seally's tag still bore Lucy's name. He'd changed that immediately, but there was no way to take back his words, to apologize, to thank her for taking the time and effort to bring Seally home.

Oh, well, she had to be a tourist, since everyone in Reno knew who Lucy McCallum was and that she was gone. The lady was probably back in Dubuque or wherever now, telling her friends about her almost-adventure in the wilds of Nevada.

"Colin!"

Scotty's voice broke his thoughts, and he headed for the bar.

" 'Evening, Scotty. How's everything?"

"Not bad for a Saturday night. Your usual?" he asked, holding up a light beer.

"Sure." At Colin's nod, Scotty popped the cap and poured the amber liquid into a waiting pilsner glass.

"Long time no see. What have you been up to?" The unspoken question: *Have you been writing?*

No. "Not a lot. I went to an estate sale, bought a box of journals—there might be an idea or two in them."

"Good to hear."

Scotty moved away without pursuing the subject, to Colin's relief. But that was Scotty, sensitive to things like that. He was just about the only person to whom Colin never had to explain himself.

And that, in turn, explained why Colin found himself sitting in Columbo's on a Saturday night, nursing a brew and trying to forget the fact that a nameless brunette with a soft spot for his dog was messing with his already meager concentration.

Scotty came back to Colin's end of the bar and rested his hip against the cooler, crossing his arms over his chest. His playful grin lifted the silver curls of his handlebar mustache.

"Number Four's here tonight, Colin. She's one classy lady, just what a guy like me needs."

"Yeah, just what you said about Gilda and Annie and Ruth." It was a running joke between the two; Scotty's public profession and generous nature, combined with Nevada's uncomplicated matrimonial laws, had led him to the altar three times, each time unsuccessfully. Now, Colin searched the bar for a buxom blonde, Scotty's usual type.

"She's in the dining room, by herself. If you look right behind you..."

It was the woman. Colin could only stare for a moment, then he blinked and refocused. The light in the restaurant was as dim as it had been inside her car, making it impossible to be certain, but something about her bearing made him sure she was Seally's rescuer.

He remembered the halo of shoulder-length, dark hair, framing a delicate, pale face. Beyond that, her features were indistinct, but there was the way she held her head, the movement of her hand through her hair...

"Some looker, huh?" Scotty's voice sounded behind him, and Colin turned back to the bar. "Think I stand a chance?"

"I want to pay for her dinner," Colin blurted, without thinking. At Scotty's raised eyebrows, he rushed to explain, "I know her, sort of, I mean, she did me a favor...." His voice trailed off. How to explain this... compulsion to Scotty, when he couldn't even explain it to himself?

"Hey," the bartender said softly, as if he understood. "It's okay. Let me get her waiter for you."

After settling her tab, Colin debated briefly whether to introduce himself or to leave. The latter would be far easier, but wouldn't ease the strange need within him. Better to meet it head-on and be done with it.

Taking a cocktail napkin, he scribbled a quick note and gave it to Scotty.

Maggie signaled for the check and sat back with a contented sigh. Treating herself to a dinner out had been an excellent idea, even if choosing to walk to the restaurant now meant that she'd practically waddle the mile and a half back to her apartment near the university. The Caesar salad and seafood pasta were worth it though, and the stroll through the neon glitter of downtown Reno would be a delightful diversion from academic tomes and newspapers on microfilm.

When her waiter laid a black leather folder on the table, she ordered, "Just a moment," and reached for her purse.

"That's all right, ma'am. Your dinner has been taken care of." At her puzzled look, he nodded to the waiting folder and moved off.

Flipping it open, she found a folded paper napkin, and nothing else. Great, all she needed was some lonely businessman making a play for her. She was tempted to ignore the note and leave, but if the guy tried to follow her home... She unfolded the napkin.

"You never call, you never write, you never visit. Love and Kisses, Seally."

Seally! Maggie scanned the room, half expecting to see the black Lab lapping up a plate of pasta. But there was no dog, no one staring expectantly at her. Until she looked into the lounge.

Maggie knew instinctively that this was Seally's owner, the man with the broad shoulders and grieving voice. He stood, leaning back against the bar, not overtly watching her, but still, she knew.

His long, denim-covered legs were crossed at the ankles, topping battered black cowboy boots. His elbows rested on the bar behind him, and one hand casually held a tall pilsner glass. Absurdly, she remembered John Travolta in *Urban Cowboy*—did cowboys the world over practice that pose? Or just cowboys with the goods to show off?

She could picture this man on a horse, his tawny hair ruffled by the wind as he rode across the plains. Or with a pick resting on one wide shoulder, then muscled arms shifting to bury its point in the rocky soil. Or in a cavalry uniform, scarf bright yellow against his deeply tanned skin...

Enough! This man, waiting so coolly, was no nineteenth-century fantasy, but a real, flesh-and-blood 1990s man who owned a black Labrador retriever, lived in a mountain cabin and could apparently afford to buy her dinner at this not-inexpensive restaurant.

And he's still grieving for a woman named Lucy.

This last thought brought Maggie up sharply. She gathered her purse and stood. Seally's owner stiffened, and as she walked toward him, he took a long, slow swallow from his beer, his eyes never leaving her face.

She stopped in front of him. "I really don't like to accept dinner from strangers," she said softly.

He shrugged. "I figure, you spend any amount of time with Seally, you're no stranger."

Maggie couldn't stop a chuckle at that notion. "I get the idea that Seally doesn't know any strangers."

An answering grin spread oh, so slowly across his face, lifting the corners of his mouth. "True enough. It's a good thing I live in the middle of nowhere, 'cause she'd make a lousy watchdog."

"No, she'd just love a burglar to death."

He laughed, an oddly rusty sound, as if he hadn't done it in a while. He offered a hand.

"Colin McCallum, Seally's human."

His grasp was firm, his fingers warm, callused. "Maggie Sullivan, Seally's chauffeur."

He still held her hand, slate gray eyes measuring, assessing. Maggie felt suddenly self-conscious under his scrutiny. She jerked her hand away, reaching up to smooth her hair to cover the movement.

"Uh, thanks for dinner, Mr. McCallum. But you really shouldn't have—"

"Colin." He gestured to the bar stool beside him. "Why don't you join me?"

The words were a request, the tone a command. Without stopping to ask herself why, Maggie sat.

After the bartender took her drink order, Maggie turned to find Colin still watching her. His examination was disconcerting. She stared back. Her mind registered the tiny network of lines around his smoky eyes—he looked to be a few years older than her thirty-two. His dark blond hair curled over his shirt collar—he was obviously the type who went too long between haircuts. A tiny scar, crescent shaped, curved up from the end of one eyebrow. For some reason, she thought he should have a mustache. His clean-shaven upper lip looked almost...naked.

Finally he spoke. "So, where are you from?"

"How do you know I'm from somewhere else?" Did it show, did a label someplace say Boston?

"They don't call Reno the 'biggest little city in the world' for nothing. Besides, most people up toward Virginia City know Seally."

The dog's name reassured her. Familiar territory. "Does she run away often, then?"

"She 'goes visiting' all the time." He shook his head. "Not usually for as long as she did this time, though." Now he looked straight at her again. "I really was grateful for your bringing her back."

"No problem." And she meant it.

A moment's uneasy silence elapsed before he spoke again. Then, "So, where are you from?"

Persistent fellow. Maggie took a sip of wine before answering. "Boston. I teach Western history at Beaton University."

"Reno must be a real joy for you after being stuck in a place like Boston."

What an odd thing to say. "It's very different, that's for sure," she agreed cautiously.

"I've been there a few times. It's too crowded for my tastes."

Ah, the lure of the wide-open spaces. She'd felt that lure since arriving in Nevada, and while she couldn't completely disagree with his assessment, she felt compelled to defend her birthplace. "I've lived there all my life. I think you get used to anyplace you live, and in Boston's case, there are attendant benefits."

He cocked a brow, sending the tiny scar skyward. "We get culture here, too." He flashed her a grin before changing the subject. "Is Reno business or pleasure?"

"A little of both, actually. I'm here for the summer working on a book on the discovery of the Comstock Lode and its larger sociohistorical connotations."

To her surprise, his eyes lit up at her explanation. "How did you come up with that for a subject?"

"I read an article in a nineteenth-century magazine about the brothers who are thought to have actually discovered silver in the region. I thought their story would make a great book."

"The Grosh brothers, right? Why them?"

Hmm, a cowboy who read. Interesting. "Because they represent every man who came West with dreams of gold. Very few struck it rich. Most became merchants, or laborers or farmers—or like Hosea and Allen Grosh, they died. But without them, the entire history of the United States would be different."

When she paused, he prodded, "Go on."

"And the Grosh story is filled with 'if onlys.' If only Hosea hadn't stuck a pickax in his foot and developed blood poisoning. If only Allen and his partner, Bucke, had left to cross the Sierras a few days earlier. If only their mule hadn't slipped its hobbles and cost them another two days. If only they hadn't lost the trail in a blizzard. If only Allen had allowed his gangrenous foot to be amputated, as Bucke did. We'd be calling it the Grosh Lode, not the Comstock, and the Nevada silver boom would have started two years earlier."

She stopped for breath, then laughed self-consciously. "Sorry, I get carried away sometimes. I'm afraid it's an occupational hazard."

Colin shook his head. "Don't apologize, Professor. I enjoyed the lecture. Your students must just love you." He could just picture her, standing in front of her class, speaking with the same intensity, her eyes sparkling, her slender hands gesturing as she made a point. Even now, her pale skin fairly glowed with her pleasure.

Maggie made a comically wry face. "Unfortunately, in my big lecture classes, no. I'll get rolling on a tangent like that, and stop to take a breath, and a hand goes up— 'Is this going to be on the midterm?' It's frustrating."

"So why do it?"

She considered carefully before she answered. "When I get tenure, I probably won't have to put up with quite so much of that. I'll be teaching more upper-division and graduate classes, with students who theoretically want to be there. And I'll have more time for research, which I love."

"So tenure's important."

"Absolutely. In academia, it's the Holy Grail. I'm already the first in my family to get a college degree, let alone a doctorate, so tenure... well—"

"Family expectations can be tough."

She nodded, waiting for him to enlarge on his comment. Something in her cornflower eyes made him almost want to. He made a conscious effort to shake the thought, and took another swallow of his beer instead.

Maybe he'd made the right choice coming here tonight, the right choice buying her dinner. He liked her enthusiasm. It reminded him of the way he used to be, before Lucy's car hit that patch of ice and rolled down the mountain. Back then, before his life went all to hell, he would find a story, a legend, a tall tale, and turn it into something much bigger. And he had fourteen novels published to prove it— fourteen bestsellers, not to mention short stories and novellas. And he'd do it again, once the right story came along.

"—do you do?"

Oh, hell. Women hated it when you didn't pay attention. Lucy had, at least. "I'm sorry, what did you say?"

She didn't look too bothered. "I was just asking about you. I think I've told you my entire life story and all I know about you is your name."

"And my dog's." She laughed again and Colin felt himself go warm all over. She had a wonderful laugh, soft and musical. "I'm from San Francisco originally, and I've lived up here for many years."

"And what sort of work do you do?"

Amazingly enough, she still hadn't guessed his identity. Maybe C. J. McCall, despite being a bestselling author, wasn't instantly recognizable outside northern Nevada. Maybe his book jacket picture was old enough. Or maybe losing the mustache had done the trick. Whatever the reason, it was a blessed relief to be simply Colin.

"Oh, I'm . . . between positions now."

She took it in solemnly, nodded once, and mercifully, dropped the subject. Points for sensitivity, too. Again, he caught himself wanting to tell her more.

"I'm actually living off my..." He caught himself about to say *royalties*. "...investments at the moment." He paused, then said in a rush, "I've been a widower for the last two and a half years."

Before he could say anything else, she reached over and touched his hand. "I'm sorry for your loss," she said gently. "And I'm sorry I pried."

He forced a smile. "No, that's okay. I'm sure you were wondering about Lucy after my tirade the other night. I had no idea her name was still on Seally's tag."

"I trust Seally is getting a new tag."

"Seally has a new tag," Colin corrected. He turned to smile at her, and something clicked. The ambient noise of the lounge receded, and for a moment, they merely stared at one another.

Colin didn't want to breathe, didn't want to break the spell. Apparently, Maggie felt it, too. She sat very still, pink lips slightly parted, the fingers of one hand resting lightly around the bowl of her wineglass.

Just when Colin felt his lungs would burst, Maggie's deep blue eyes shifted away from his, and the moment was lost. She picked up her wineglass and took a healthy swallow, a movement that didn't quite hide the fact that her hand shook ever so slightly.

Neither of them spoke for another minute. They stared out the window at the river, and Colin knew she wondered the same thing he did. What the hell had just happened?

She looked at her watch. "It's getting late, I'd better go."

"Let me walk you to your car."

"Thank you, but I'm on foot tonight. It's such a beautiful evening, I wanted to enjoy it."

"Then I'll drive you home." For some unfathomable reason that he really didn't want to analyze, Colin did not want this interlude to end.

"No, really. I need the exercise, especially after that big dinner and a glass of wine. I'd prefer to walk."

"Then I'll walk with you." He tossed some bills onto the bar, trying to figure out why it mattered whether they said good-night now or later.

"Don't be ridiculous. I'm perfectly safe. We're not in Boston, after all."

"Maybe I'd like the exercise, too."

She eyed his rangy form skeptically.

"Okay, how about—" He stood and hooked his thumbs through his belt loops, leaned back and drawled down at her, "It's the Code of the West, little lady, and you'd best not be arguing with me."

She grinned, conceding defeat. "All right, we'll walk."

Strolling up Virginia Street was safe enough, Maggie reasoned. Lots of people, lots of noise, lots of neon—no chance of the world around them disappearing, like it had in the restaurant. Her logical mind wanted to identify what had happened, catalog and file it under the appropriate feeling, and be done with it. To do anything else was just too unsettling, and she didn't have time to be unsettled this summer.

As if she even stood a chance of identifying that feeling. So far, her logical mind hadn't found one that quite fit what had happened back in the restaurant; the world around her had never disappeared before tonight.

She slid a sidelong glance at Colin; his scrutiny mirrored her own. Embarrassed to be caught in the act, she cast about for a topic.

"What kind of gambling would you recommend for a rookie like me? It all looks so overwhelming."

Colin stopped in his tracks and stared at her. "You mean you've been here for at least two weeks, and haven't indulged? Shame, shame, Professor, where is your intellectual curiosity?"

He grabbed her arm and led her across the street, into the inviting glare of a hotel's casino. Maggie stopped and gazed around the room in amazement. Vegas Night at the Faculty Club had never been like this! Flashing lights, ringing bells, wailing sirens all assaulted her senses. Rows of slot machines stretched before her, their players' determined faces underscoring the gravity with which they pulled the levers. Beyond them, she saw horseshoe-shaped tables staffed by young tuxedo-clad women expertly dealing and flipping cards, smoothly scooping up and paying out chips with equal ease.

The din of conversation fought with the canned music for supremacy, and through it all moved as diverse a group of people as Maggie had ever imagined. Young, old, thin, well fed, clothing ranging from the shabbiest jeans to the most elegant dinner jackets, united in the quest for a little luck.

Colin pulled her to a slot machine and dug into the pocket of his formfitting jeans.

"Here." He handed her three quarters. "Go for broke."

"I don't know..."

"They're very user-friendly. Just stick the coin here—" He paused while she followed his direction. "Now pull the arm."

She did as he ordered, and watched in awe as cherry, cherry, orange came up. When she realized she'd lost, she made a little face. "Darn."

Colin laughed at her expression, and urged her to try again. Her second try was equally unsuccessful.

The third time, bell, bell, bell! Maggie squealed as quarters dropped into the receptacle.

"I won! Look, I won!"

She tried to scoop the quarters into her hands, but they kept spilling over. Colin found her a casino bucket, obviously taking great pleasure at her glee.

"Oh, I want to do it again!"

"I've created a monster," he observed dryly, but Maggie didn't mind.

"If I put more than one quarter in, I'll get a bigger jackpot, right?" She started to feed the machine again, and Colin stayed her hand.

"Pick a different machine, one on the end of an aisle."

"What?" Maggie didn't understand.

"This one won't pay out again for a while, and the ones on the end pay more frequently. Draws people in."

"Oh." Maggie pondered this. "You mean, it's not just luck?"

Colin chucked her under her chin, and she instinctively jerked her head back. He ignored her response and answered, "There's nothing in life that's just luck, Professor, and you'd do well not to forget that."

His words took away some of Maggie's enjoyment. She started to hand him the bucket, but he pushed it back to her.

"Come on, let's find a couple of winners."

They found machines side by side, and for the next half hour, they fed the one-armed bandits. Maggie found herself developing a rhythm: the clank of the coins dropping, the clunk when she pulled the arm, the whir of the barrels, and their thump, thump, thump as they settled, revealing fruit, bells or bars. Seesawing between winning and losing, she and Colin eventually found themselves back to three quarters, Colin's original stake.

"Here." Maggie handed the coins back to Colin.

"You don't want to put them all on one more try?"

"Nope." Maggie shook her head cheerfully. "We've come out even, and had fun doing it. That's all anyone can ask, right?"

"Right. Makes an interesting philosophy for life, don't you think?"

On that note, they left the casino and continued their walk up Virginia Street. Soon, they left the hustle and bustle of downtown Reno behind, entering a residential area near the university.

Away from the glare of neon, the full moon shone brightly.

"You know, this is probably a cliché, but you don't see the moon shine like this in Boston."

"Or New York, or Los Angeles, or San Francisco, or any big city. You ought to see it from my cabin sometime. There's nothing like it."

Was that an invitation? Maggie tried to read behind his casual words. They'd had an enjoyable evening, and she hadn't met very many people since she had arrived. It might be nice to have someone with whom to socialize. But was he still mourning his Lucy? She didn't think she wanted to be the one he experimented with while he figured it out.

Too soon, it seemed, they reached the tiny front porch of her garden apartment. She unlocked her door, then turned to offer her hand. "Colin, I really enjoyed this evening. Thanks for the dinner and the company."

"I enjoyed it, too. I'd like to see you again, soon."

"I'd like that, too."

He tugged her toward him. "Good." She looked up, he hesitated for a moment, then lowered his head to brush his lips softly against her cheek, his touch tickling her skin.

He straightened and smiled down at her. Stroking his thumb against her jawline, he whispered, "Good night, Professor."

As he turned and sauntered down the walkway, Maggie could only whisper, "Good night," after him.

Her research through nineteenth-century photo files would progress much faster, Maggie concluded, if she didn't keep superimposing Colin McCallum's face over that of rough-and-tumble miners and cowboys of another age. That angular, almost craggy face, that little curved scar which kept his eyebrow perpetually cocked.

She couldn't help it. Three days had passed since their evening together, three days, and not one word. He'd said he wanted to see her again, but left without her unlisted number. He was unlisted, as well; she'd checked. She could drive back up to his cabin, but that seemed so... forward. Not her style at all.

Sighing, she returned her thoughts to the research at hand. The box of photos in front of her held nothing of value to her—time to exchange it.

Carrying it to the counter, she requested another, and absently brushed a spot off her white walking shorts while the librarian went to a back room.

A cold, wet thing pressed itself into the back of her knee and she yelped, then whirled to face her attacker. Seally and Colin stood there, Colin grinning like a fool and Seally with an oddly similar look.

Colin held up his hands in mock terror at her expression. "She got away from me, honest. It wasn't my fault."

"Yeah, right. She's not supposed to be in here anyway, is she?" He looked good, just like she remembered. Jeans, boots and a chambray shirt again; entirely masculine, entirely tempting. Her heart sped up a little at the sight, and she reminded herself to breathe.

"Seally's a special case. She knows the powers that be."

A voice behind them confirmed that fact. "Seally! And Colin! It's been too long!"

"Hello, Evelyn. It's good to see you, too." He leaned over to kiss the wrinkled cheek of the white-haired volunteer.

Other staff members gathered to greet the pair. The librarians looked delighted, Colin looked discomfited at the attention and Maggie was increasingly puzzled. Why was Colin on such familiar terms with the staff of the Reno Historical Society library?

"What are you working on, Colin?" "Have you got a new project started?" "Are you here doing research?" The questions flew.

Finally Maggie voiced one of her own. "Colin, what are they talking about?"

When Colin hesitated, Evelyn answered for him. "Don't you know? He's C. J. McCall, the Western writer!"

Oh. C. J. McCall. She began to understand; it all made sense now. The grieving widower, his knowledge of Western lore, his reticence regarding his own life, his isolated cabin in the mountains. Even the mustache she'd imagined him having, just like the book jacket photos. How could she have not figured it out earlier?

She'd read all about him in *Personality*—about his beloved Lucy's tragic death, and how he'd shut himself away, no longer writing the books that leapt to the top of bestseller lists, the books that gave a human face to the West, the books that inspired a renewed interest in Western history.

"No," she whispered. "No, I didn't know."

Now they were all staring at her. Before anyone could say anything else, she forced a bright smile. "Well, I'm sure you'll all want to catch up with each other, so I'll just get back to work."

As she turned and walked away, she prayed no one could tell how unnerved she really was. She forced herself to walk steadily back to her table to gather her things, promising her racing mind and thudding heart that they could take off just as soon as she got outside.

Chapter Two

Maggie headed for the exit, ignoring the curious stares she could feel following her movement. The library staff would turn their collective attention back to Colin the moment she left the building.

Colin. C. J. McCall.

She needed air, and time to absorb this news. She felt like an idiot, not recognizing him. It wasn't as if his appearance had changed that much. Even clean-shaven, she should have known him. She had every one of his books on her shelf.

And her lecture on the Grosh brothers! His book *Silver Sage* had been all about the heyday of Nevada silver mining. He knew the subject, probably even better than she did.

And as for seeing him socially, well, how could she have thought him remotely interested in her, when the memory of his beloved Lucy still haunted him?

She walked quickly, despite the noonday heat. Moisture formed and slid down her neck, saturating the cotton T-shirt she wore. This corner of the University of Nevada campus offered no shade, no hiding place, so she didn't ease up as she headed down the long slope toward the main body of the campus. She needed to get away, to surround herself with the anonymity of a crowd of people.

"Maggie, wait!" Colin's voice called behind her.

She continued without slowing, not looking back, unwilling to face Colin, reluctant to let him see her disappointment, her confusion. She had to pull herself together before she could face him.

A hand on her arm stopped her midstride. She whirled, opened her mouth to tell him—what? If she couldn't identify what she felt, how could she articulate it to him?

"I didn't lie to you." His face wore a pleading expression.

Maggie shook off his restraining hand, and turned to walk on.

"Not overtly. You just forgot to tell me something, something important."

He shrugged, his eyes on Seally prancing along the walkway ahead of them. "It's not that important."

"But you're C. J. McCall!"

"No, I'm Colin McCallum. I write as C. J. McCall." He whistled, and Seally circled back to join them.

And one had nothing to do with the other? "But I didn't know."

"Of course you didn't." He made it sound so reasonable, which it wasn't, of course.

"But I should have," she persisted.

"Why?"

"Because I've read all your books." Maggie punctuated her statement with an expansive sweep of her arm. "Your picture is on the back cover. You're famous!"

"So what?"

"So, your books are wonderful. So full of life. They're one of the reasons I got into Western history."

He stopped and eyed her skeptically. "Oh, come on, now."

"No, really," she insisted, stopping, as well, wanting him to understand. "I read your first book, *Winchester Justice,* when I was eighteen, and it captured something for me. I had to learn more. Why didn't you tell me?"

"Because of...this." He shoved a hand through his hair.

"This?" Because she wanted to know who he was?

"You're babbling on about my books, and my name, and I'm no longer Colin, the guy who taught you to play the slots."

"But you're not." He was much more.

"Yes, I am."

"Well, yes, but once you start writing again—"

"And that's the other reason." He shoved a hand through his shaggy hair again, taking a deep breath before he spoke again. "I get awful damn sick of people wanting to discuss my books, and asking when I'm going to write again!"

"But I didn't—"

"But you do want to know, don't you?"

She opened her mouth, then shut it. She knew the answer was in her eyes.

Maggie trudged up the street toward her apartment, the enticing vision of a steaming tub her only impetus to keep moving. Her eyes stung, her neck ached and her right hand still bore the strain of clutching a pencil too tightly, for too long a time.

What a rotten day. After her run-in with Colin, after Colin had stalked off in anger, she'd gone back to the library to continue her work, with little success.

To her surprise, Evelyn had approached her. "I seem to have let the cat out of the bag, dear. I do apologize."

"It's not your fault," she'd reassured the older woman. "It was a surprise to me, though."

"I assumed you knew. Everyone around here does."

"So I see," she'd responded. "I'm afraid I don't usually keep up with that kind of gossip—"

"Oh, I'm so happy to hear that, dear." The older woman leaned closer. "You know, for a while some of those reporters wouldn't stay away. As if we would be telling tales about our Colin!"

Her words had made Maggie abandon any thought of attempting to glean insights into Colin from his library acquaintances, and she'd tried to return to her research. But her mind kept returning to Colin's face, and she kept seeing that combination of frustration, annoyance and, yes, disillusionment, that he'd worn.

Why he should be disillusioned with her, she didn't know. *He* was the one who'd neglected to tell her everything about himself, that he wasn't just Colin the cowboy....

No, she'd been incredibly insensitive to press him on an issue he obviously had no desire to discuss. If he wanted to pretend C. J. McCall didn't matter, she should have dropped the subject. Period.

Self-chastisement did not improve her mood. By the time she entered the courtyard of her apartment building, she wasn't sure even a soak in the tub would cure her. Then she saw Seally.

And behind the dog, leaning against her porch railing, the man who'd ruined her day. She found no comfort in the fact that he looked as unhappy as she felt.

She moved closer, trying to assess his frame of mind. Would he be angry? Apologetic? If anything, he looked a little nervous.

"Hi," he said cautiously.

"Hi," she returned, equally cautious.

Colin pushed away from the rail and took a deep breath, studying the woman before him. Maggie didn't exactly look thrilled to see him. She looked tired and cranky, instead. Even her bright pink T-shirt drooped. This wasn't going to be as simple as he'd hoped.

"I, uh, felt bad that we left things the way we did. I thought we could talk."

Her face lost some of its wariness. She hesitated, then offered, "I owe you an apology, Colin. It was none of my business—"

He held up a hand, cutting her off. "That may well be true—" He grinned at the annoyance that flashed across her face, and the knot that had twisted up inside him eased, just a little. "—but I want to try to explain anyway."

Maggie studied him, her gaze frankly assessing. Colin hoped his face showed none of the trepidation he felt. He wanted to clear the air, not make a big deal of this. "Okay," she agreed at last. "Why don't you come in and we'll talk."

When she brushed past him to unlock her door, Colin started at the sliver of awareness that shot through him. Bedraggled as she was, the lady still packed a wallop. Lord help him if she decided to put some effort into it.

Inside, Maggie bustled about, opening blinds and windows, allowing the afternoon heat to escape and the cool evening breeze to enter the room. She still looked jumpy, and Colin took pity. "Why don't you wash up? I kind of barged in on you here—I'm sure you weren't planning on entertaining as soon as you came home."

Maggie gave him a grateful smile. "If you really wouldn't mind..." Her voice trailed off. She looked toward the hall and back at him.

Her uneasiness bothered him. He was no threat. "No problem, really," he reassured her. "Seally and I will be fine out here. Go." He turned her around and steered her toward the hallway. Her shoulders stiffened slightly under his hands, so he squeezed briefly and released her.

As Maggie moved down the hall, Colin examined the room around him. He knew from their Saturday-evening conversation that Maggie had sublet this apartment through her academic connections, so he expected little of her personality in the decor. But Maggie was everywhere.

A table in one corner held a computer and printer, a stack of notes awaiting transcription beside them. Framed photographs were clustered on a bookshelf, and he stopped to study them. Family, obviously. A woman who looked like Maggie would look in thirty years, with streaks of gray shooting through her deep brown hair; four big men, one a generation older than the other three, each with a shock of red hair and the requisite accompanying freckles; a gaggle of children, their hair varied shades of red, from strawberry blond, through carrottop, to the auburn mane of one particularly enchanting little girl. Maggie obviously valued her family a great deal. He wondered if she missed them, being so far away.

Finally he turned to the bookcases. They were filled with books on the American West—either the apartment's regular tenant was also a Western enthusiast, or Maggie had brought her own collection with her.

He grinned at the sight of his book, *Placer Dreams.*
Flipping it open, he found to his surprise the inscription To
Maggie—Happy Trails, C. J. McCall.

Too bad he had no recollection of signing the book for
her. Ironic, really, since Lucy had accused him of sleeping
with practically every female fan he encountered on his
publicity tours. Not that he'd ever taken advantage of that
kind of encounter, but if he'd been looking, chances were
that he would have at least noticed Maggie.

As if underlining that sentiment, the sound of the
shower he heard through the wall elicited a vision of Maggie, naked, water coursing over her smooth flesh, flowing
down her slim legs to pool at her feet. His groin tightened, an uncomfortable but welcome sensation. It had
been a while since he'd had that elemental male reaction to
an interesting woman.

Still pondering that notion, he wandered into the
kitchen. Through the sliding glass door he could see a
small barbecue on the patio outside. He peered into the
refrigerator and smiled in satisfaction. Moments later he
was lighting the grill and determining the best formula for
a half-hour marinade for chicken.

Maggie emerged from the bedroom feeling immensely
refreshed, indeed, almost human again. She wore tur-
quoise leggings and a floral-print oversize shirt, their
bright colors invigorating her. Taking the time to dry her
hair and dab on a small amount of makeup gave her the
added boost she needed to face Colin.

The odor of burning charcoal drew her to the kitchen.
Flames danced in her barbecue, Seally sprawled over the
remainder of her small deck and Colin stood at her sink,
ripping romaine lettuce into a wooden salad bowl.

"You do make yourself at home, don't you?"

Colin wiped his hands on a dish towel, lifted a glass of white wine off the counter and presented it to her with a flourish.

"I try to. Where do you hide the anchovies?"

Maggie didn't even attempt to hide her amazement. "How did you know?"

"Romaine, Parmesan, olive oil, garlic," he ticked off. "Doesn't take a detective to figure this one out."

Digging into a corner cupboard, Maggie chuckled. "So now you know my secret vice. I live for Caesar salads."

"Just another thing we have in common."

His hand met hers as he took the anchovies, sending tingles up Maggie's arm. He, on the other hand, didn't seem to be affected at all, darn him. Maybe it had been too long since she'd been around an interesting man.

Colin refused her help, ordering her to sit and entertain him while he worked. Maggie obliged, amused but discomfited by this role reversal. In her mother's house, the women worked, the girls helped, the men watched television and the boys played football. Division of labor at its finest.

Conversely, Colin looked perfectly comfortable with a garlic press in his hand, evincing an ease that surprised her. *Why* she should be surprised, she didn't know. After all, she knew practically nothing about this man.

But this evening presented the perfect opportunity to change that state of affairs.

She found she enjoyed watching him cook. There was something elementally masculine about the way he performed duties she'd always perceived as feminine—stirring, chopping, even setting the table.

He kept up a light stream of conversation as he carried out these chores, inquiring about her day, commiserating over her lack of progress.

"Some days are just like that, Professor. You have to think of them as laying the foundation for other days, the ones when everything gels, when you find the one source you've been pursuing."

His understanding made her itch to ask about C. J. McCall, but she held back, reluctant to spoil the easy mood they shared. Her patience would eventually be rewarded, she admonished herself.

At last, everything was ready. Colin fed Seally slivers of barbecued chicken and ordered her into the living room to lie down. He then served Maggie and himself. As they ate, Maggie searched for a topic to keep the conversation light, to keep from bringing up the subject that interested her most.

"Seally certainly is well trained. That surprised me."

Colin nodded, swallowing a bite before answering. "Yeah, Lucy did a great job with her."

"Lucy?" Here was an opportunity to find out something about his late wife. "She was mainly Lucy's dog, then?"

"Yeah. I was usually pretty busy—writing, doing book tours or just doing research. You know how that is." He looked expectantly at Maggie, waiting for her agreement before continuing.

"Anyway, Lucy was lonely, so I bought Seally for her— right before I went on a book tour. *Rio Blanco,* maybe?" He paused to recollect, then shrugged. "Not important, right? Lucy thought she looked just like a baby seal pup, all sleek and black and wiggly, so Seally got a name and Lucy got a new friend."

"What a thoughtful gift," Maggie said, and meant it. She pushed aside the questions that had immediately popped into her mind, such as why Lucy apparently didn't have her own interests to occupy her while Colin worked, or why they lived up on a mountain if Lucy didn't like to be alone. Those issues were none of her business.

"Yeah, well..." Colin looked discomfited by her praise, and abruptly changed the subject. "I couldn't help looking over your books. I now believe that you're a longtime fan, but you never told me we'd met some time ago."

Maggie almost choked on a piece of lettuce. "Excuse me?" Meeting Colin wasn't something she would have forgotten, and knowing who he was would have saved them both a great deal of aggravation.

"My John Hancock's in your copy of *Placer Dreams,*" Colin answered, a twinkle in his eye.

"Oh, that." Maggie waved a hand dismissively. "A gift from one of my brothers, while I was a starving grad student."

"One of the redheads."

After a moment's puzzlement, Maggie realized he'd examined the photos in her living room. How odd that he'd studied them so closely. "Yes, the middle one, Brendan."

"Good Irish name."

"Oh, yes. There's Rory Michael, Brendan Conor and Sean Patrick. I'm the baby of the family, and the only daughter."

"And you're Margaret what?"

"Mary Margaret, please. My mother still insists on calling me that for the most part, though I've managed to train everyone else in the family."

He shook his head, causing a lock of tawny hair to fall over his forehead before he shoved it back. "Being an only child, I can't imagine being surrounded by brothers."

"It was a trial." Maggie laughed. "My Barbie dolls were beheaded, I was forced to play army from the time I could walk and worst of all, they knew all the boys in high school, and none of them was good enough for me."

The lighthearted conversation set the tone, and their easy camaraderie continued through dinner. Maggie learned that Colin had grown up in San Francisco, spending summers with his grandparents at their mountain cabin. Colin learned that except for brief research forays to Colorado and California, Maggie had spent her entire life in Boston. They discovered they had mutual acquaintances in libraries and historical societies throughout the West.

When the conversation turned to their respective life's work, Maggie couldn't hold back any longer. She just had to know.

"Do you miss it? I mean, writing was your life for a long time. You've spoken tonight of the research, and tours, but not of the writing itself."

"Do I miss it?" Colin echoed. He paused, gathering his thoughts before speaking. "Yes, sometimes, maybe. It's sort of hard to tell, the past two and a half years have been pretty strange for me."

"Go on," she coaxed, pushing her empty plate forward and resting her arms on the table.

Once again, Colin hesitated. Maybe she wouldn't understand. She acted as though she charged through life, as though she never had a moment's doubt about anything once she set her mind to it. "'Writer's block' is too simple a tag to put on it. Used to be, I'd read something in an old newspaper, or hear a story, or the words of a song would trigger something, and off I'd go." He shook his head sadly. "The spark isn't there—that's the only way I can explain it. When it comes back to me, I'll write again."

Maggie pursed her lips, obviously unable to grasp this idea. "But your stories come from reality, they're based on historical accounts," she argued. "I mean, when I read Richard Bucke's story in the *Overland Monthly,* something just compelled me to learn more about the Grosh brothers. And once I did, I just had to tell that story. Doesn't that happen to you?"

Colin shook his head again. "Nothing's sparked that compulsion in me for a while now. You certainly don't feel that way about every story you hear, do you?"

"No, but—" She paused, frustration written on her face. "You just need to find the right story, right?"

"I wish it were that simple." How to explain something so intangible, so elementally unexplainable that even he didn't quite understand it? He only knew what he felt.

"Let me try a different tack. I saw something once on creativity that compared it to a cow chewing its cud. People might call it downtime, or wasted time, but that cow is making milk. It's not only when the farmer is milking the cow. I guess it's taking me a long time to chew that cud."

"You've never said anything like that in the profiles I've read about you. I mean, like that piece in *Personality*—"

He cut her off. "You don't believe that garbage, do you?"

"No, of course not, but—"

"They never spoke to me or anyone I'm close to. My friends respect my privacy. Anything you read, those hacks made up!"

"I'm sorry I brought it up." Maggie looked so chagrined that Colin regretted his forceful words. He struggled for the words to explain his feelings to her.

"It's okay—it's just a subject I get a little hot about. I don't like my personal life being analyzed in some sleazy tabloid, especially when they didn't get it right. Truth is, things weren't the greatest between Lucy and me—not that we were contemplating divorce or anything—"

The phone rang just then, interrupting his speech. Maggie rose with a murmured apology and crossed the kitchen to answer it.

Colin gathered the dishes and carried them to the sink. He couldn't believe that he'd said that about Lucy. Maggie didn't need to know anything about that. And telling her what things had been like, well, it was almost disloyal. After all, it had been his fault Lucy had been so unhappy.

Maggie turned her back to him and lowered her voice, the movement returning Colin to the present. Who was she talking to, and why didn't she want him to hear her?

Straining, he could just catch some of the conversation.

"No, today wasn't such a productive day. Look, Edmund, you've caught me at kind of a bad time." She glanced back over her shoulder.

"No, nothing like that."

Colin forced a smile and made himself busy with the dishes.

"Yes, someone's here." Pause. "A neighbor." The rest was unintelligible.

Colin made no effort to wash dishes quietly. Flatware banged against china, the wooden salad bowl slipped from his soapy hands with a loud clatter. Maggie turned and glared at him, as if she could quiet him with a frown. She was having trouble following the conversation and frowning at him simultaneously.

"Of course I'm still planning to stay through the summer.... No, I miss...Boston, too, but my research is important. You know that."

Dishes done, Colin made no pretense of ignoring her conversation. He turned, leaned against the counter and watched her, arms crossed against his chest. Maybe he was acting like a jerk, but she was supposed to be paying attention to him, not to some guy across the country.

Maggie finished the call and recradled the phone. Damn it! Edmund's timing had been less than perfect, and Colin's candid appraisal wasn't making things any easier.

"Who's Edmund?" he inquired politely—too politely.

"A colleague of mine, in Boston." There. Let him think what he wanted.

Especially since she wasn't quite sure how to label Edmund, anyway. Certainly less than a boyfriend, maybe more than a friend. It was one of those things she was trying to figure out this summer. So far, a continent between them wasn't helping. And neither was the man standing across the kitchen from her.

"He always call this late?"

"Late? It's only eight o'clock!"

"It's eleven o'clock in Boston—past his bedtime, isn't it?" The tone hadn't changed, but the words annoyed Maggie.

"That's when the rates go down." He couldn't argue with that, could he?

"Tight as a tick, huh? Can't be much fun on a night on the town." His twitching lips betrayed his amusement.

Maggie opened her mouth to utter something rude, then snapped it shut. She wouldn't give him the satisfaction of rising to his bait. After all, what business of his was it who she talked to?

He grinned openly now. "I know it sounds like a line, but you're cute when you're mad, Professor."

"I think it's time for you to go," she said through clenched teeth, resisting the urge to respond to his needling.

"Awfully cute," he whispered, moving closer. Maggie tried to move away and felt the counter edge press into her lower back, stopping her.

Colin caught her jaw in one hand, tipped her head back and paused before lowering his head. She felt, more than heard, the words *Damn cute* breathe across her face before his mouth covered hers.

The first kiss was soft, inquiring. Her answering response must have pleased him, for the next kiss was different. There was no hesitation this time. He used his lips and his tongue to devastating effect, stroking, teasing, until she opened her mouth under his, allowing him a leisurely exploration.

He ran his thumb along her jawline, then moved his hand to the back of her neck to urge her closer. His other hand slipped around her waist, pulling her up against him.

Maggie's arms clutched his muscled shoulders, almost desperately. He was hard all over, she registered in some small corner of her mind. His broad chest flattened her soft breasts. His arousal pressed against her stomach, his torso paralyzed her. She was powerless to move, to react, to do anything but allow his mouth to continue its slow, thorough plunder.

Slowly his grip eased, and he shifted, trailing his lips along her jaw and down the column of her neck. His arms loosened and he pulled back to allow a fractional gap between them. He rested his forehead against hers, clasping his arms loosely at her waist.

"I'd better leave, while I still have the option," he whispered, his breath hot against her skin.

Maggie nodded, once. Anything else would have required too much effort.

Colin straightened, giving her a quick hug before letting her go. He made quick work of gathering Sealy and heading to the door, stopping on the front porch to bid Maggie good-night. She didn't know whether to be sorry or grateful that he made no move to kiss her again. Instead, he briefly saluted and vanished into the darkness.

Closing the door softly, Maggie rested her forehead against the wood, willing herself to stop shaking. She'd come to Nevada this summer to work, not to get waylaid by her libido, not to contemplate getting involved with a cowboy whose silvery eyes got sad when he talked about his late wife. She couldn't afford to get sidetracked; she had too much to do and too little time in which to do it.

She would go back to Boston with her heart intact and her notebooks full, and she'd carry the seeds for a book that would ensure her professional future. There was no sense getting mixed up with a man whose life lay across the country, and whose heart was buried in a Virginia City cemetery.

Colin awoke the following morning feeling unaccountably cheerful. It was a gorgeous day. Sunshine streamed blindingly bright through the shutters, birds squabbled in the trees and Sealy nuzzled his face, begging to go out and enjoy it all.

He stretched lazily, coming fully awake bit by bit, contemplating his good fortune. It was almost as if he were emerging from a deep slumber, from hibernation. The past two years and change had been a time for healing, but perhaps it was time to get on with life.

And he didn't know why, but he had a dark-haired college professor to thank for the push from the nest. Maggie had something about her, a mind that challenged his, a curiosity that refused to accept simple answers. Meeting her had given a new edge to his staid, isolated existence, had given him a desire to show her the world beyond her Boston experience.

Something about the way she approached her subject, as if she could learn everything from the written records left behind, made him want to shake her, to drag her out and show her the scars in the earth, the trails still pressed into the soil, the evidence that these people had lived, had loved, had died and had left more than books behind them.

He wanted her to feel what he'd felt, back when he was writing. This in itself was a startling revelation. He hadn't felt that involved with anything in too long a time. Perhaps it wasn't the same kind of thrill he'd felt when a book was happening, but it was close.

And kissing her had been a revelation all its own. He'd forgotten what it was like to enjoy the simple heat, to lose himself in the sheer pleasure of physical contact. She'd kissed him as if they were made for each other, her lips fitting his perfectly, her body molding to his as though it had been waiting for him to come along.

The thought occurred to him that maybe he and Maggie could both learn something this summer, before she headed back to Boston, and her classes and her real life, and he settled back down with his journals and diaries, looking for an idea to turn into a story.

After looking at the clock, he decided six in the morning was a little early for a wake-up call, no matter how much he wanted to talk to her. So he bounded out of bed, threw on a pair of shorts and took Scally for a run, reveling in the fresh mountain air, the scent of juniper and pine, the steady rhythm of his running shoes pounding the dirt trail.

Returning to the cabin, he showered and made coffee, catching himself humming as he did so. He prowled around the house, willing the clock hands to move faster. Just what time was it permissible to call, anyway?

Eight o'clock finally came, and he couldn't wait any longer. He picked up the phone and dialed her number.

"'Lo?" Her voice was low, sleepy, sexy.

"Good morning, sunshine. It's a beautiful day."

"Don't tell me you're one of those obnoxiously cheerful morning people," she growled.

"Well, if you put it that way..."

"You are, aren't you?"

"Okay, I am," he admitted. "But I have many other redeeming qualities."

"Thrifty, loyal, hardworking," she muttered.

"All of those," he agreed readily. "Look, this isn't just a wake-up call. What are you doing today?"

"Mmm...same old stuff. Back to the library."

"Can I talk you out of that?"

She hesitated, and when she answered, her voice sounded more awake. "I don't think so, Colin. I have a lot to accomplish, and a very short summer in which to do so."

"This is work. You've only been up the hill once, right?"

"Twice, if you count Seally."

"That doesn't count. You really need the grand tour, to see Silver City and Dayton, where the Overland Trail ran— the atmosphere will add a lot to your book."

A pause. "You're right, of course, but I don't necessarily have to do it today."

Despite her words, Colin could sense that she was tempted, so he pressed his advantage. "Wouldn't you like to see where the Groshes had their cabin?"

"What?" Now she was wide-awake. Colin could picture her sitting up in bed, her dark hair tousled about her face, her hand reaching up to push it out of her eyes. She was probably the football-jersey type, at least when she was alone—

"Colin, are you still there?"

"Uh, yes, of course."

"What are you talking about? You know where the Groshes' cabin is?"

"*Was*," he emphasized. "From descriptions and to-pos—"

"Oh, I'm hopeless at topographical maps," she said mournfully.

"Nonsense. All you need is a good teacher. Come up and spend the day with me, and you'll go home with a superb knowledge of map reading, as well as a new appreciation of Silver City." *And of me,* was his unspoken hope.

There was silence on the other end of the phone, but Colin resisted the temptation to play his trump card. It would be better as a surprise.

"Sounds like a constructive way to spend the day," she finally answered. "What's the weather like?"

"Gorgeous," he replied. "Warm and sunny. Bring a sweater for later, but you'll definitely want to wear shorts." He tactfully refrained from mentioning that he wanted to see those legs again.

They set a time, and Colin hung up the phone with a satisfied smile. A gorgeous day indeed.

She hadn't really wanted to come, Maggie reminded herself as she drove up Geiger Grade to Colin's home. The only reason she'd said yes was that Colin had promised to take her to the Grosh cabin site. If it weren't for that, she'd be in the library working, where she belonged, and not fantasizing about a man who kissed too well for her own good.

But she would be working here, too. She had to remember that. It wasn't a date, after all. Her camera, her notepad and her pocket tape recorder sat in her tote, waiting for action, serving as tangible, physical reminders of why she was really here. She would be friendly, businesslike even. No danger of a repeat of the scene in her kitchen.

Besides, she wouldn't be up here all that long, no matter what Colin said. When she'd driven this road before, she'd seen just about everything there was to see. Silver City was little more than a wide spot in the road, scarred hillsides and falling-down buildings the only reminders of its former glory.

And Virginia City! "Queen of the Comstock," indeed. Queen of the Tourist Traps was more like it. All the way up the mountain Maggie had seen signs for the "Suicide Table," some curiosity catering to the mass conception of the rough-and-tumble, savage, shoot-'em-up West. The town itself had been a garish mixture of saloons, curio shops and dubious "museums," designed to separate visitor from dollar, no doubt.

To be fair, there were several elegant restored Victorian mansions, and a truly fine old spired Catholic church gracing the hillside, but Maggie had been so disappointed by the overall effect that she hadn't even stopped the car. She couldn't imagine anything Colin could do to make Virginia City more charming.

Arriving at her destination, she pulled in beside a forest green Bronco, and got a good look at Colin's "cabin." In daylight, she could see that this was no rustic log dwelling, but a vision in cedar, stone and glass, built low and sprawling to blend in with the forest.

Seally came bounding out the open door, Colin following behind her. He paused to shut the door and lock up, giving Maggie a chance to appreciate his rugged good looks again.

Today he'd dropped the chambray for a light blue knit polo shirt that fit his muscular shoulders and arms exceedingly well. Whatever else he was doing with his time these days, he worked out. He wore jeans again, but instead of boots, he wore dusty, once-white running shoes. The look said he could have been out for an afternoon at Fenway Park, instead of running around the Nevada backcountry.

"Hi. I'll give you the grand tour—" he gestured to the house behind him "—later. Time's a-wastin'." He suggested they take his truck—"We might go off-road a little." He didn't give Maggie time to object to his itinerary, but loaded her and Seally into the truck and pulled out.

To her surprise, instead of turning up the mountain toward Virginia City, Colin turned down the hill, back the way Maggie had just come. Geiger Grade was becoming altogether too familiar, Maggie thought wryly, although she had to admit that the drive was far less threatening with someone else behind the wheel. Even if that someone made shifting gears a sexy ballet of muscular legs and pedals. She shook off the thought.

"Where are we going? I thought we were going to Silver City."

"We are, eventually. I promised you the grand tour, yes?"

"Colin—" she started. She'd had no intention of spending the day tooling around the countryside with this man.

"Relax, Professor," he said with a grin. "Think of this as soaking up atmosphere for your book."

Maggie decided that since he was behind the wheel, all she could do was give in gracefully and hurry them along until they reached Silver City.

When they reached the highway, he turned the truck south, explaining, "I like to take visitors this way, because you get to see a great transition, from mountain to valley, to lake, to desert."

"I've been to the State Library in Carson City a couple of times, so I've driven this road," Maggie replied, trying to sound less petulant than she felt.

Either she succeeded, or he didn't care. "So you know I'm right," Colin countered.

No, she didn't know any such thing. "Actually," she was embarrassed to admit, "I didn't really notice much— I was too busy trying to figure out where Grosh and Bucke crossed the valley."

"I can give you a general idea on that," Colin promised. He reached over and patted her bare knee, his warm touch startling her. "But you really need to pay attention to the topography. It's a big part of the story."

"I'm a historian, not a geologist," she corrected.

"And what is geology but a history of the earth?"

When she failed to respond, he shot her a triumphant smile and began pointing out natural and man-made landmarks.

The road curved around a tiny lake, and Colin took a fork off the highway. Maggie was content to watch Colin as he spoke, admiring his easy movements and equally relaxed speech. She liked the way the ends of his mouth lifted when he smiled, the way his shaggy hair ruffled against his shirt collar. She felt surprisingly comfortable with him, even though he was nothing like the men she usually saw in Boston.

Like Edmund. Edmund Brock was a professor of literature at Beaton, and as unlike Colin as any man could be. She'd never seen him in a pair of jeans; to his mind, "informal" meant skipping the tie. He knew all the right people, ate at the correct restaurants, attended the appropriate lectures and had been a great adviser to Maggie as she moved beyond the South End and into the academic whirl.

But he'd never kissed her like Colin had, a little voice reminded her, and Maggie felt herself flush at the memory. True, Edmund's infrequent embraces had never caused her to…lose herself as she had the night before, but that was because of Edmund's basic restraint and refinement, not because of anything lacking on his part, or on hers, for that matter. She just wasn't the type for a passionate, forget-everything, throw-caution-to-the-wind kind of relationship. Last night had been an anomaly, nothing more.

Belatedly, she realized Colin had stopped the car. He sat with his left arm draped across the steering wheel, studying her.

She blinked and looked around her. They appeared to be on the outskirts of a housing development nestled in the foothills, the fire road before them running into the hills. "Sorry, I was just thinking," she said, feeling her face flush as she remembered what she'd been thinking about. A lady of restraint and refinement probably didn't compare gentlemen's kisses. "Why are we stopped?"

"This is probably about where our boys started climbing up the Sierra Nevadas. Come on. I'll show you."

He led her a short way up the fire trail, then turned to motion over the land. "They probably came down from the Virginia Range right in that area, then skirted south of Washoe Lake before climbing up somewhere in here. I'd have to look at Bucke's account and at the topos to be sure," he said, "but most of these fire roads follow earlier trails, so this is as likely a spot as any."

Maggie looked out over the valley, trying to imagine what it had looked like in 1857. The Virginia Range had still been covered with piñon and juniper forests, so the view across the valley would have been green. Take away the houses and the roads, and you could almost see it.

"Now you're getting it!"

Maggie didn't realize she had voiced her thoughts until Colin spoke. She turned and was surprised to see something close to approval on his face.

"Getting what?"

"The idea that the story you're telling is so much more than the books in the library. You're starting to feel it."

"I don't know what you're talking about."

"Sure, you do," he responded. "Your book isn't just about what other people have said about the Groshes. It's about the land, the dream those brothers had and how—"

"I'm writing an academic treatise based on scholarly research, not some pop culture history based on fuzzy 'feelings.'" His criticism hurt. Her family's lack of understanding she could tolerate, since they simply didn't comprehend the nature of her research, but for Colin to jump on the bandwagon stung deeply.

"I'm certainly not suggesting that you abandon your scholarly research. I'm merely—"

"Trying to tell me how to write, and I don't appreciate it. You have absolutely no concept of the requirements of academia."

In a now-familiar gesture, Colin ran his hand through his tawny hair, leaving it more disheveled than before. "No, I don't," he conceded. "Come on, let's go."

Chapter Three

Colin was silent as they resumed their drive, and Maggie had time to regret her sharp words. All the joy of the day had gone out of him, it seemed. He kept his eyes fixed on the road ahead, his hands firmly clenched on the steering wheel.

He probably hadn't meant any censure of her work, even if it sounded like it to her. For the thousandth time, Maggie wished she weren't so thin-skinned.

You'd think that with as often as I've had to explain my work, I could be a little less defensive about it, she thought. Her family, Edmund, her colleagues—it seemed as if everyone in her life had an opinion about what she was doing as well as how she was doing it, and none of them was the least bit shy about sharing those opinions with her.

She recalled the consternation that had resulted when she'd announced her summer plans.

"I don't understand why you need to go all that way," her mother had protested. "With all the universities in Boston, you're telling me that none of them has the books you need for your project?"

Brigid Sullivan hadn't been satisfied with answers about special collections and historic papers available only in local archives. "Why didn't you choose something you could work on here?"

As if it were that simple. Maggie hadn't even tried to explain how the Grosh brothers had called to her, how their story begged her to retell it.

Edmund had been even worse. "Going to play cowboys and Indians for the summer, Maggie?" His gibe, delivered in a wry, pseudo-sophisticated manner, had contained more truth about his attitude toward her work than she wanted to admit.

He didn't respect her research. While damning from a colleague, that sort of opinion was even more hurtful coming from someone whom she presumed to be her friend, someone who supposedly wanted a deeper relationship with her.

At least Colin believed in what she was doing, even if he disagreed with her methods, Maggie realized, hazarding another glance at the man next to her. To her disappointment, she saw no change in his stiff bearing.

After a few miles had elapsed, Maggie couldn't stand the strained silence any longer.

"I see what you mean about the topography," she offered cautiously. "We're coming into the desert, right?"

"Uh-huh." A stiff nod punctuated his brief reply.

Undaunted, Maggie tried again. "How far is it to Silver City from here?"

"About twelve miles."

Four syllables. They were making progress.

"Are we going to stop in Dayton?"

He turned and glared at her. "I don't know, Maggie. Do you suppose you could risk my pushing some unknown button again? I'd hate to upset you again without even having a clue as to why!"

Maggie recognized the hurt behind his sarcastic words. She hated the idea that she'd wounded him when he'd only been trying to convey to her his feelings about the region.

"Look, I'm sorry I snapped at you about my work. It's something I'm a little sensitive about."

"No fooling."

Colin's dry reply struck Maggie's funny bone, and laughter bubbled out.

"All right, I'm a lot sensitive. Can we call a truce?"

Colin eased his death grip on the steering wheel. Maggie's laughter melted the little lump that had developed in his chest when she'd cut him off so abruptly. Perhaps the day wouldn't be a total loss, after all. Sure, she'd overreacted to his suggestion, but maybe he needed to be a little more subtle in his approach.

He'd been so thrilled to find someone who loved the history of the region as much as he did that he'd made the mistake of thinking she saw that history the same way he did. And nobody did that. He'd learned that lesson with Lucy.

There was no way he could have gotten Lucy to spend the day driving around the county, just soaking up ambience, unless that ambience included a new boutique, or a trip into Reno for a night of casino hopping. She wouldn't have wanted to see the Overland Trail.

Once again he wondered how he could have been so blind to their incompatibilities. What he'd done to her, forcing her to live up here when she'd wanted to live in

L.A. or San Francisco, making her so unhappy, was something he'd have to live with the rest of his life....

But he couldn't change all that had happened. He could only try not to repeat the same mistakes. He wouldn't try to make a woman fit into his life again.

Shaking his head to dismiss the past, Colin turned east at the outskirts of Carson City, and took a deep breath. He'd leave the day's itinerary to Maggie, and stop trying to push his own expectations. "So, to Dayton or not to Dayton?" His deliberately light tone belied the tension he felt.

"To Dayton, please," Maggie answered. "You said we could see the Overland Trail there."

Colin's tight chest eased a little at her words. He recognized Maggie's agreement for the peace offering it was, and he vowed to enjoy it for as long as it lasted.

By the time they reached Dayton, Colin's bad mood had vanished entirely. Once again, he transformed himself into the consummate tour guide, entertaining Maggie with anecdotes about this once-bustling, now-sleepy town. They wandered around the town, Seally pulling impatiently at her leash whenever they stopped for too long a time.

"Other than the paved roads and the cars, this place hasn't changed much since the 1870s. You really get a feel for what some of these small towns looked like."

Maggie nodded absently, engrossed in the historic plaque in front of her. "The pony express came right through here, did you know?"

He loved her enthusiasm. When she got going, her sapphire eyes sparkled, her hands made sweeps encompassing the world around her—in short, she came alive. Unlike when she talked about the demands of academia.

If she wrote the way she spoke, she could reach so many more people than she did in the classroom. And she'd love that connection to the public, he was certain. He knew it was one of the things he missed most about writing, that offering of a new experience to a perfect stranger. Sometimes he still got fan mail, thanking him for his stories, telling him he'd helped someone through a bad time, and of course, asking when he was going to write again.

"Which way now?" Maggie's question brought him back to the present.

"We're making our way eventually to the top of that hill."

"Why?"

He smiled enigmatically. "It's a surprise." A tug on the leash reminded him that his beast would not stand for much more sight-seeing. "Let's head on. Seally's getting antsy."

Colin caught Maggie sending him sidelong glances as they strolled through town; if she'd expected a repeat of the previous evening, his casual behavior probably puzzled her. Today, he made sure that the only times he touched her were when a guiding hand was needed—on her lower back as he ushered her into a museum, or at her elbow to lead her across a less-than-busy street.

The kiss they'd shared had obviously unnerved her; she'd been more than a little skittish about spending the day with him. He'd have to work on earning her trust, her friendship, before pursuing anything else.

It was amusing, really. There had always been a lot of women who wanted C. J. McCall, who pursued him. Having to plan a pursuit was a funny turnaround. He could probably learn to enjoy the challenge, if he worked at it. Perhaps Maggie would cooperate.

Maggie glanced at the man striding up the slope beside her, wondering what deep thoughts he pondered. Maybe his were similar to hers, that this ... whatever it was ...

seemed to be moving too fast, that they needed to back off. Maybe last night had been an experiment, a way for him to see how he felt about being with a woman again. If that was the case, it had obviously worked altogether too well.

Not that she had a lot of experience in that area with which to compare it. Thanks to the curse of three over-protective brothers, she hadn't done much dating in high school, so by the time she'd hit college she'd found herself way behind the pack, and between her upbringing and the demands of her discipline, she'd had precious little time or inclination to experiment. Now she had her professional goals to consider, and those goals left her no time at all to play.

That was why her relationship with Edmund had functioned so well, at least until he'd started making nasty cracks about cowboys and Indians. Although she suspected he'd done that because he didn't want her gone for the entire summer, that it was his not-so-subtle way of letting her know he'd miss her. In the long run, however, he understood the rigorous demands of academia, understood her drive to succeed and didn't leave her guessing as to the meaning of a kiss.

Fortunately, if his behavior was any indication, it looked as if Colin had reached the same conclusion as she had about that kiss—that it was a mistake, and that friendship would be a far better notion. Now, if she could only forget the way she'd lost her head completely in the scorching power of his caresses, in the hard heat of his body against hers...

The body in question came to an abrupt halt beside her, and Maggie stumbled a little as she, too, stopped. Seally, unleashed at last, went romping away, flushing birds from their cover, sending them screaming into the sky.

Maggie and Colin stood at the crest of a gently sloping hill overlooking the town and the cemetery. A soft breeze tousled Maggie's hair and cooled her flushed cheeks, ruffling the knee-deep grass surrounding them.

"It's beautiful," she breathed. "What a wonderful view."

"Ah, but I didn't bring you here for the view. Look over there." He pointed across the hillside.

Maggie's eyes followed his gesture, but what he wanted her to see didn't immediately register. Then she saw the parallel lines pressed into the slope.

"Oh!" she gasped. "It's the trail."

"Yep, it's the Emigrant Road, the overland route to California and the gold fields."

"When you said we could see it, I thought you meant some preserved section in a park. I had no idea it would just be—" she flung her arm out in a sweeping gesture "—out there. Why hasn't the grass grown to cover it?"

"So many wagon wheels have pounded the dirt that nothing will grow there."

Belatedly, Maggie remembered the camera hanging over her shoulder, and started snapping pictures. They would serve as a reference point for her work. She made Colin pose with Sealy, the dog looking adoringly at her master. If the photo turned out well, she would frame it as a thank-you for what was turning out to be a lovely day.

Perhaps sensing Maggie's excitement, Sealy was all-aquiver by the time the Bronco reached American Flat. Colin let her loose, ordering, "Don't go far, now." The Labrador retriever looked over her shoulder, as if in assent, before bounding off into the trees.

Colin spread a map on the hood of the truck. "Okay, Professor, school's in session."

Obediently, Maggie came to stand beside him, looking at the map and then at the canyon surrounding them. "Good luck, Colin. I warn you, I'm hopeless."

"Five minutes with Dr. McCallum and you'll be an expert," he promised.

"Yes, Doctor," she replied solemnly, but spoiled the effect by bursting into laughter.

"You mock me. I'll have you know I hold four honorary degrees. Now, pay attention."

He pointed to the map in front of them. "Now, the basic difference between a highway map and a topo is the amount of detail."

"That's the part that confuses me. All those squiggly lines."

"Those squiggly lines are called contour lines. On this particular map, the distance between them represents twenty-five vertical feet. So, the closer together the lines are, the steeper the grade, the farther apart, the more level."

"Show me where we are."

"Sure. We're right here." He pointed to a spot, and Maggie moved closer to see. "Here's the road, and where we turned off."

She bent to peer over the map. A light, flowery scent hit Colin's nostrils, and he breathed deeply as she spoke.

"So, this is the hill to our left."

He leaned over her, his arms bracketing her body. "Correct. See that little bulge on the map?"

"Yes." She nodded intently, sending her dark hair swaying. Little wisps tickled his jaw, sending an answering tingle down his spine. She didn't seem to notice how close they were, or what effect that closeness was having on him.

He was finding it increasingly difficult to concentrate on the map. "Find it on the hill."

Maggie studied the hillside for a moment, then grinned triumphantly. "Look, there it is!"

Colin resisted the urge to hug her. She looked so pleased with her discovery.

"And look, this is the stream over there." She pointed at the map and then across the road. "This is a lot clearer than trying to figure it out from a book."

That's what I was trying to tell you. Colin bit back the thought before he voiced it. "It takes some practice to translate the two-dimensional map surface to the three-dimensional space around you," he agreed instead.

"So, where was the cabin?"

"One description said that it was at the foot of American Flat, near an old mine shaft." He pointed to a hollow in the hillside. "That depression looks as if it could have once been an adit, so I'd guess it's right up there. Let's go take a look."

They climbed a short distance and wandered around. While no remains of a stone cabin were evident, there was enough trash from various eras to indicate long-term habitation of the site. Maggie stared around in awe.

"They were here, weren't they? This looks just like the descriptions in the books. I'm standing where they lived. It makes all this so much more real."

Once again, Colin refrained from commenting. His words wouldn't make her understand; this was a discovery she needed to make on her own. He hoped she would allow him to be there when she made it.

From American Flat it was only a short drive along a dirt road to the main purpose of Colin's tour.

"Silver City Cemetery." Maggie read the faded sign aloud. She turned to Colin, eyes wide. "You don't mean it's still here, do you? Hosea's grave?"

"Of course it is. Why wouldn't it be? Where's he gonna go?"

She ignored his joke as she gazed about her. "Well, look at this place. It's all broken-down, fences have collapsed, stones have fallen, markers have rotted. I've read enough about ghost towns to know what kind of shape their cemeteries are usually in. It's really here?"

"Yes, Maggie." Colin smiled gently. "It's still here."

In her excitement, Maggie fumbled with her seat belt, unable to release the catch. Colin leaned over and caught her hand, stilling it before he unlatched the belt. "Relax, Hosea's not going anywhere."

"Right." She took a deep breath before opening the car door.

He understood her excitement; he really did. God knew he'd felt it enough times himself—walking where his heroes had walked, reading a schoolmarm's description of a land so utterly foreign from the home she'd left behind, seeing a grave like the one awaiting them.

Maggie stood at the cemetery gate, waiting, looking. Colin shook off his thoughts and moved to join her. Even Seally seemed to understand the solemnity of the moment; she padded along softly behind him, the jingling of her tags the only sound in the quiet afternoon.

"What are you waiting for?"

She turned to him, her eyes soft, her face earnest. "Do you know where exactly where Hosea is?"

Colin nodded and, unable to resist the unspoken plea on Maggie's face, took her hand in his. "Come on. Let's go see him."

Clutching his hand as if it were a lifeline, Maggie followed him into the cemetery.

"Wait. Don't tell me where," she ordered. "I want to walk around a little first, and absorb it all."

She led him to the bottom of the hill, their shoes sinking into the soft earth. Walking along a row of graves, she paused every so often to read a name, a date out loud.

"So many babies, Colin, and so many young women."

"It was a hard life, Maggie. No romance about struggling to make it with poor food and no medicine. The men didn't live much longer than the women. See?" He pointed to a gravestone indicating that the man it honored had died at the advanced age of twenty-nine.

Maggie nodded, then dropped Colin's hand, intent on photographing the scene in front of her. Colin absently rubbed his hand against his jeans, missing the warmth of their intimate contact.

Maggie started walking again, leaving Colin and Seally to trail along behind her. He didn't mind her preoccupation; it gave him a chance to study her.

In the sunlight, her wavy hair revealed auburn highlights, proof that she was related to the red-haired behemoths in the photographs. Her skin held a delicate glow that made him want to taste it.

Maybe she should have a hat, he fretted, remembering how she had smoothed sunblock into her fair skin while in the car. She wasn't accustomed to the altitude; the sun shone far stronger here than in Boston. Despite her efforts, the tip of her upturned nose was turning pink.

He'd buy her a hat.

Maggie moved slowly up the hill, snapping pictures as she went. She was getting closer, and Colin quickened his pace to catch up with her. He wanted to watch her face, to see the mixture of awe and delight that had accompanied

Now, if she could only stop dwelling on last night, she'd be just fine.

If his intention was to keep her off-balance, he'd succeeded admirably. She was still trying to absorb all she'd seen, all she'd felt, all that Colin had shown her today, not only about the Comstock, but about himself. Now, in his cabin, she was learning more.

He was sentimental. Sepia-toned pictures were scattered through the room, grouped on tables and hanging on the walls. Several of the subjects bore a strong resemblance to Colin; Maggie presumed them to be ancestors.

He liked his creature comforts. Far from the rustic shelter she had envisioned, Colin's bilevel cabin was a shrine to the latest in high-tech and high-indulgence gadgetry. His office held a curious combination of old and new: a state-of-the-art computer in a huge antique rolltop desk, a cherrywood armoire housing a desktop copier and facsimile machine. The bookshelves lining one wall contained a mixture of first editions, bound manuscripts and bestsellers of all genres.

In the living room, Persian rugs covered the hardwood floor. Oak paneling and a pair of black leather couches flanking the massive stone fireplace gave the room an undeniably masculine aura. Between the couches, more books and magazines were scattered on a glass-topped coffee table.

Colin had invited her to explore, so Maggie wandered downstairs, where she found a fully equipped exercise room adjoining what was obviously Colin's bedroom.

A black lacquer entertainment unit holding a complete stereo system, videocassette recorder and giant-screen television dominated the wall opposite a king-size bed. The bed itself was a work of art, its frame a modern, swirling interpretation of brass, its black sateen comforter contrasting with cream-colored linens. The mass of pillows against the headboard invited Maggie to burrow into them, to snuggle up with one of the books from the stack on the nightstand.

A little unsettled by that image, Maggie stepped out onto the wide porch to discover a redwood hot tub. A vision came to her: soaking there on a cold winter's evening, enjoying a mountain view through the steam rising from the water.

Snuggling, soaking. This place was making her imagination run amok. Time to head back upstairs to a more relative tranquillity, she decided.

The tantalizing odor of garlic sautéing in olive oil pulled Maggie toward the kitchen; Colin was cooking dinner once again.

Maggie had accepted his invitation, not only because she was reluctant to let the day end, but because she was eager to put all the pieces together. She'd hoped his home would hold the key, and to some extent, it did, revealing aspects Colin had only hinted at, or omitted entirely.

For instance, although antique photos abounded, there were no pictures of Lucy. He'd said that they'd had problems; had those problems been serious enough to warrant his banishing her image from his home? Or was her pictorial exile the product of a grief so sharp, he couldn't bear any physical reminder or her existence?

She had too many questions about Lucy.

The only contemporary photograph in Colin's home, in fact, was a formal portrait of a couple Maggie assumed to be his parents. The man looked like an older, more conservative version of Colin; short haired, wearing a well-cut, expensive suit. The silver-haired woman beside him wore an emerald silk dress and carefully coordinated, understated makeup. The overall effect was of money, old money. Very far away from South Boston.

And from Virginia City, for that matter. What sort of relationship did Colin have with his parents? She couldn't quite picture this couple visiting a cabin at the end of a gravel road, even a cabin as luxuriously appointed as this one.

When Maggie entered the kitchen, she found Colin at the stove, stirring something in a pan; the anise bouquet of basil rose from it to tickle her nose. He turned and smiled, cocking an eyebrow in inquiry. "What do you think?"

"You're very self-sufficient, aren't you?" What she really meant was *alone,* but she didn't quite dare voice that thought.

How could he live out here, by himself, away from family and friends? She couldn't imagine living such an isolated life. Back home, in Boston, she was at her parents' every Sunday for dinner with the whole family, and usually went by sometime during the week. If she didn't, she heard about it.

He shrugged. "I'm comfortable. All those books were good for something."

"They were good for a lot, Colin," Maggie protested. "Your books have influenced a whole group of Western writers, who have been trying to catch up ever since."

"Yeah, nice of me to give them a break, huh?"

Something in his sarcastic tone made Maggie wonder if perhaps he missed writing more than he cared to acknowledge.

Colin spoke again, this time in a tone so calm, so casual, that she almost thought she'd imagined his bitter words. "Dinner will be ready as soon as the water boils. Fresh pasta only takes a couple of minutes."

"Fresh? I'm impressed."

"Don't be. I make it once a month and freeze it."

"I'm still impressed. When I prepare something from the freezer it comes in a plastic tray. Homemade pasta is beyond my imagination."

"Does your culinary expertise extend as far as putting a salad together? You can use whatever's in the crisper."

Maggie set to work, inventorying the kitchen as she had the rest of the house. Like the other rooms, the kitchen was modern, well-appointed and oriented to offer sweeping views of the surrounding mountains. The windows above the sink looked out over the Washoe Valley; as the sun went down, the bright lights of Reno cast an unearthly glow in the distance. Across the valley to the west rose the Sierra Nevadas, snow still dusting the higher peaks despite the fact that it was mid-July.

Maggie decided that it would be no chore to do dishes while taking in this scenery, and she said as much to Colin.

He responded with a chuckle. "Maybe I've lived here too long, then—I always use the dishwasher."

"How long have you been here?"

"Fourteen years. My grandparents owned this land and had a small cabin here. They left it to me, and when I sold *Winchester Justice*, I moved up and started building. With every book contract, the plans got a little more elaborate."

"It's a wonderful place, Colin. You're very fortunate."

"Probably." His skeptical tone belied his response, and he didn't say anything else as he dumped fettuccine into the boiling water. Maggie placed the salads on the table and stopped to watch the sun settling into the mountains. The loss of light caused the sky to slip from palest coral to a softer pink, finally fading into a lilac haze.

Colin's dining table sat in a corner of the kitchen, a perfect place to view Mother Nature's show. Maggie felt no need for further conversation as she watched the sun descend. She was still getting accustomed to everything about Nevada, with its wide-open spaces a contrast to Boston's congestion.

The whoosh of splashing water and a cloud of steam punctuated Colin's movements as he drained the pasta. He poured it into a bowl, added the sauce and brought it to the table, sniffing his creation appreciatively.

He lifted his wineglass and tapped hers lightly. "To a lovely day."

One of many to come, I hope. The thought popped into Maggie's head, surprising her. While she had found Colin intriguing from their first encounter, she hadn't planned on simply *liking* him so much. That could complicate things; she had too little time this summer to devote any of it to romance.

Still, she dismissed the wayward thoughts and returned his toast. "It was a wonderful day, thanks to you, Colin. I have to admit, I wasn't exactly impressed with Virginia City before your tour."

"Watch those first impressions, Maggie. They'll get you every time."

She sighed. "You're right, of course. I set myself up. I wanted something noble, something perfectly preserved, and Virginia City isn't quite like that."

"Don't kid yourself. Even in its heyday, by no stretch of the imagination could Virginia City be described as noble. It was rough-and-tumble, filled with men and women trying to make a buck, people unwilling or unable to live within nineteenth-century America's narrow boundaries. Those people had dreams, yes, but don't mistake dreams for nobility."

Colin caught Maggie looking at him as if he'd revealed some deep, dark secret, instead of talking about miners and mining. He picked up his fork and attacked his pasta. Sometimes he said too damn much for his own good.

Sure, dreams hurt people sometimes; he'd learned to live with that. But that was his own business, not Maggie's.

Her next query indicated she hadn't gotten the "own business" issue straight yet. Not that he'd spelled it out to her.

"Can I ask you kind of a personal question?"

His immediate impulse was to say no, to cut her off now. He wasn't sure he was ready for "kind of personal" questions. He took another bite of pasta, delaying his answer while he thought about it.

She gazed across the table at him, bright eyed, obviously curious. Finally, he nodded. He could always sidestep her query. He'd had lots of practice over the past two and a half years.

"Why did you shave your mustache?"

Of all the things she could have asked, he'd never anticipated this one. Too surprised to evade the issue, he said the first thing that came to his head. "It made it much easier to avoid C. J. McCall questions."

She blinked, and considered. "You mean, now that you're clean-shaven, people like me don't recognize you."

"In a nutshell, yes." *And they don't ask when my next book will be out, or how I'm doing, or if I'll critique their manuscript....*

He really didn't want to talk about this.

He changed the subject abruptly. "So, now that you've seen the Comstock, where do you go with your research?"

If the conversational shift surprised Maggie, she didn't show it, but merely considered his question for a moment before she answered. "It doesn't change my basic game plan, really. I'm still looking for primary sources, particularly manuscripts and letters from people who knew the Groshes."

"Like who?"

"I have some names mentioned in early works. One citation that particularly intrigues me is a manuscript written in the early 1860s by a man named Francis Hoover. He was a lawyer and surveyor in California about the same time as the Groshes were here."

"What's so special about his manuscript?"

"He knew the Groshes, he corresponded with them and he probably had a pretty good idea where their claim lay."

"And why is that so important?"

"The Groshes are credited with being the first to discover silver in any quantity, but most historians stop short of crediting them with discovering the Comstock Lode. I think they did discover it, and I think that their place in history is far greater than the footnote usually accorded them."

"And you want to prove it."

"I'd love to. Allen Grosh abandoned his papers during that last trek over the Sierras, but there's plenty of other evidence out there. I just have to find it."

"I wish you luck. Just remember, don't lose sight of the story by burying yourself in the facts."

Maggie opened her mouth to argue, then apparently thought better of it. "Yes, Colin," she said meekly.

"Why do I have the feeling you're saying that merely to placate me?"

She grinned unrepentantly. "Probably because I am. You just heard my 'yes, Sister' voice, the one I used on the nuns in high school."

"Had them fooled, huh?"

"For the most part."

Colin heard the unspoken *but* and prodded her on.

She shrugged and lowered her eyes modestly. "But I got bored. College was a shock. I actually had to study."

"And thus began an illustrious academic career."

"Right. Which will come to a grinding halt if I don't get tenure."

"You strike me as a very determined woman. If you want tenure, you'll get it."

She shook her head. "Unfortunately, it's not necessarily up to me. Besides having to come up with a really good book, be an inspiring teacher and perform loads of community service, I'm sort of at the mercy of departmental and university politics."

"So why do it?" he persisted. "Why put yourself through all that trauma?"

"My parents instilled in all of us a very strong work ethic. They taught us all that we were to do the best we possibly could with our God-given talents. To do anything less would be a disservice."

"To whom?"

"To them and to myself."

That answer didn't tell him anything at all, but when he opened his mouth to question her statement, she shook her head and smiled gently. "I have a feeling that we could really get into a disagreement here, so why don't we change the subject? I don't want a repeat of this morning's scene."

She was probably right, Colin conceded as they resumed eating. He found he wanted to dig deeper, to really understand what drove her, professionally and personally, to learn what made her tick. Was she pursuing these goals for herself or for her parents? It was hard to tell from what she'd said.

He forced himself to swallow his curiosity and focused instead on the unconsciously sensual picture she made—inhaling the rising aroma of the pasta, flicking a bit of basil off her lower lip with the tip of her tongue, tearing a chunk of bread with long, graceful fingers.

She caught him studying her and smiled self-consciously. "Eat," she ordered. "You're making me feel like a glutton, watching me like that."

"I'm enjoying it. You show such... delight."

Maggie's sunburned cheeks turned a shade pinker. "You're embarrassing me. Let's talk about something else."

"Fine," Colin agreed readily. "Why don't you tell me about Edmund."

"Edmund?" Her face went blank for an instant. Obviously not a subject she'd anticipated.

"You know, Edmund, the guy you were talking to last night while your *neighbor* did the dishes."

Maggie rolled her eyes at the memory and groaned. "Sorry about that—I just thought it would be easier if— Oh, never mind." She shook her head in confusion.

"Are you serious about him?"

"Serious?" Her lowered head shot up. "No. He's a good friend, someone I see socially. He's very fond of me."

Colin had to push aside the quick rush of jealousy that nudged his middle. It was too soon for that kind of feeling; he had no right to it. At this moment, he wasn't even sure quite where he and Maggie were headed, even if he had his ideas. "Then why not tell him I was there?"

She pondered a moment before she answered. "Because it could become awkward if he thought I was becoming involved out here."

What did she think was happening here? He wasn't exactly thinking about her as a *buddy*, for goodness' sake. "But, Maggie, aren't you?"

Her forehead creased. "Aren't I what?" she echoed.

"Becoming involved."

A quick shake of the head punctuated Maggie's rejection of that notion. "I can't, Colin. We both know that."

No, he didn't know that. "Why not?"

"Because I'm going back to Boston at the end of the summer, and you're... you're still..." She made a vague gesture with her fork.

"I'm still what?"

Maggie sighed. "Lucy."

Chapter Four

She looked relieved to have said it, a relief that Colin didn't share.

Oh, great. Someone else who thinks I'm still living in the past, based on the garbage they'd read in Personality. He was damned tired of people assuming they knew all about him, thinking they knew the inner workings of his psyche based on the slime written in some rag.

And that it was Maggie making those assumptions disappointed him even more.

Not that he'd been as forthcoming about his feelings as he could have been, but he wasn't used to wearing his heart on his sleeve. Still, he thought he'd shown her that he was moving on, that Lucy was a part of his past, not his present or future. He thought the time they'd spent together would have told Maggie that he was no longer mourning Lucy, that that particular circle of his life was closed.

Obviously, he was wrong.

Colin sighed, thinking of the things he didn't want to say, of the things he would have to say so Maggie would understand. For Maggie, he'd spell it out.

He reached over and took her hand. "She's gone, Maggie. I've accepted that, and now I'm trying to live my life again. And along the way, I'm finding myself attracted to you."

"Maybe you think I'm safe—maybe that's the attraction," she countered, pulling her hand away.

"Safe?" Not from where he sat. She was the most dangerous thing to come down the road since Lucy had died. Completely sidetracked from where he'd intended to go with this discussion, he asked, "What do you mean by that?"

"Safe." She shrugged, suddenly fascinated by the flatware resting on the table. She toyed with the butter knife before she continued. "No risk. You can try out your relationship wings on me, kiss me, maybe even talk me into your bed, and know that no matter what happens between us, I'll be gone by the middle of September. There's no real danger for you."

Colin stood and strode across the room, feeling his jaw clench, his insides tighten at her casual words. How could she possibly think . . .

It was a moment before he could speak.

"I'm insulted," he finally got out.

"Look, Colin, I'm sorry if I struck a nerve, but—"

He whirled and stalked back to the table. Resting his fists on the surface, he leaned over until his face was inches from Maggie. When he spoke, his voice was taut, his words clipped. He wanted no misunderstanding.

"No, you didn't hit a nerve, you insulted me. Lady, if I wanted to—" he chose a mildly crude epithet and watched Maggie blanch "—there are any number of women in

Storey County who would be more than happy to oblige. I don't use women, period. If I want to pursue a relationship with you, it's because I thought that there was something between us, although at the moment I'm not so sure!''

Maggie stared at him, unblinking, uncowed by his tirade. He slapped his palms against the table's pine surface before he straightened and began pacing the room.

''I don't know what's with you, Professor, what you're afraid—''

As soon as he said the words, he knew. He leaned back against the counter, crossing his arms over his chest.

''That's it, isn't it?''

''I don't know what you're talking about.'' Maggie's voice was cool, collected, but she betrayed her inner agitation by gazing anywhere in the room but at him.

''Maggie, look at me,'' he ordered softly, and waited.

After what seemed like an aeon, Maggie turned her cornflower eyes to meet his.

''You trying to make me mad?'' he asked, keeping his voice soft.

''No, Colin, but—''

''You don't really think you're an experiment to me, do you?'' he persisted.

''No, Colin, I—''

''Then why would you accuse me of such a terrible thing?''

Something akin to chagrin flashed across Maggie's face. She rose, and crossed the room to stand beside him, imitating his pose.

''I'm sorry, Colin. What I said was uncalled-for.''

''Then why did you say it?''

She shook her head. ''I don't know. Fishing, I guess.''

Her answer didn't surprise him. Still, he reached over and turned her chin with his index finger until she was forced to meet his gaze.

"Maggie, you should know me better than to accuse me of something like that."

"I don't know you very well at all," she countered.

"And I'd like to change that."

She stared up at him, caution warring with desire on her face. "I don't indulge in summer flings, Colin."

Neither did he. All he was suggesting was that they spend some time together. Just because he couldn't start a serious relationship didn't mean he wanted a fling, either. He wasn't quite sure what he wanted, but he did know one thing. "I'm not proposing a summer fling."

She straightened and shifted her eyes away from his. "Whatever you call it, we'll be going our separate ways at the end of the summer. It's not practical for us to start something that we only know is going to end."

"Why not?"

"It's not productive."

"You measure your relationships by their productivity?"

Maggie jerked her head away and glared across the room. "Oh, stop it, Colin. You know what I mean."

"No, Maggie, I don't," he persisted. "You're acting as though our spending any time at all together will necessarily end in heartache, or derail your project. Neither of those is my intention, believe me."

She shook her head, sending her dark mane swinging. "Face it, Colin, despite any intentions you or I may have, if I spend my remaining time in Nevada playing with you, I won't be getting much work done."

"Not necessarily," he argued. "You forget, I know quite a bit about your subject. I know where to look, I know who to talk to. You could think of me as your research assistant, if you will."

Maggie burst out laughing. She couldn't help it. The idea was ludicrous. "Colin, my research assistants are traditionally young and starry-eyed—"

"So I don't exactly qualify on either count, do I?" he said wistfully.

"No, you're far more the eccentric-professor type."

"Hmm, interesting role reversal," he teased. "We could have fun."

They could, too, she realized suddenly. His knowledge, her drive. A thought tickled the back of her mind, tempting her. Maybe they could share something here, maybe she could offer him a different outlook....

She knew he missed writing. The things he'd said, the things he hadn't said, all pointed to that.

The man needed to work again. However beautiful and comfortable his home, it couldn't make up for such a large gap in his life. However much he worked out, or tackled new recipes or cataloged his manuscripts, they weren't substitutes for the satisfaction of creating, producing.

She knew it from her own experience. All her life, she'd worked, studied, accomplished. She knew instinctively that Colin had a similar need to work, however he sublimated it. Why else would he be spending so much time with her, showing her his vision of the West?

Whatever his protests, he felt the lack.

Maybe she could help him. He got excited showing her his West; maybe this could translate into excitement for his own work. Maybe in showing her the West through his eyes, he would see it anew himself. Maybe, just maybe...

Maggie awoke the next morning still contemplating Colin's rehabilitation. As she stretched sleep-tightened muscles, she hit upon the obvious solution. He wanted to spend time with her, she needed to work. All she had to do was say yes. Colin would trail along behind her, finding renewed inspiration in her zeal for her research.

To her sleep-muddled brain, it appeared to be a simple fix.

The ring of the telephone on the nightstand interrupted her musings. Colin? She shook her head and cleared her throat before she answered.

"Hello?"

"Maggie, sweetheart, I'm so glad you're there. I tried and tried last night. Where were you?"

As always, her mother sounded breathless, as if she'd raced to the phone and couldn't wait to spill her words.

Maggie didn't really want to discuss her evening, so she tried to skirt the subject. "So you were the hang-ups on my phone machine, Ma. How are you?"

No good. "Don't ignore my question, dear. Where were you?"

She tried imprecision. "I went out to dinner."

"Oh, that's nice, dear. With whom?"

So much for subtlety. "Ma, forgive me, but it's a little early for me. Could we slow it down a bit?"

"Of course, dear. I always forget the time difference. I've been up for *hours,* and been to Mass, and weeded the garden and..."

Maggie half listened to her mother's chronicle while trying to focus her thoughts. How much should she tell her mother about Colin? Would she worry, or start looking for a mother-of-the-bride dress?

"Are you awake now, dear?"

No point in putting it off any longer. "Yes, Mother."

"Good. Tell me about your date."

Her mother's choice of words sent a tremor of alarm up Maggie's spine. She'd deliberately tried to avoid thinking of the time she spent with Colin in any traditional man-woman terms, reluctant to place any expectations on it, beyond a summer friendship.

"I wouldn't exactly call it a date, Ma. I spent the day exploring the area with a writer who knows a lot about the history of the Comstock, and we had dinner together." No point in mentioning that dinner was at his house, or that he cooked or that he kissed like a dream....

"You're being evasive, dear. Spill it."

That was her mother. Just when she thought she could get away with generalizations or equivocation, her mom called her on it. It was a talent that had served her well raising four rambunctious children, and she seemed to have perfected it over time and grandchildren. There was no use obscuring the issue any further. With a little luck Colin's name wouldn't mean anything to her, since Western fiction wasn't her mother's cup of tea anyway.

"His name is Colin McCallum, he writes novels as C. J. McCall—"

"Not that poor man who can't write because his wife died!"

So much for luck. "That's what the tabloids say, Ma. What are you doing reading those kinds of rags?"

Once again her attempt at diversion failed. "Don't change the subject, dear. Is it true?"

Maggie considered carefully before she answered, trying to balance Colin's right to privacy with her mother's natural inclination to worry. "He hasn't said a lot about it, but I gather it's taken him some time to recover from his wife's death."

"Have you asked him?"

"No, Ma, I haven't," she said, suddenly impatient with her mother's questions. "I've only known him a week, and I've only seen him on three separate occasions, so it seems a little forward to ask him to spill his deepest, darkest memories." Too late, she realized her mistake.

"Three dates? In one week? Just what do you think you're doing out there, Mary Margaret?"

Oh no, the double *M*. Now she was in trouble. Feeling ten years old again, being called on the carpet for passing notes in Sister Bernadette's class, Maggie struggled to come up with an acceptable answer.

In the silence, she reminded herself that she was not that ten-year-old, but a mature thirty-two-year-old college professor who no longer needed her dates vetted. Saying as much to her mother, she was surprised when the older woman backed off.

"Of course you're a grown woman, dear. I'm sorry. It's hard being across the country from you, and your pop and I can't help but worry. We want you home, where you belong."

Slightly ashamed of her petulant outburst, Maggie fought to ignore her mother's reminder of home and hearth. They went through this every time her mother called. She softened her tone, counseling herself that her mother's concern was only natural. "I know, Ma. I'm sorry I snapped."

"Quite all right, dear. I understand. We'll talk about something else. How is your research progressing?" Her voice still held just the merest hint of hurt, but Maggie accepted the proffered olive branch.

"Very well, actually, thanks to Colin. The reason I've seen so much of him is that he's helping me with my research. He knows the area and the literature quite well. I'm making excellent progress, and I'll come home with more than enough material to complete my book.''

Her mother's voice brightened, and their conversation continued on a more even keel. While Brigid Sullivan didn't even pretend to comprehend Maggie's obsession with the West, she was truly proud of her daughter's professional reputation, and so had no difficulty in praising her work.

After a flurry of verbal hugs and kisses for and from the rest of the family, Maggie ended the conversation and headed for the shower.

The rush of water beating down soothed her ruffled spirits, allowing her to place the phone call into its proper context. Her mother loved her, but didn't quite understand her. This made for a certain gap in communication.

To a woman who had married a neighborhood boy at nineteen and never looked back, the path Maggie had chosen was an alien one, but one that she expected Maggie to fulfill to the best of her abilities. After all, hadn't the nuns at St. Colum's predicted big things of her? And hadn't her pop told everyone at the station that Maggie would run that college someday? And wasn't Maggie getting—

Maggie was getting annoyed again thinking of her mother's expectations, she acknowledged ruefully. Not to mention wasting water trying to wash tension down the drain along with the cream rinse. Resolutely, she wrenched the shower off and stepped out, feeling goose bumps rise on her wet skin.

She was blotting her dripping hair when the phone rang again. She considered letting the answering machine pick up, but this time she was certain the caller would be Colin.

Wrapping the towel sarong-style around her torso, she rushed to the bedroom.

"Hello?" Even to her ears, her voice sounded breathless, eager. She should have let the machine answer.

"Hi. Am I interrupting something?"

"No, no," she was quick to deny. "I'm just out of the shower, that's all."

"Ah. Now, that's an interesting vision. Are you dripping?" Colin's voice had darkened, become more intimate.

Maggie felt her nipples bead up, tighten. She'd never realized a man's voice alone could do that. She tried, unsuccessfully, to ignore the sensual lure. "Just my hair. The rest of me is safely swaddled."

"Hmm, too bad."

Maggie judged her earlier projections overly optimistic. If their relationship continued on this level, rather than on an academic footing, she'd spend the rest of her summer in hormonal hysteria, instead of finishing her research. That would not do at all.

She changed the subject. "Are you still interested in working with me? I was thinking of driving over to the California State Library later in the week."

Even as she spoke, Moira Ford's words from high school came back to haunt her. *"Boys don't like grinds, Maggie. How do you ever expect to have a date if you spend all your time at the library?"*

It had been her senior year in college before she'd discovered that there were men who actually liked the library, but she'd never quite cast off those high school memories, never quite abandoned the notion that "boys don't like grinds."

"Sounds great." To her relief, Colin sounded sincerely enthusiastic. "I haven't been there in ages."

They set a date, and ended the call.

As the day progressed, Maggie found her mind wandering from her work to Colin. Was she a fool to allow their relationship to continue, even on a casual level? Was she setting herself up for heartache?

Colin McCallum was a man she could fall for, no doubt. There was too big a pull there for her to dismiss it, for her to pretend that nothing was going on between them.

But unfortunately, in the end, her life and Colin's were separated, not only by a continent, but by vastly disparate hopes and dreams. She could see that it would take a geologic cataclysm to move Virginia City closer to Boston, and she suspected that in the long run, it would take a similar force to unite her with Colin.

"Shave and a haircut" echoed through Maggie's apartment, and she uttered a short curse as she eyed her unruly mane in the bathroom mirror's reflection. The anticipation of today's trip had kept her awake late into the night, which in turn had caused her to shut the alarm clock off this morning and go back to sleep. She'd awakened a scant half hour ago and rushed through her morning ablutions, the result of which was this Medusa-like mess.

As the knock sounded again, she hurried through the living room and plastered what she hoped was a nonchalant smile on her face before opening the door.

"Good morning. I'm sorry to have kept you waiting."

Colin turned from studying the courtyard to greet her. "Hi. I like your hair."

Oh, God, was he making fun of her? Or did he really like the messy look? Maggie couldn't say she was thrilled with either option.

On the other hand, he looked great. He'd abandoned denim for a dressier look—slacks in a gray, tweedy material, topped by a cream oxford shirt that accentuated his deep tan. Black penny loafers completed the ensemble. He looked like the wealthy author she knew him to be.

Maggie was glad she'd chosen a dressier outfit herself for their day together. She knew her rose jacket over paler slacks and blouse accented her fair coloring, making her look delicate, as her mother would say.

She stepped back and invited him in. "I'm running a little behind—I overslept. There's coffee in the kitchen if you want some. I have travel mugs so we can take it with—"

Colin stopped her rush of words with a firm kiss. "Good morning, Maggie. Why don't you go finish getting ready, and I'll handle coffee detail." He disappeared into the kitchen before she could reply.

Shaking her head over his high-handedness, Maggie returned to the bathroom and the problem of her hair. Funny how the racing of her heart could make her hair seem like a minor worry. She finally opted to pull the whole mass back into a tortoiseshell clasp at the nape of her neck, allowing a few of the more unruly curls to escape and frame her face. There. Now it looked as if she'd planned this effect—almost.

Rose quartz "door knocker" earrings completed her outfit, and she studied her reflection carefully. Feminine, but professional—that was the look she'd wanted, and she decided she'd succeeded.

Even if her face was still a touch pink from Colin's kiss.

Returning to the living room, she found Colin sprawled on her couch, paging through a day-old newspaper. He looked up when she entered, and smiled, his eyes inventorying her outfit, his warm expression conveying his approval.

"Very nice. Are you ready?"

"I just have to get my briefcase."

She saw he'd gathered mugs and her insulated carafe, and after she'd collected her things, they left. She caught herself breathing a sigh of relief when they exited the apartment; his presence seemed to fill her tiny apartment, using up all available air.

She looked for his dusty Bronco, but instead, to her surprise, he opened the passenger door of an immaculate, powder blue, vintage Thunderbird convertible. She stopped dead in her tracks and stared: a '56, she decided, remembering her brothers' lessons about vintage cars; the Continental kit holding the spare tire gave the year away.

"I'm surprised," she said finally. "I never would have guessed you had it in you."

Colin looked abashed, and made a great deal of work rubbing a smudge off the door handle with his thumb. "Yeah, well, you know . . ." His voice trailed off, then he shrugged. "It's just a little indulgence."

"*Little* indulgence? This car's a cream puff, Colin. It's in perfect shape." Maggie slid into the white leather seat and stroked the dashboard. "You've even got the original radio in here."

Colin laughed as he rounded the hood and slid behind the wheel. "Look in the glove box."

Following his command, she found a tiny but elaborate stereo system. Colin was still chuckling as he started the car. "It's not vintage—I like comfort too much."

Remembering his cabin, Maggie silently concurred.

"When I was a kid, I always wanted one of these babies. After *Sierra Sunrise* hit the bestseller lists, I realized I wasn't a 'one-book wonder,' and that I could afford my dream car. I've put a little work into it since then," he finished modestly.

"Hmm." Maggie sighed. "Fame and fortune must be nice."

"Fortune, at least," he agreed. "What's your dream car?"

"Me? I live in Boston. We have crazy drivers. I'd never drive a car I valued that highly there."

"But if you didn't live in Boston," he persisted.

Maggie knew what her choice would be, but hesitated before she answered. Why wish for something she would never have?

"Well?" Colin prompted her.

Maggie tipped her head back and closed her eyes. "Mmm, a 1966 Mustang convertible. Red."

For a moment, she allowed herself a vision of driving along a winding mountain road, her hair flying free in the wind. She knew it was a pipe dream—living someplace else, owning her imaginary Mustang, cruising the highways. Ties of career, ties of family, ties of tradition held her to Boston as surely as any physical tether. She made the red Mustang drive out of her mind, and slowly opened her eyes.

Colin was watching her as he drove, a smile lifting the ends of his mouth. "Nice dream?"

"Nice *dream*," she echoed, her emphasis on the second word.

"You've got to follow your dreams, Professor. Otherwise, life's pretty empty."

He was a fine one to talk, she thought uncharitably. Perhaps he should practice what he preached, instead of criticizing her.

She ordered herself to shake the sour thought, and concentrated instead on the scenery surrounding them. Now that they had left Reno behind them, the highway rose steeply as it followed the eastern slope of the Sierra Nevada mountains. The hills on either side of the road were covered with cedar, lodgepole pine and red fir. The breeze increased along with the altitude, whipping Maggie's dark curls about her face, threatening her tidy ponytail.

"Here." Colin thrust a soft white object into Maggie's hands. "I forgot to give this to you earlier."

"This" turned out to be a white baseball cap, and Maggie bundled her hair underneath, grateful for the protection.

"I was worried about you getting sunburned, so I picked it up for you yesterday." While he'd done his best to sound casual, the edge of proprietary interest in Colin's voice told Maggie otherwise.

"Thanks, it's just what I needed," she said, squelching the flash of annoyance that ran through her. A little of his "Colin knows best" attitude, in everything from cooking dinner to how she should write her book, could go a long way.

Maybe it was to make up for the lack of direction in his own life. The idea crept into her mind unexpectedly, but perhaps it was a reasonable explanation.

And she could provide the cure. The thought of Colin writing again pleased her. She allowed herself an idle fantasy of Colin dedicating his next book to her, and smiled at the notion as she focused her attention once again on the passing landscape.

Colin caught her smile out of the corner of his eye, and smiled himself, wondering at the source of her pleasure. She'd liked the cap enough; she probably wasn't used to men doing things for her. She probably saw herself as the self-sufficient type—not that she wasn't—but every woman liked being taken care of now and again.

It was great to have her beside him, cruising along the interstate, enjoying the sunshine and fresh air and the prospect of a day together. He loved the way she looked, all pink and feminine, those dark curls blowing against her fair skin. She'd tip her head back to look up the mountain every now and again, as if she wanted to memorize it all, to engrave it in her memory forever.

A roadside mileage sign told him they were halfway to their destination, and he glanced at the dashboard clock in surprise. An hour had elapsed and he hadn't even realized it. Funny how traveling with the right person could make that happen.

A comfortable silence. For what felt like the first time in his life, Colin understood the meaning of the phrase. Maggie didn't fill the car with idle chatter; her silences weren't a result of strain or awkwardness.

Lucy's behavior the few times they'd taken long road trips together came back to him. She nattered on about anything that came to sight or mind, from the number of fast-food restaurants along their route to a state license plate she'd never seen before. If Colin was unresponsive, lost in thought, plotting a scene or pondering a character's motivation, she talked to Seally instead. Lucy hadn't valued silence.

The past two and a half years had given Colin the measure of silence's worth. It didn't mean empty, it didn't imply any deficiency; it held a fullness, a completion in itself.

Maggie seemed to understand that notion. Perhaps it was her role as an academician, perhaps it was simply her nature. Whatever the reason, he found her presence comfortable, considering their short acquaintance. He glanced over at her again and decided she probably felt the same way about him; she'd fallen asleep.

As they approached their destination, Maggie awoke and oriented herself, asking questions about the towns they'd passed and about Sacramento itself. She wanted to know everything he knew about the area, about the communities that had survived the gold rush, and those that had not.

"We can stop in Auburn on the way back if you'd like. It's got an Old Town section dating back to the gold rush, and it's not too touristy."

"I suppose it depends on how long we're at the State Library. I have a feeling we'll be there a long time, they may have to kick us out to close."

"Well, we could always get a seedy motel if we wanted to stay in the area," Colin offered.

"I don't think so, Colin," she said with a dismissive wave. "I don't do seedy."

If she only knew that he'd only been half kidding with his offer, she probably wouldn't have treated it so casually. While his brain realized it was far too early in the relationship for a physical commitment, his body thought otherwise. So far, his brain was winning—just barely.

Exiting the freeway, Colin negotiated the network of one-way streets leading to the State Capitol complex. The library was located in a massive marble edifice across from the gold-domed Capitol building, and Colin chose his route to give Maggie an optimal view of the area.

"Colin, this is lovely. So majestic. This has a very different feeling from Boston."

"The Massachusetts Capitol building was constructed in an earlier period. By the time they built this, Neoclassicism was in vogue, especially for 'important' buildings like this."

Maggie shook her head. "I don't know why I'm ever surprised at the extent of your knowledge. You're really a Renaissance man, you know."

"That's me, jack-of-all-trades, master of none," Colin quipped as he eased the convertible into a parking space.

Her open admiration embarrassed him; it wasn't as if he were doing anything with the talents she so lavishly attributed to him at every turn.

He shook off the dark thoughts as they entered the library; he had other days in which to dwell on his shortcomings.

Maggie stopped at a glass-encased directory, but Colin grabbed her hand and tugged her toward the elevator. "I know where we're going, remember?"

He led her to the elevator, told the waiting attendant, "Three," and upon their arrival took her down a long hallway to a doorway labeled California Room.

Maggie gasped in delight when she saw the size and scope of the destination, a huge room with a high, vaulted ceiling, lined with bound volumes. Computer terminals cataloged the library's holdings; in addition, extensive card files held further references. A separate, dimly lit room held microfilm readers and metal file cabinets full of California newspapers on microfilm, some dating back to the early days of Spanish settlement.

She would have rubbed her hands together in glee, she realized, but for the fact she was still clutching Colin's. He toured her through the facility with a familiarity that made her ache for all that he'd lost. She guessed he hadn't been here since Lucy's death, and his obvious pleasure made her wonder why he'd made himself stay away for so long.

"So, where do we start?" he asked after their survey.

Here was her opportunity. "Oh, Colin, why don't you just do your own thing for a while?"

"But I'm supposed to be your research assistant," he protested. "We agreed."

No, *he* agreed, Maggie argued silently. To Colin she said, "I know, but there's so much stuff to look at here that I need to get myself situated before I can think of anything else." She offered him a placating smile. "So I'll just start digging around, okay?"

Colin looked as if he'd have liked to argue, but instead nodded his assent. "Okay, but you speak up if you want me to do anything. *Anything,*" he repeated sternly.

Eager to send him on his pursuit, and equally impatient to begin her own research, Maggie promised and shooed him off before she settled in front of a computer terminal and typed in a command.

Hours later she arched her back, stretching her arms overhead to relieve the tension in her shoulders. Research was physically harder than one would guess; muscles tensed from sitting in one position too long, eyes ached from straining to read tiny print.

Colin hadn't come looking for her once, she realized with pleasure. Thinking of him as absorbed in his research as she was in hers gave her a heady feeling of accomplishment. She'd had the right idea inviting him along.

When she saw him coming toward her across the long room, her heart gave a little jump. He looked excited, as if he couldn't wait to tell her about the sheaf of papers he carried in one hand. As his eyes met hers he raised the bundle with a triumphant flourish.

"You wouldn't believe all that I've found!"

"Shh!" a nearby patron warned, eyeing them reprovingly.

Maggie waited until Colin was beside her before she whispered, "What?"

He dropped the stack in front of her and leaned over her from behind, his arms bracketing her. "Look at all this."

For a moment, Maggie was too overwhelmed by the sense of being surrounded by Colin to do anything. She inhaled his fresh masculine scent and fought the urge to incline her head slightly and rest her temple against his jaw.

"Isn't it something?"

"What is all this?" she asked, riffling the stack of papers.

"All the newspaper references to the Groshes I could find."

She couldn't believe it. She fought for words. "Oh, my," was all she could manage in the end.

"There's quite a bit of material there, spanning for the most part about the twenty-five-year period immediately following their deaths, when their father was trying to establish his right to the Comstock claim."

"Oh, my," she repeated.

"Maggie—" he started, but she interrupted.

"Just give me a moment, Colin. Please."

He shut up.

Conflicting emotions, excitement and frustration, warred inside her, each fighting for expression.

When she'd seen Colin's animated expression, she'd been certain he'd found some inspiration, some catalyst of his own. To discover that he'd spent the day studying newspapers for her was a tremendous setback.

"I thought you'd be pleased." His voice held puzzlement, dismay even. Maggie looked up at him and saw the doubt on his face.

"Oh, no, Colin," she rushed to say. "I'm honestly speechless. I never expected you to find all this." That, at least, was the truth. She'd been so sure he would find his own diversions....

But it wouldn't do to hurt his feelings, not when he'd done so much. "You've done quite a bit of work, Colin. Thank you." She forced a smile. "I can't wait to start going through all this."

A muffled gong sounded just then, followed by an announcement that the library would close for the day in fifteen minutes.

Maggie stared at her watch. "I can't believe we've been here since ten, and it's already quarter to five."

"Time flies when you're having fun," Colin quipped.

Maggie studied him seriously. "Did you, Colin? Did you really have fun?" She needed to know.

"Yes, Maggie. I did."

Well, it was a start. If he'd gotten so much pleasure researching for her, perhaps creating his own work wouldn't be too far behind.

Buoyed by that thought, Maggie stood and gathered her materials. "I just realized why I'm starving. We haven't had a thing since breakfast. Let's grab some dinner before we head back to Reno."

Colin was still eyeing her quizzically, but merely nodded his agreement and followed her out the door.

Even as her feet kept a steady pace, Maggie's mind raced ahead. She wasn't a good enough actress to fool him if he persisted in questioning her reaction to his research; she'd just have to keep the dinner conversation steered in a different direction.

That shouldn't be too hard, she concluded. With a little luck, he'd forget all about it before they were done with their appetizers.

Chapter Five

"So, what happens now?" Colin asked.

They were seated in a narrow restaurant near the Capitol, the kind of place frequented twenty years earlier by lawmakers and lobbyists—dim and cozy, lined with red leather booths. The bartender at the immense mahogany bar probably still knew how to make a decent martini.

The menu certainly hadn't changed at all in those twenty years—steaks and chops dominated, with a daily fresh fish the only concession to California's nouvelle cuisine. The restaurant was one of Colin's favorite places, and normally, after such a prolonged absence, he would have been delighted to find himself dining there once again.

But he had other, more important things to think about right now. Like trying to figure out what was going on in Maggie's pretty head.

He didn't understand her reaction to his work today. He had thought she would be thrilled with all the material he'd found for her, in fact, he'd thought it was the point of his coming to Sacramento with her. Hadn't they discussed his playing research assistant only days ago?

And he'd probably dug up every reference available from every two-bit mother lode newspaper and broadsheet in the library. It added up to a wealth of material for her to work with.

Maggie had attributed her reaction to speechlessness, but Colin could tell that it was something more. Something akin to disappointment had been written on her face before she'd recovered her bearings and thanked him prettily for his assistance.

And she'd been quiet, preoccupied, on the way to dinner. He couldn't ascribe that to exhaustion alone. True, they were both tired, both feeling the effects of working for seven nonstop hours, but he could almost feel her holding something back from him.

While the prospect of a long drive home after such a day might have bothered him another time, he found himself looking forward to having Maggie as captive audience tonight. He'd find out just what she'd been thinking, just why his work had so obviously displeased her.

Meanwhile, she was answering his question. "Now I can really start what I like to call my treasure hunt," she said, leaning forward and absently toying with the handle of her coffee cup. "I've got tons of information now, so I'll spend the next few days sifting through it, sorting it into groups and topics. Some of it will be just what I'm looking for, and some of it will probably send me back to one library or another to find something else, some other piece."

She paused and took a sip of coffee. "It's like searching for buried treasure—you take a clue and try to decipher it. If you do it right, you're one step closer to your reward. If you take the wrong path, it may take you a while to backtrack and find your way."

"Buried treasure," Colin said, considering her words. "I like the analogy."

"I came up with it years ago to explain to my brothers why I was wasting my time reading books, instead of doing something important, like perfecting my roller-hockey technique. They're all very literal, so they needed that sort of concrete example in order to understand."

"Your brothers aren't scholars, then?" Colin felt as if he were on his own treasure hunt.

Maggie snorted. "Not hardly. All three of them got through high school by charming the Sisters and being good football players. They're bright, but 'unmotivated,' as we say in the education business. They thought I was a changeling."

"And your parents?"

"What one would call 'salt of the earth.' Pop's a police officer—" She responded to his knowing grin with one of her own. "Yeah, I know, Boston, Irish, cop—it's too clichéd for words, isn't it?"

The waiter arrived with their entrées, and Maggie attacked her lamb chops before continuing. "My mom believes, to this day, in cooking meat until she has personally ensured that it's dead." She waved the bit of meat on her fork for emphasis. "She couldn't allow lamb to be served this rare if her life depended on it. She's very traditional, home and hearth and all that sort of thing."

She painted a picture very different from the one he'd imagined. "So how did they get you?"

"Heck if I know. God knows they've probably asked themselves the same thing more than once. I've always thought the changeling theory had a certain amount of charm." Her shrug was nonchalant, her voice told of the strain of being different, of not fitting in their narrow world.

Colin remembered the photos. "But you love them."

"And they love me," Maggie said fiercely. "I may be a changeling, but I'm their changeling."

They both laughed then, and Colin paused his interrogation so they could eat. The more he knew about her, the more he wanted to know. He found it difficult to refrain from asking for her entire life story, but Maggie was too cautious to spill it all at one time.

Not that he was exactly forthcoming with the details of his own life. So far, Maggie had respected the "off-limits" signs he'd posted in certain areas—Lucy, work, the past— but if their relationship continued, or *as* their relationship continued, he mentally corrected, she'd want, and deserve more.

And what could he tell her? That he'd been a selfish, preoccupied husband who might as well have driven his wife off that precipice? That he'd so immersed himself with his precious work that he and Lucy had evolved into virtual strangers by the end of her life? That he would live every day of his life knowing that if he'd been a better husband, Lucy might have died a happier woman? That he'd only felt guilt, and not grief, at her death?

Yeah, she'd love to hear those things about him. That would ensure the relationship would go no further before she went back East. Hell, she'd probably pack up and head home early, just to put the continent between them.

"Is something wrong with your steak?" Maggie's voice broke into his dark thoughts. "You're not eating, Colin. You should be starved."

Colin forced a smile, and shook his head. "No, nothing is wrong. It's just that sometimes my mind wanders.

Lucy used to hate that." He held his breath, awaiting her disapproving response.

"You, too?" Her cornflower eyes widened in amazement. "When I get working on something, I have a one-track mind. It drove my folks crazy when I lived at home. I was so happy to move into my own place, where I could immerse myself in my work for days if I wanted."

Colin consciously unclenched his tightened muscles and picked up his fork. She understood. Imagine that.

Maggie chatted on through the rest of dinner about the work she'd done, and what lay ahead. If she expected more than the occasional "Really?" in response, she gave no indication of any annoyance.

As they headed for the car, Colin still hadn't figured out the best way to ask her why she'd been so disappointed by his discoveries. He was contemplating the finesse route—he'd wait until she was nice and relaxed, maybe an hour or so into their drive home, and slide into the subject. She wouldn't have adequate warning to come up with another half-baked excuse about speechlessness. Yes, that was the best way—he'd take the subtle approach.

When they reached the car he took sweatshirts out of the trunk for both of them. "Here, it's bound to be a little chilly on the drive home."

"Thanks." Maggie pulled the sweatshirt over her head, and Colin almost laughed at the picture she made. The sleeves stretched past her fingertips, and the hem hung past her slender hips, hiding their curves completely.

Maggie looked down and chuckled. "When I was a kid I used to swipe Brendan's sweaters. They fit me about like this, big and cozy. I feel quite protected."

"That's me," Colin said. "A protective kind of guy." Although at that particular moment he felt more like the guy she should be watching out for.

Maggie cocked her head to one side and studied him for a long moment before she spoke. "You are, Colin, whether you realize it or not. You're very protective—nurturing, caring—whatever you choose to call it."

She opened her car door and slid in, pausing to pull her baseball cap from her tote bag and tuck her hair up underneath it. "I appreciate everything you've done for me today. You've been a real sweetheart. This cap, coming with me, doing my research . . ."

Ah, her research. So much for finesse. Colin shut her door and leaned over, resting his crossed forearms against the frame. He was close enough to taste the hint of coffee on her breath, see the slight widening of her pupils as he drew closer.

"Ah, yes, Maggie, your research... Tell me, won't you, why I got the distinct impression you didn't want me doing any of your research for you today."

She drew back into the seat, but not far enough to escape his probing gaze. "It wasn't like that, Colin—" she began, but he cut her off.

"When I brought you those papers, your surprise wasn't that I found so much information, but that I was working on the Groshes at all, right?"

Maggie sighed, her breath warming his face. "Why don't you get in the car, Colin?" she suggested. "We can discuss this on the way home."

He smiled, feeling a little wicked now. "Oh, I don't know, Maggie. I kind of like having you pinned here, sort of at my mercy."

Closing her eyes, Maggie counted almost inaudibly to ten. Only the little puffs of air escaping her parted lips told Colin what she was doing. Then she looked him straight in the eye, and said, with more asperity than Colin would have expected at that moment, "Let's hit the road, Colin.

I assure you, sharing a car for two hours will have me equally at your mercy, and I'd like to get home sometime tonight."

She fixed him with an unblinking stare. Colin resisted the urge to cry "Bravo," and merely straightened, walked around the car and got behind the wheel.

He didn't look at her again while he drove toward the freeway, didn't say another word until they'd left the lights of Sacramento behind them and were ascending into the Sierra foothills.

Maggie spoke first, her voice soft, low, rushed. "I didn't mean to upset you. I thought that if you were with me while I was working, you wouldn't be able to help it—you'd start doing research of your own."

"I beg your pardon?" Colin made a halfhearted attempt to keep the incredulity from his voice. Surely she couldn't be saying what he thought she was saying.

"I think you want to write again, Colin. I know it's in you, that you just need the right story."

He *had* heard her right. He just didn't believe it. "Let me be sure I understand you. You've appointed yourself a one-woman committee to get C. J. McCall writing again?"

"Well, when you put it like that . . ."

He turned and stared at her.

"Well, sort of," she finished lamely.

Colin shook his head. "Maggie, sweetheart. No offense—you're a brilliant woman—but that's the stupidest thing I've ever heard."

Maggie bristled at his less-than-tactful words. "I think that's going a little far, don't you?"

"Not at all. Unless you want to call it the most egocentric, rather than stupid," he countered.

Ouch. A direct hit. Maggie sank lower in her seat, recalling her fantasy of his next book, dedicated to her. "No, let's go with stupid," she said with a sigh.

"You want to explain it to me?"

"Why don't I apologize and we'll drop it," she suggested, without much hope.

"No, I don't think so. It's a long drive, and I could use the entertainment." His stiff voice told her he wasn't as amused as his words suggested.

She tipped her head back against the seat, searching for words in the blanket of stars hanging above them.

When she'd driven from Boston to Reno at the end of June, she'd been entranced, awed even, by the sheer number of stars visible in the rural sky. Since then, she'd left the neon lights of Reno any number of times to recapture that experience, and it never failed to inspire her.

Until now.

The heavens revealed no secrets to her, showed her no way to distract Colin from his dogged determination to understand her questionable scheme.

Even without looking at him, she could sense his growing impatience. Still, he drove on, silent, waiting.

"It isn't what you think, you know," she burst out at last, unable to endure his unspoken criticism.

He cocked an eyebrow in reply. "And what am I thinking?"

Maggie replied before she lost the little resolve she possessed. "That I care more about C. J. McCall than Colin McCallum."

A noncommittal snort was Colin's only comment, but it told Maggie she was on the right track. She scanned her mind for the right words, the right way to explain how she felt about him and his work.

"I care about you, Colin, I really do."

Silence.

"And because I care, I worry. You seem a little—" she paused, her mind unable to summon the appropriate word "—lost," she finished lamely.

Again, he made no reply.

"Help me out here, Colin," she pleaded after what seemed like an eternity.

"Oh, I think you're doing fine," he replied.

"Oh, hell, Colin," she snapped at last. "I'm sorry if I stepped on your precious toes, but I can't imagine what kind of relationship you expect us to have when whole areas of your life are off-limits."

"True enough."

She was on a roll now, and continued as if he hadn't spoken. "So I think you should write again. That doesn't make me a bad person."

"I never said you were a bad person, Maggie."

"But you're angry."

Another snort.

"And you feel betrayed."

"Uh-huh."

"But I only want what's best for you."

Colin laughed then, a rich, rolling sound entirely at odds with his stern demeanor. "Maggie, you would not believe how many people have wanted what they imagined to be best for me over the past couple of years. Only, it's funny. Their definition of 'what's best' hardly ever matches mine."

Maggie felt as though she'd been slapped. He was laughing! Here she'd had the best of intentions, the best of all motives, and he found them funny. She didn't deserve this.

He tapped her chin lightly with a closed fist. "Come on, Professor, lighten up. You've got to admit, it's pretty funny. I can see the headlines—'Boston Woman Inspires C. J. McCall to Create Again.' Just think, you could make the cover of *The Tattler*.''

Maggie pulled the brim of her cap lower, grateful for the cocoon of darkness surrounding them, hiding her crimson face. "You're not being fair, Colin. I'm not about to go running to some sleazy tabloid with your story."

"No, of course not. But you'll have to forgive me if I'm a little suspicious of your motives. Nobody wants to help me out just because I'm such a great guy. There's usually something else going on."

If not for the warm breeze ruffling the treetops and swooping over the windshield to caress her skin, the next half hour would have been silent. Colin was lost in his thoughts while Maggie tried to come to terms with what he'd said, and hadn't said.

People had used him in the past. That much was obvious. He'd spoken of it so easily, so casually, but it had to pain him a great deal. Was she one of those users? Did she want him to write again so she could claim she knew him when? Maggie sighed and settled back into her seat to think about her own motivations.

When Colin spoke again, his question, delivered in an oh, so casual tone, wasn't at all the one Maggie had thought he'd ask her.

"Just why is it so important to you that I write again, Maggie?"

It wasn't one she'd fully answered, either. She said the first thing to come to mind, almost flinching at its inanity.

"Because you're a wonderful writer, Colin. You have so much talent, so much to say."

Unfortunately, Colin wouldn't allow himself to be put off with such silliness.

"But what if it's not there anymore?" he said gravely.

"That's not possible!"

"But it might be."

"No, it's not." It couldn't be. "You're just blocked."

An exasperated shake of his head punctuated his reply. "Maggie, writer's block lasts a couple of hours, or a couple of days. This is a little bit bigger than that."

"So what is it?"

He was silent for a long time before he answered. "The stories are gone."

She waited for him to continue, to explain. He didn't.

"Do you suppose you could enlarge on that for me?"

Colin sighed, a ragged sound that blended into the night wind. "What I mean, Maggie, is that whatever was inside me when I was writing has vanished. I had a compulsion to create from the time I picked up my first crayon, and that compulsion is gone."

"But why?"

"A lot of reasons. Maybe it was the pressure I put on myself to produce a book a year—a *good* book a year," he stressed. "I was working myself into a major case of burnout when Lucy died, and I suppose her death sort of brought things to a head."

He stopped then, but Maggie filled in the blanks. The grieving widower, the inspirational light of his life extinguished.

But that didn't explain now. He seemed, if his pursuit of her was any indication, to be recovering from his loss.

"Are you still mourning Lucy?"

The smile he sent her was sad, ironic. He shook his head slowly. "No, Maggie, I'm not."

Maggie twisted in her seat to face him. "You're not grieving, you've certainly had rest to recover from what you call burnout—what's stopping you?"

He shook his head again. "When I write—*wrote*—" he corrected "—the stories came from my heart. Every word came from my soul, and my soul is empty. The words are simply no longer there."

His voice reminded her of that first phone conversation they'd had, when he'd told her Lucy was gone. Empty, hollow, aching. Making her want to comfort and run, all at the same time.

For once, it seemed, Colin was being completely honest with her. No cryptic notions, no cynical observations, no sidestepping her questions. He was really trying to be open with her, to explain his feelings to her.

She felt flattered, warmed by his trust, closer to him than she'd ever been.

And she didn't understand him at all.

Maggie spent the next few days trying to make some sense of what Colin had told her. His words dominated her days, disrupted her sleep with vivid dreams of desolation and blank pages. His voice echoed through her mind—sad, empty, final.

He mourned his loss, but had come to some sort of peace, some sort of acceptance, at least until she'd come along and interfered with his life, stirred things up with her questions, her ideas.

And that situation left her with a dilemma. Should she continue to see him, or gracefully exit his life, allowing him to recover at his own pace?

She was...fond of him. They shared interests, enjoyed each other's company and generally got along quite well. She would only be in Nevada another six weeks; if she put her mind to it, she could probably keep her mouth shut about C. J. McCall for that length of time. It wouldn't be easy, but she could if she had to.

But their relationship was going to end at the end of the summer anyway, so ending it now would just move up the inevitable. If they stopped seeing each other, then there would be nothing messy to tie up in September. No recriminations, no emotional upheaval. No worrying about saying the wrong thing to him, or wanting more from the relationship than they could have.

Besides, she'd opened a Pandora's box with her probing, her plotting, her outspoken desire for him to be what he once was. Why should he ever trust her again?

Adding to her confusion was her weekly phone call from her mother. Brigid Sullivan hadn't needed to directly address the possibility of Maggie getting sidetracked; she could be far more subtle than that.

"Your friend Edmund sent a lovely bouquet of flowers for my birthday, dear. He's such a nice man, and he misses you almost as much as we do."

Remember, you have commitments here in Boston.

"I certainly hope you're accomplishing all you set out to do this summer."

Remember why you're there.

"Someday, you'll look back on this summer as quite an adventure."

Remember, you're coming home in September.

Maggie stopped answering the phone after that. If it wasn't her mother calling, it was Colin, and she knew that his voice alone could sway her, tempting her to a course she might otherwise resist.

His messages made her miss him. Some were matter-of-fact: *"Hi, Maggie. Call me."* Others were curious: *"Maggie, you there? Are we not speaking?"*

So far today, he hadn't called. Maggie had made up her mind that when he did, she would express her concerns to him, and tell him of her midnight decision that they not see each other again. Surely he would understand. Shoot, he'd probably be grateful to her.

When the knock on her screen door sounded, she knew instantly who it was, even before his voice called, "Professor? You home?"

She'd missed his voice, she realized. When she listened to him on the answering machine, she could pretend a distance, but here, in person, his deep tenor could unstiffen her spine if she allowed it to.

Goodbye would have been much easier to handle over the telephone, she acknowledged as she eyed his shadowed form through the screen. In person was going to be much tougher.

She invited him in, but remained seated at her computer, as if his visit would interrupt her work briefly at best, as if this were just another visit.

"Hi."

"Hi," she responded, not turning around. "Let me just finish this thought." As if all thoughts but those of Colin hadn't completely abandoned her. She typed in the command to save her file and swiveled her desk chair, facing him with a bright smile.

"So, what brings you down the mountain today?"

"Is your answering machine broken?"

Well, he certainly got right to the point. "No, Colin, I've been busy. I'm sorry I haven't—"

"I've always believed the ownership of a telephone answering machine carried with it the obligation to return calls."

"You're right, and I do apologize for my rudeness. But I've really—"

"Been avoiding me, right?"

Maggie closed her eyes for a moment. Maybe when she opened them again he wouldn't take up quite so much of her living room, use up so much of the available oxygen. Perhaps he would prove to be a fantastical illusion summoned by her overactive imagination.

No such luck.

"Yes," she said at last. "I needed some time to think about things." As explanations went, it was pretty weak, but it was the best she could come up with.

He nodded. "I figured as much. Trouble is, when you think too much, you make funny decisions."

"Is that 'you' a generic term, or are you referring specifically to me?"

He shrugged. "If the shoe fits..."

He was going to be difficult. The telephone would have been far easier, she thought regretfully.

She took a deep breath, trying to summon the perfect words.

"Colin, I've thought of little else but our situation for the past four days—"

"Probably talking with me would have helped."

"And I have come to the inescapable conclusion that the best, the only solution to our problem—"

"We don't have a problem."

"Is if we don't see each other anymore."

"See what I mean? Funny decisions."

This wasn't working. Colin's mouth was twitching.

"Colin, I'm serious. I'm obviously not good for you."

The twitching stopped. "What are you talking about?"

Maggie twisted her fingers together and pressed them against her abdomen to steady herself. "Colin, I don't like stirring things up. I hurt you, I can tell, and I don't like knowing that. I feel helpless."

He moved closer, until he towered above her seated form. She tipped her head up, and looked earnestly into his silver eyes, trying to memorize them for the time when he was gone.

"Colin, you're still recovering from Lucy. Whatever effect I have on you, it's temporary at best. I can't keep myself from asking about things that are none of my business, and I see what that does to you. When you talked about the stories being gone, you were so sad, and it was all my fault. And on top of it, I don't understand, so I can't help you. It seems futile to bring up all these hurts when whatever we might start here is ending in six weeks, anyway," she ended on a low sob. She bowed her head to collect herself.

Colin hunkered down beside her, and gently wiped the trickle of tears away with his thumbs.

"Maggie, I'm touched by your concern, really touched, but don't you think you're jumping the gun just a bit?"

Her head came up. "I don't understand."

"You've got us together and broken up and me with a busted heart, and we haven't even figured out where this thing is going yet. Why don't you let me make my own decisions on what I can handle right now?"

She shook her head and sniffed. "I'm not sure you can make a logical decision, Colin. I think my way is for the best, really."

"And if I don't agree?"

"Then you'll have to respect my decision."

"Or I could try to make you change your mind." He leaned closer.

"I really don't think this is a good idea, Colin," she said in a whisper.

"What? I can't hear you," he murmured.

"I said." She realized she was still whispering, and tried to raise her voice. "I said—"

Colin cut her off with his lips, his mouth absorbing whatever words she tried to utter. He didn't touch her in any way, other than the soft, gentle caress of his lips on hers. But still Maggie was ensnared, frozen, unable to pull away from him.

The kiss continued forever, yet somehow it ended too soon. He trailed his lips over her cheek to trace the delicate shell of her ear with his tongue, then traveled down her throat to explore the intriguing line of her collarbone. He moved back up her jawline to brush her lips again, softly, gently, persuasively.

He pulled back a fraction of an inch to whisper, "Do you want to give this up, Maggie?"

"Yes—I mean, no. I mean . . ."

"You don't know what you mean, Maggie. You think you need to do what's best for me and, sweetheart, that's the nicest thing a woman's ever offered me, believe it. But you're fighting yourself on this, Maggie, and I'll fight you, too. So you might as well forget it. It's two against one."

"Colin," she tried again, but he cut her off with another kiss.

"Maggie, you're afraid that you're hurting me, but the way I see it, I'm feeling something again, feeling alive in a way I haven't felt in the past two and a half years. Don't take that away from me."

His whispered plea spoke to her, made her look at their situation in a way she hadn't considered, and almost caused her to say an immediate "Yes." Some doubt must have still shown in her eyes, because Colin stopped her lips with a single warm finger across them, and said intently, "Please, think about it, at least. Think about what I've said."

Gazing at him, seeing the determination, the confidence on his face, made Maggie realize that she didn't need to debate the issue any longer. "It's all right, Colin. I don't need more time. If you can handle this, I won't try to second-guess you."

Chapter Six

Colin shifted gears and prepared to pass the slow-moving camper on the winding Mount Rose highway. Maggie sat beside him, half turned toward the Bronco's back seat to fondle an adoring Seally.

Steve and Devon Thorne's invitation to spend a few days with them at their Lake Tahoe home had come at an opportune time, Colin reflected. Maggie needed a break; her face bore the strain of too much work, of too many hours spent in libraries or in front of her computer.

More importantly, they needed to spend some time together, some time simply to get to know each other on a deeper level. She seemed to imagine him to be some sort of emotional basket case, and what better way for her to learn otherwise than a few days spent with lifelong friends who understood and tolerated every foible?

Not that it had been easy to persuade Maggie to go. She'd argued her work load; he'd reminded her about all work and the legendary Jack's fate. She argued the tenuous state of their relationship; he promised separate bedrooms and the buffer of other people. She argued the imposition; he told her that Steve and Devon couldn't wait to meet her.

When he'd discovered she'd never seen the world-famous lake, he'd filled her head with stories of the blue water and the legends surrounding its shores, and had finally threatened kidnapping if she didn't come willingly.

She'd given in at last, though he wasn't sure which of his arguments had worked. Maggie didn't give much away.

Which had made her revelations the other day all the more surprising. When she'd told him that her reasons for wanting to end their relationship had been based on concern for his well-being, he'd been floored, almost speechless.

People didn't worry about his comfort. It was assumed he could take care of himself, or that at least the earnings of C. J. McCall could. Maggie's simple act of caring was an utterly alien experience to him. He wasn't quite sure how to handle such a thing.

"How much longer?" the woman occupying his thoughts asked, and he turned to smile at her.

"We're almost to the summit. You'll be able to catch glimpses of the lake right after that."

Satisfied with his promise, she returned her attention to Seally, affording Colin the opportunity to study her without interruption.

As always, she looked wonderful. Her flowered sundress's thin straps bared her delicate shoulders to his gaze, and he'd bet money she wore no bra under its cotton bodice. Her firm breasts shifted with every move she made, eliciting a corresponding tightening of his loins.

She'd pulled her hair back into a clasp at the nape of her neck, and while Colin preferred it unbound and free flowing, he couldn't help admire the way this style accented her delicate bone structure, highlighting her sculpted cheekbones and almost pointed chin.

And he was going to be in trouble if he didn't get his mind off her physical appearance, he warned himself. He wasn't bringing her to Tahoe to seduce her, but to see if they could come closer to knowing each other.

This in itself was chancy. How much of himself did he care to reveal to her? She wouldn't settle for half-truths and evasions much longer, not if she bared even a portion of her soul to him.

Through the trees he caught a glimpse of azure water. "Look, the lake!"

By the time Maggie turned around, it was too late. The expression on her face was precious, like a kid who'd just lost her ice-cream cone.

"Don't worry. It's not going anywhere," he reassured her. "Just pay attention to the road, instead of my dog, and you'll see it before we're on it."

"The fact that I'm paying attention to your dog is the only reason she's not in the front seat with us," Maggie reminded him. "So don't knock it."

She gave as good as she got. That was his Maggie.

"Tell me about Steve and Devon," she continued, changing the subject. "You've known them forever, you said. Precisely how long is that?"

He laughed. Funny how much more of that he'd been doing since Maggie had driven into his life.

"Steve's parents and my parents are old and dear friends. He's two months older than me, so we really have known each other all our lives. Devon didn't come along until preschool. We were a bad imitation of the Three

Musketeers all through school, and somewhere along the way the two of them fell in love."

"So they've been together all that time. How sweet."

"No, not at all. They broke up during college, and both married other people. I stayed in touch with both of them, and since they never stopped asking about each other, I invited them up to the cabin for a weekend following their respective divorces."

"A little matchmaking?" Maggie suggested.

"Well, I'd neglected to tell either of them the other one was coming, or that Lucy and I would be in Los Angeles for a few days."

"Oh, Colin, you're an evil man."

He shrugged cheerfully. "Can't knock success. They've been married three years, and they're still speaking to me."

Maggie's chuckles subsided, and she studied him seriously. This was a whole side of Colin she hadn't seen before now. Maybe a weekend with his friends was a good idea. "So, you're a closet romantic, Colin."

"Not so closet, if you read my books."

"Oh, no, Colin," she disagreed. "Your books are very real, gritty, even tough. That's one of the things I enjoy most about them—you don't buy into some sugarcoated vision of the Old West."

She was sitting up now, blue eyes snapping, and Colin couldn't resist egging her on. "So you don't think romance and reality can coexist?"

The tendrils framing her face trembled as she shook her head. "It depends. Take my field, for instance. The revisionist interpretation of Western expansion says that it wasn't brave men taming a continent, but rather men *and* women of all ethnic persuasions who systematically plundered its resources."

Now they were getting into it. "Don't you think reality could be somewhere between that and the romantic vision?"

"What do you mean?"

Colin had started the discussion just to get her going, but somehow he was caught up in it, as well. "Allen and Hosea Grosh came out here with dreams of riches, yes, but certainly not with visions of raping the land."

"Of course not," she conceded. "And yes, if you break it down to individual cases, you see a different picture. But the result is the same, nonetheless. We cut down whole forests that will never be replaced, we gouged giant holes in the earth that will never be filled, we hunted the buffalo nearly into extinction—"

"And that's why I prefer to stick with those individual cases. It's too easy to look only at the big picture, and come up with some facile conclusions. For instance, those great gouges in the earth? The ones in Nevada and California financed the Union victory in the Civil War, enabling us to remain one nation."

And I'd better shut up, or Maggie's going to want to head back to Reno right now.

"Okay, I'm convinced, you're a romantic," Maggie assented cheerfully. "God, I'd love to get you into a faculty meeting sometime. You would set some of those pompous asses on their ears."

Colin was beginning to feel a tad self-conscious about his fervor. "Sorry. I got a little heated—"

"No, no, I love it. The fact that you're able to defend your position so eloquently makes it even better."

"But I stomped all over yours."

"Not at all. I called it the revisionist position, if you recall, not my position. I tend to side more with you."

She'd had him fooled. Of course, it had been a while since he'd had that kind of adrenaline-inducing, pulse-raising discussion. Probably since the last time he'd seen Steve and Devon, and that had been a year ago or more. There was something about seeing happily married people when you weren't too happy yourself...

Maggie's presence would make for some interesting discussion in the old hot tub, he decided. "Did you bring your swimsuit?" he asked abruptly.

"Now how did we get from romanticism versus reality in the West to my swimsuit?"

"Steve and I usually have this kind of argument in the hot tub late at night. You'll fit right in, provided you remembered your suit or are casual about that kind of thing." Not that he was; he just liked to try and get a rise out of her.

The only rise he got was of her eyebrows as she studied him in mock annoyance. "Colin, I remembered my suit. You must have reminded me three or four times over the past three days to bring it."

"Can I help it if I can't wait to see you in something skimpy?" he said with a deliberately comic leer.

She blushed. With her fair skin there was no disguising the rosy glow that spread from her cheeks to color her entire face.

"It's not skimpy. It's a one-piece," she said, looking resolutely out the window.

"Skimpy, my dear, is in the eye of the beholder."

When they arrived at Steve and Devon's lakefront home, the couple met them in the driveway with enthusiastic hugs and kisses for Colin, and welcoming smiles for Maggie.

"I thought we'd have lunch on the terrace," said Devon, a petite, effervescent blonde who rushed enthusiastically through her sentences, as if her words couldn't wait to escape. "Steve, why don't you show Colin the new boat, and Maggie can help me pull everything together."

Maggie felt an automatic stab of annoyance at being relegated to the kitchen, just like at Ma's, but as soon as the men left them, she realized Devon had an ulterior motive in getting her by herself.

"Now you just sit. There's really nothing for you to do except tell me all about how you met Colin. He was remarkably closemouthed when we spoke on the phone, other than to say he wanted to bring a friend along with him. We've been dying of curiosity."

Warmed by Devon's enthusiasm, Maggie related the story of her initial encounter with Seally, explaining her summer sojourn and how she and Colin shared an enthusiasm for Western life and lore.

"So you're only staying for the summer?" Devon echoed, disappointment written on her face. "Too bad. Colin could certainly use a woman like you in his life."

"A woman like me?"

"Oh, you know," Devon answered, waving a hand in her general direction. "Obviously intelligent and self-sufficient, sharing interests. Lucy was all wrong for him, I always thought."

Lucy. Maggie couldn't pass up the chance to learn something about Colin's late wife. "You knew her, then?"

Devon nodded. "Of course. Colin wasn't always so cut off, you know."

"What was she like? Colin doesn't say much about her, not directly, at least."

Devon considered for a moment before she spoke. "I have to admit I didn't have much use for Lucy, so anything I say is bound to be a little biased."

Maggie persisted. "If you don't mind, I think whatever you can tell me will help my relationship with Colin."

Removing a stack of plates from the cupboard, Devon placed them on a rattan tray before she spoke. "Lucy was a beautiful woman, very striking. She was tall, model slim, a platinum blonde—she and Colin looked stunning together."

Great. A gorgeous blonde. Did she really want to hear this? "How did they meet?" she asked anyway.

"At the wrap party for the television-movie version of *Rancho Real,* down in Los Angeles. Lucy was working as a model and actress, and had a walk-on part in the production. Even though her part was minuscule, she got invited to the party because the producer thought she would make him look good." She shook her head ruefully. "Sounds pretty silly to me, but then, I'm not the glamour type myself."

Maggie had to bite her tongue to keep from urging Devon to move the story along. It would come in its own time.

"Anyway," Devon continued, "it was head over heels at first sight. All of a sudden, Colin was making a lot of trips to L.A., which, of course, was distracting him from his work. I think he proposed so he could settle down and write again."

"And she said yes."

"She did. I was pretty surprised. She didn't seem the type for a cabin in the mountains. They got married at his parents' house in San Francisco. Have you been there yet?"

At Maggie's shake of the head, she nodded. "Well, you'll see it. The house is gorgeous, in Pacific Heights— very old San Francisco, very old money and it was a very high-society wedding. I'm sure Lucy thought she'd landed in clover."

"So what went wrong?"

"Oh, I think Lucy wanted to be Mrs. C. J. McCall, not Mrs. Colin McCallum. She never understood what being C. J. McCall entailed for Colin. When she found out it wasn't all glamour and parties, and that he liked living in the mountains, and that he worked awfully damn hard on his books, it came as a shock to her."

"If things were so bad, why did they stay married?"

"Colin's a very nurturing man, and Lucy was a very needy woman. The two of them settled into a routine."

Maggie couldn't stop a frown. "I still don't see it. Colin's too strong to settle for that kind of a life."

"The capper was when Lucy found out she couldn't have children. She was devastated."

"Hmm. No outside interests, no career, other than being Mrs. C. J. McCall. I can see how that would affect her."

"She stopped complaining so much after that. Like Colin would dump her or something."

"Do you think he wanted children?"

Devon paused to consider the question, arranging and rearranging the flatware on the waiting tray. "Well, he didn't want to bring them into a bad marriage, that's for sure. Before that, I think his attitude had been 'one of these days.' You know, the kind of thing you take for granted when you get married."

Maggie tried to picture a miniature Colin, and smiled at the image of a little towhead with silvery eyes and a slender build. Or a little girl with those eyes and her dark hair....

Stop that, she ordered herself.

"We'd better take this stuff out. The boys will be wondering where we are."

For an instant, Maggie envied Devon her lifelong knowledge and familiarity with "the boys." Oh, to know what motivated Colin, to know the secrets of his past.

Lunch, consisting of a spread of salads—from an exotic tabbouleh to an elegant seafood Louis—was a relaxed, casual affair. The Thornes' terrace overlooked the picturesque lake, providing a setting more exclusive than that of the most expensive restaurant in the area.

The company was equally impressive. While the "Three Musketeers" reveled in their longtime friendship, they took care not to exclude Maggie from any of the conversation, explaining inside jokes and long-ago events as necessary.

She learned that the Thornes were both attorneys in San Francisco, who managed their practices so they could spend at least three days a week at the lake. After occupying their twenties and thirties in search of professional rewards, they were now concentrating on less tangible, but more fulfilling goals, like making up for the fifteen-year gap in their relationship. They were openly grateful to Colin for his interference on their behalf.

After the meal, insisting the only way to tour the lake was by water, Steve suggested an afternoon's cruise on their ski boat.

Maggie went downstairs to change into her swimsuit and a covering pair of shorts, feeling no small amount of trepidation at the notion of Colin seeing her so scantily clad. How would she measure up next to his late wife, the stunning blond model?

Every forgotten doubt from adolescence sprang forth anew, and she had to rebuke herself sharply before she could turn the knob and exit her room.

Colin, awaiting her on the terrace in shorts and a T-shirt, could have been reading her mind. "Hmm, I knew I'd like skimpy," he murmured, bestowing a warm kiss on her bare shoulder. "Dibs on your back."

"I beg your pardon?" she asked, absently running her fingertips over the spot his lips had branded.

"I get to be the one to put lotion on that luscious skin," he explained. "I'd be happy to do the parts you can reach, too."

His praise banished her self-doubts. Of course, he didn't look bad himself. His T-shirt, though loose fitting, draped over well-defined muscles, and the shorts he wore revealed well-toned thighs and calves. His daily run obviously did him some good.

They joined Devon and Steve at the boathouse, and after a minimum of preparations, lowered the boat into the water and were on their way.

Colin made good his promise to cover her back with sunscreen. The touch of his slightly callused hand against her smooth skin sent shivers playing across her shoulder blades. "Cold?" he inquired politely, the gleam in his eye telling her he knew perfectly well why she trembled.

It was a perfect afternoon for boating, crystal clear and hot, the water's spray cooling them as they bounced along the lake's surface. Colin, Steve and Devon had agreed that Maggie had to see Emerald Bay, so they headed south from the house at the very northern tip of the lake.

Steve, as lanky as Devon was petite, played tour guide, ably steering the boat and pointing out landmarks as they rode along.

Thick, lush evergreen forests tumbled down the surrounding mountains, ending just short of the lake itself. Steve explained that these wooded groves hid some of the most expensive and exclusive of Lake Tahoe's properties.

As they neared a promontory he identified as Rubicon Point, the atmosphere changed dramatically. The air temperature dropped a good five degrees, and Maggie shivered in awe as the water changed from a pale azure to an intense blue-black.

"What happened?"

"I love to bring people through here," Steve answered. "Rubicon is the deepest point along Tahoe's shoreline. It's a little over fourteen hundred feet here, and Mother Nature wants to be sure we notice it."

Even as they spoke, they rounded the promontory and moved into lighter, warmer waters. Maggie twisted her head to stare back at the indigo depths.

"Amazing," she concluded. "It's so dramatic."

"And wait until you see the bay," Devon enthused. "It's the most wonderful place on the lake."

As they navigated the curve into the bay, Steve cut the engine back and they drifted slowly into the vivid blue-green waters, a reflection of the surrounding pine forest.

"I could give you the whole geologic explanation of how the glaciers carved this out, but I find most people don't really care," Steve said wryly.

"You're right, I don't," Maggie whispered, and for a few moments, the only sound was the slap of waves against the boat's hull.

The bay was as enchanting as promised. Encircled by steep, forested hillsides, sheltered from the lake's breezes, it was an intimate, tranquil respite from the hustle of speedboats and cruisers on the lake itself.

Rising from the center of the tiny cove was an even tinier island, crowned by what appeared to be a miniature stone house. Indeed, the only contrast to this Lilliputian scale was the massive Scandinavian house, Vikingsholm, dominating the end of the bay.

"Do you want to go see it?" Devon asked. "They'll let us dock if we want to."

"I vote no," Colin answered before Maggie could speak, resting his feet on the side of the boat. "I, for one, am too relaxed to fight tourists." He slipped an arm around Maggie's shoulder and pulled her close. "Okay with you?"

Maggie agreed that she was perfectly comfortable, and they opted not to stop, drifting around the island. A speedboat hurtled past them, rocking their craft in its wake and sending water spraying.

"Damn hotshots," Steve grumbled. "The speed limit here is fifteen knots, but there's always one boat to pull a stunt like that. They should leave it on the lake."

"Now, sweetheart, don't let it bother you," Devon soothed, rubbing his shoulders. He reached up to squeeze her hand, and Maggie caught the silent communication.

"It's always been like that between them," Colin murmured into her ear, sending a delicate tremor down her spine. "He blusters, she calms. They were made for each other."

And yet it had taken them years to discover that, Maggie recalled. How did couples make their relationship work if they weren't so obviously "made for each other"? Goodness knows, she'd never been able to sustain one long-term relationship, but she'd always blamed it on not meeting the right man. Perhaps there was more to it.

Not that Colin had "right man" potential, she reminded herself. Between his past and her plans, it looked as though there were too many obstacles in their future to even consider putting him in that category.

"What's wrong?" murmured Colin, giving her neck an affectionate squeeze.

Maggie started to equivocate, but thought better of it. "I was just contemplating the hoops couples jump through to stay together."

"You make it sound as though it's an impossible task," he objected.

"Sometimes I think it is," she countered.

"Oh, that's not true at all." Devon leapt into the conversation. "Look at Steve and me. We've been through an awful lot, but we're together now, which is all that matters in the end."

"But you were apart for a lot of years, and if Colin hadn't pulled his stunt—"

"If Colin hadn't pulled his stunt, it might have taken us a little longer, but I truly believe that Steve and I were meant to be together," Devon replied.

"If Colin hadn't pulled his stunt," Steve corrected, "it would have taken us a *lot* longer, because we're two of the most stubborn people on the planet."

The discussion continued back at the house through a dinner of grilled fish and salad, and into the promised assembly in the hot tub overlooking the dark expanse of the lake. Steve took the position that one made sacrifices to sustain a relationship; Devon, sitting on the side of the tub and dangling her legs in the water, said that when love was involved, there was no sacrifice entailed, but rather a matter of setting priorities. Colin argued that Devon's notion was a semantic distinction at best, and Maggie sat and absorbed the words and emotions flying around her.

Colin was right, she concluded mentally. Calling it "setting priorities" shrouded the fact that choices had to be made, that both parties couldn't have things the way they wanted them to be.

"So, what do you think, Maggie?" Devon turned the focus of the conversation to her. "What will happen in the fall? What are your priorities?"

"Devon, that's not fair," Steve objected, but Colin interrupted.

"No, I'd like to hear Maggie's answer."

"Only if we get to hear yours, too," she countered, bargaining for time to come up with an answer, as well as for Colin's opinion.

"No problem. I'll go first, even." Colin took a sip of his wine before he continued. "I think," he paused dramatically, "that Maggie will go back to Boston and miss me terribly, and I'll miss her, too. She's got a sabbatical coming in January, so she can come back here for a few months, until the spring quarter begins. After that, we'll do the long-distance relationship thing for as long as we can—I'll visit her, she'll visit me and we'll see if she gets tenure."

Wow. Colin had thought this relationship much farther along than she would have imagined. She wouldn't have dared to project so far into the future, not with her book and tenure riding in the balance.

"And what if she gets tenure?" Steve persisted.

"We'll cross that bridge when we come to it."

Steve looked to Maggie. "Your turn."

Unwilling to commit herself as far as Colin had, but not wanting to embarrass him in the process, she strove for a neutral answer. "I think we'll have to see where we are at the end of the summer."

It worked. The others respected her unspoken wish to avoid the emotionally charged issue, and the conversation shifted to less serious subjects.

When a decent interval had passed, Maggie stepped out of the tub and grabbed her towel. "I don't know about you guys, but I'm beginning to feel like a prune."

"Wimp," Colin said playfully, splashing water onto her feet.

"Hey, I haven't had the years of training you've had." She crouched at the edge of the tub and splashed him back before rising and wrapping the towel saronglike around her torso. "It's bedtime for me. If we're going hiking tomorrow, I need my rest."

"I'll be down in a few minutes." Colin's words held a careless promise Maggie had no wish to address.

"Makes no never mind to me, as long as I get the shower first." She trotted off, eager to be out of the shared bathroom before Colin came downstairs.

Standing under the shower's hot spray, she visualized her tensions washing down the drain, and felt herself slowly relaxing.

Colin's semirosy view of their future together had surprised her, had shaken her even. How he could predict such a hopeful future when they hadn't even gotten the present straight was beyond her. She couldn't see that far ahead, no matter how she looked at it.

She felt a little funny too, that he was sharing his optimism with Devon and Steve.

Not that Devon and Steve weren't wonderful people. Warm, open and caring, they exuded the kind of love any couple would envy. Maybe that was part of her problem. It was difficult comparing your life to paragons like that; you always came up lacking. Perhaps tomorrow she'd discover some flaw, some chink to indicate that their relationship wasn't absolutely perfect, either.

While she dried off, she could hear Colin moving around the adjoining bedroom. Though he'd come through with his promise of separate rooms, she couldn't say she was completely satisfied with the arrangement, since their bedrooms shared a bath located between them. It would be altogether too easy for Colin to slip into her room on whatever pretext, and between the relaxation of being on vacation and the vision of Colin in his swim trunks, she was feeling a little too close to seduceable this evening. It wouldn't take much of an effort on his part to put her over the edge.

A knock sounded on the door. "You almost done in there, Professor?"

She hurriedly pulled her Patriots jersey over her head, calling, "I'll be out in just a minute!" Grabbing her brush, she opened the door to her room and called over her shoulder, "It's all yours," and slipped out before he could reply.

Climbing into bed, she attacked her toweled hair with a wide-tooth comb, resolutely ignoring the sound of the shower in the next room. She tried, without success, to ignore the image of a naked Colin standing under the running water, his skin shiny and slick, the hair on his chest sleeked by the spray, dark, smooth, narrowing to a pencil-thin point at the waist. But that point wouldn't disappear into swimming trunks as it had in the hot tub.

He'd caught her staring, of course. And had been amused. And hadn't, thank goodness, said a word in Steve and Devon's presence.

Clothed, he had a fine figure, but bare chested . . . well, he was simply magnificent. Obviously, the exercise room in his home didn't go to waste. He had the kind of well-muscled, well-shaped form other men wished for.

Another knock. "Maggie, may I come in?"

She'd been half expecting him to come to her, even though she had no idea how she was going to handle it. *Here goes,* she thought, steeling herself.

"Sure," she replied, her voice cracking just a bit.

Colin strode in, naked but for the towel wrapped carelessly around his waist. He was combing his wet hair as he came across the room, and Maggie could only watch, her mouth suddenly parched.

"We didn't say good night," he said in a low, intimate voice, sitting down on the bed beside her.

Drops of water glistened on his tan skin, begging Maggie to lick them up. The hair on his chest was just beginning to fluff up, begging her to lace her fingers into it and explore the muscled contours underneath. She recognized the scent of the soap she'd used; it smelled different on him—masculine and enticing.

She swallowed, and touched her lower lip with the tip of her tongue to moisten it. Before she could say anything, Colin whispered, "Ah, Maggie, that's not playing fair."

He lowered his head oh, so slowly, as if giving her an opportunity to pull away. As he came closer, she noticed his silvery eyes had flecks of darker color in them. The tiny laugh lines around those eyes disappeared as she closed her own in anticipation of his kiss.

He didn't disappoint her. His warm, hungry mouth engulfed her, overwhelming her, devouring her. It wouldn't settle for a passive response. It demanded her full participation, nothing less than a complete and total engagement, an absolute and honest reaction.

She gave him that response. She opened her mouth under his, her tongue joining his in an intimate dance that left them both impatient for more. She touched his smooth shoulders, slid her hands onto his hair-roughened chest, burying her fingers in the surprisingly soft, surprisingly crisp pelt.

He bracketed her face with his palms, turning her head one way, then another, altering the kiss with every movement, first pressing deeper, then pulling back to plant warm, wet kisses all over her face. His hands slid down her torso to fondle her waiting breasts, finding her nipples hard through her shirt, making them more so with his touch. He teased them, lightly brushing the tips with his thumbs before succumbing to their invitation and rolling them between thumb and forefinger.

He lowered his head to her left breast, pulled the aching point into his mouth, and wet it through her jersey. Maggie let out a moan, shocking herself with its intensity, but she was too far-gone to protest. When he lifted his head, she guided it to her other breast, pleading silently for the same relief.

His movement gradually slowed, and he trailed his mouth back up to hers, pressing kisses the entire journey. The motions of his hands soothed now, rather than aroused, and slowly he pulled back just far enough to look at her.

Maggie became aware of the sound of their heavy breathing, of the tingle of breasts heavy with desire, of her own heady abandon.

Before she could react to these intense emotions, Colin ordered, "Don't," caressing her flushed check with a rough thumb. "I really didn't bring you here to seduce you, Maggie," he whispered. "And although there's nothing I'd like to do more at this moment, I believe I'll do the noble thing and go back to my room. Good night." He brushed a kiss across her forehead, and left her alone.

Great, Maggie thought dumbly. Just when she was ready to throw caution to the wind, the man had to turn into a gentleman. What absolutely, positively, utterly rotten timing.

Maggie... issued a cheery... good morning... to really... to the table... and side to back who... He... When he grumbled... helping... simply true... morning.

Chapter Seven

When Maggie planted a firm kiss on his lips and issued a cheery "Good morning" to the table at large, Colin didn't know whether to be more surprised or outraged. *She* didn't look as though she'd lost any sleep last night. *She* obviously hadn't spent the night pitting conscience against libido. *Her* meager slumber hadn't been filled with vivid dreams of their bodies twisting, touching, loving.

"Can I get anyone anything?" the object of his resentment asked, helping herself to coffee from a thermal carafe on the sideboard.

"More coffee," he grumbled, and held out his cup.

"Oh, did we wake up on the wrong side of the bed this morning?" she inquired sweetly, ruffling his hair as she filled his cup.

"*We* certainly did." He emphasized the first word. If they had awakened in the same bed, there would have been no wrong side. "You're supposed to be grumpy. I'm the morning person, remember?"

Maggie waved a hand airily. "Must be something in this mountain air. I feel great." She shot him a triumphant smile and turned to Steve and Devon, who were watching the scene in open amusement.

"So, what's wrong with him?" she asked, cocking her head in Colin's direction. "And more importantly, will he get over it before we go hiking?"

"I'm not sure," Steve considered seriously. "The last time I saw him like this was after my bachelor party before my first marriage. Then, at least, he could blame it on one heck of a hangover."

"Yeah, it was the same when Richard and I split up," Devon offered helpfully. "Colin helped me drown my sorrows, and we both felt pretty miserable the next day."

"Tsk, tsk. I had no idea this was part of his nature," Maggie murmured, shaking her head.

"Would you please stop talking about me as if I'm not in the room?" Colin burst out. "Those are the only two hangovers I've ever had in my life, thank you very much, so I'd appreciate it if the two of you wouldn't make me out to be a habitual drunkard."

"There, there," Maggie soothed, stroking his hand. "We all know that—we're just having a little fun at your expense. Why don't you tell me what I can do to make you feel better?"

Colin considered doing just that, but ultimately recalled the old saw about discretion and valor, and refrained. "Another cup of coffee, and I'll behave," he promised instead.

"Good boy." Maggie gave the back of his hand a final stroke before retrieving the carafe once again and refilling his cup. Back at the table, she took a muffin from the waiting basket and bit into it with gusto.

Forgetting his pique, Colin instead concentrated on the picture she made. It was good to see a woman eat like that. Too many ate as though they had to look like a runway model—no breasts, no behind, no shape.

Not Maggie's problem, Colin granted, recalling the previous evening. Her breasts had filled his hands perfectly....

"So, what's the plan?" she asked between bites. "Breakfast, then Squaw Mountain?"

Get your mind out of the gutter, McCallum, Colin ordered himself sternly. *Maggie's not going to want to spend the day with a man who's thinking solely with the southern portion of his anatomy.*

"Sounds fine to me," he managed. "Steve, Devon?"

"Um, we're going to pass, I'm afraid." Devon sounded a little hesitant.

"Oh, no. How come?" Maggie's voice betrayed disappointment. What, after last night she didn't want to be alone with him? Had he rushed things too much, pushed things too far?

"Yeah, why not?" he echoed.

"I'm afraid it's my fault," Devon explained. "I'm feeling a little—" she looked at Steve "—under the weather."

"Nothing serious, I hope." She didn't look ill, Colin thought. In fact, she looked positively glowing.

Devon and Steve exchanged glances again, and Colin could almost hear the silent "Should we tell them?" that passed between them. He figured it out.

"You're pregnant, aren't you?"

They both beamed, and Steve squeezed Devon's hand. "Yes, we are. After three years of practice, we got it right."

Colin suppressed the twinge of envy that hit his midsection. He'd always imagined he'd have kids, but now that he was forty, it seemed like more of a pipe dream....

Idiot. Steve and Devon were the same age, remember? It wasn't too late. For an instant, an image of a dark-haired little girl flitted through his mind.

He forced the thoughts aside, and joined Maggie in congratulating the couple. When they all calmed down, Devon explained that while she might be overreacting, she was feeling too cautious for a strenuous hike. "So I hope you don't mind if the two of us beg off."

"No, of course not. But we could skip the hike and do something less taxing, if you'd like," Maggie offered.

Steve and Devon exchanged glances once again, and Colin began to suspect a plot afoot. Well, turnabout was fair play, and he'd done a good job three years ago.

Maggie gave in with good grace, but the raised eyebrow she sent his way indicated she harbored similar suspicions.

"We'll tell you all about the hike," she promised.

Well, maybe not all, Colin amended silently.

"Wait, Colin," Maggie gasped. "I need to breathe." she stopped midpath and forced her lungs to take deep, slow breaths. Gradually she felt her heart rate drop from a gallop to a steady trot, still too fast, but she wasn't in imminent danger of collapsing anymore.

"Why didn't you tell me we were going too quickly?" Colin's tone echoed the concerned expression on his face. "We could have gone slower."

"I know. I didn't realize it myself until it caught up with me, all at once, on that last rise." Words came a little easier, now that she wasn't fighting for every last molecule of oxygen in the thinner air of the mountain.

"Do you want to stop?" Colin's worried look touched someplace deep inside Maggie, and her heart melted just a little more.

"No, actually, I think we can continue, as long as we take it slow." She squeezed his hand briefly, enjoying the momentary contact. "Come on, let's go."

It was another gorgeous day. *I could get very used to this,* Maggie conceded internally. It was worth taking a couple days off from her work to experience this beauty, for such a graphic reminder of the world outside the library.

An achingly blue sky hung overhead, wisps of angel-hair clouds punctuating its depth. In front of them, Squaw Mountain stretched upward, its green slopes dotted with bright wildflowers, and light snow dusting its peak.

Maggie turned and walked backward; not only did it give her already aching quadriceps a much needed respite, but it gave her a splendid look at the mountain below them.

Thank goodness they'd made the first half of the journey via the aerial tramway. She'd never have made it all the way up on foot.

"Tired again?" Though keeping to an easy pace, Colin evidently wasn't taking any chances.

"No," she was quick to reply. "I wanted to see the whole thing. What a view."

"It's even better from the top," he said smugly.

"If that was meant as a carrot, don't worry. I won't wimp out on you." She turned around again to walk beside him. "It's awfully hard to imagine this mountain in a blinding snowstorm, isn't it?"

"Not if you've lived through a good winter here, I assure you." He shook his head ruefully. "Our Grosh brothers wouldn't have been able to see the trail in front of them coming up this slope, much less the surrounding peaks for orientation. It's no wonder they headed up the wrong mountain."

"Which do you think it was, oh map reader mine?"

Colin pointed south to a much steeper peak. "I think it was that one, although I don't envy them the climb."

Despite the heat of the day, Maggie shuddered at the vision of the two men struggling up the ragged slope in a howling blizzard. "No, me neither. I feel like I'll barely make it up this hill."

Folding her hand in his, Colin made as if to pull Maggie along. "Don't worry about it, sweetheart. You're doing fine. I'm more used to this altitude. Remember, I run most days at six thousand feet."

His body showed it, too. He had runner's legs—long, lean, with sinewy muscles defining their form. His khaki shorts exposed enough of his tanned thighs to make Maggie itch to explore the sculpted mass, investigate the strong lines. Beside him she felt short, soft and hopelessly out of shape.

Still, she made it to the top of the mountain, where a stone memorial marked the crest of the Emigrant Road. Here the trail's remains were obscured; winter's ravages had erased the twin tracks of wagon wheels, and the passage of time had softened the evidence of men's journeys.

Despite this lack of physical reminders, despite the contemporary intrusions of ski lifts and tow bars, Maggie felt curiously in touch with the past. Maybe it was the pristine alpine meadow spreading out before them, untouched by modern man. Maybe it was the almost silent *tramp, tramp of* long-gone feet she sensed, the shudder and creak of wagon wheels straining to reach the summit.

Or maybe she'd been hanging around Colin too long, she thought wryly. She was starting to see ghosts everywhere.

"Why don't we head down the hill and find a spot to picnic?"

Abandoning her ghosts to their past, Maggie followed Colin partway down the slope to a green semisecluded bowl a little ways off the trail. They spread their blanket and opened their day packs before Maggie sprawled out with a heartfelt "Oof!"

"Here." Opening her eyes a crack, she discovered Colin wagging a bottle of mineral water above her head. When she made a halfhearted grab for it, he pulled the container just out of her reach. "Uh-uh."

"Sadist." With a groan, Maggie let her hand flop back down on the blanket.

"How bad do you want it?"

"Name your price, McCallum."

"A kiss, Maggie, a kiss."

She pretended to consider. "Cheap enough, I suppose. Do your worst."

To her surprise, Colin rolled over on his back. "You kiss me."

Maggie hesitated, then steeled herself with the vow she'd made the previous night, after he'd left her alone and frustrated. She and Colin didn't have a lot of time left. They could dance around each other for the rest of the summer, or they could close their eyes and jump in, and take advantage of the time they had left.

Somewhere in the middle of a restless night, Maggie had come to a decision. If Colin wouldn't seduce her, she'd just have to seduce him.

Of course, it had seemed a good idea at midnight, and teasing him this morning had been fun. But now, in the full light of day, she realized she'd never seduced a man. She wasn't sure she knew quite how to go about it.

"Decided you weren't thirsty?"

So she'd do whatever occurred to her, she decided with a sudden burst of confidence. She couldn't imagine Colin would complain too much. "No, just gathering the strength to do it properly."

And she did just that. Sitting up, she leaned over him and brushed her lips against his. He remained motionless, so tentatively, her tongue darted out to moisten his lips, then her own. Pressing her lips more firmly against his, she was rewarded with a response. He opened his mouth under hers, inviting her to explore. Her tongue tasted his, playing hide-and-seek around the smooth barriers of his teeth. Gradually she pulled back, leaving his lips with a final soft caress before she took the water bottle from his outstretched hand.

"Thanks," she said cheerfully, and tipped the bottle to her lips, gratefully swallowing the quenching liquid, feeling her heart's pace slow once again.

"My pleasure," Colin finally responded, in a slightly strangled voice.

Maybe this seduction stuff wasn't so tough after all.

Colin recovered quickly enough, and they set to work unpacking their picnic. Their conversation stayed away from touchy subjects, such as writing, and Lucy, and tenure, and the end of summer. Instead, they focused on the kind of man-woman, getting-to-know-you conversation of favorite music, sports teams and television shows. Just like a real date, Maggie realized, and just as Colin had promised, they were getting to know each other better.

To be sure, sexual innuendo was never far from the surface, but it was a more relaxed, more . . . intimate kind of teasing, one that left her with a warm glow and a renewed certainty that she'd chosen the right course.

After lunch, they settled back, watching fluffs of clouds scud across the blue sky. Maggie dozed off, replete with food and the taste of Colin's kiss.

She awoke slowly, feeling the warm sun against her eyelids, a pesky fly tickling her nose. She batted at it, but the pest persisted, until she at last opened her eyes and saw Colin lazily waving a blade of grass across her face.

"Do you know," he said conversationally, leaning closer, "that your nose wrinkles in the cutest way when I tickle it?"

A shake of her head was the only response she could muster. Still groggy from sleep, she could focus her senses on nothing more than Colin's proximity. An intoxicating odor of maleness, soap and sweat, tantalized her nose. The tiny lines around his eyes that deepened when he smiled loomed as miniature valleys close up. That little scar above his eyebrow caught a tiny trickle of moisture descending from his temple, inviting, begging her to capture its salty flavor with her tongue.

"I'm thirsty."

He paused above her. "You know the tariff."

He was talking about far more than a swallow of water, but Maggie only nodded. Slowly, slowly, his head descended, his lips brushing hers with aching softness.

His hand reached up to brush aside an errant curl, and remained, tunneling into her hair to hold her head still as he continued his gentle, ruthless assault.

He half sprawled on top of her, and his left hand moved up to mimic its partner. The feel of his fingertips, massaging, soothing her scalp while his lips aroused her was the most erotic sensation Maggie could have imagined.

Her hands reached up to explore his muscled back, measuring its breadth, marveling at the controlled strength felt in every movement. She pulled him closer, pressing his torso against hers, seeking surcease for breasts tender and aching. His chest flattened hers, and his kiss deepened. Colin rolled over onto his back, taking her with him, never breaking their contact.

Above him now, Maggie discovered whole new areas to explore. Free to move her head, she experimented, changing the angle of their kiss, sucking an earlobe to arouse him further.

Her hands continued their survey, sweeping over his chest, memorizing his shape, his strength. She could feel his hard nipples through his polo shirt, but that wasn't enough for her anymore.

Tugging at the hem, she pulled the shirt from the waistband of his shorts, allowing her hands access to the warm skin underneath. Stroking, petting, searching, her fingertips found the hard nubs they sought, nestled in the soft springy hair covering his chest.

"Lord, Maggie," Colin breathed, and his mouth seized hers again, suckling, nipping, probing. He rolled her over onto her back again, his arms still around her, grinding his pelvis into hers, making her feel the hard length of him, his desire, his need.

Finally he lifted his head and whispered, "We have to stop."

"Why?" Maggie whispered back. Her voracious hands had moved from his chest to explore the hard contoured planes of his back, tracing the bumpy line of his spine from neck to waistband and back up again.

"Because if we go on much longer, I won't care that we're on a mountaintop, in full view of a hiking path that hasn't been empty all day."

"Oh." She'd forgotten where they were. The feel of Colin's strong, hard body against hers had driven all thoughts of propriety clean out of her mind. "Guess I should get my hands out of your shirt, then."

"No hurry." Colin gave her a lazy grin and kissed the tip of her nose. "I just meant we'd better cool it a little, not pour ice water over it."

That should have done it, Maggie thought irritably, worrying the thin strap of her new silk chemise later that evening. He wanted her, she'd made it obvious she wanted him. So why was she alone, in her bed, with Colin asleep in the other room?

After their picnic, after their heated interlude on Squaw Mountain, she'd been certain Colin would abandon his gentleman's stance and come to her tonight. She'd been certain enough that she'd asked Devon about the location of the nearest lingerie shop, only to have the other woman insist on accompanying her on her shopping trip.

Choosing the appropriate garment had been a trying experience. Devon's eye went automatically to the ultra-seductive: the high-cut teddies and sheer-lace camisoles designed with her petite figure in mind.

When Maggie had explained that she only wanted something a little sexier than a football jersey, Devon had pooh-poohed that idea and continued rifling through racks of brightly colored silks, pausing only to hold one or another up to Maggie's reluctant form.

"Nonsense. You want to knock his socks off, don't you?"

They'd finally compromised on the garment Maggie wore now, a thin silk chemise, with a rose-hued print reminding Maggie of a Monet garden scene. It was long enough for her comfort, and the spaghetti straps holding it up revealed enough bare skin for Devon's taste.

Lingerie shopping had been embarrassing enough; more embarrassing, however, was that Devon had to remind her about protection.

"I don't want you to go through what I did," she'd explained matter-of-factly. "When Colin got the two of us up to his cabin, we ended up... together, and since we hadn't planned on it— Let's just say I spent the next three weeks in a slough of uncertainty, with Steve dogging me, which did not do wonders for the relationship."

Protection. Maggie eyed the package on the bedside table wrathfully. She'd felt like a teenage idiot, not even thinking of the consequences of her decision, another idea which Devon dismissed.

"You've got more immediate things to think about, right? Who knows, maybe Colin's already taken care of it. You just can't be too careful, that's all."

So here she was, all dressed up and no place to go.

No, she did have a place she could go. She could get out of bed, pick up her little packet and march into Colin's room. Surely, faced with that, he wouldn't still cling to his gentlemanly posture. Would he?

Idiot. Colin rebuked himself as he flipped another unread page of the magazine he held. Maggie wanted him, he wanted her. So why was he alone in his bed, and she alone in hers?

It wasn't because they were guests in Steve and Devon's home; the Thornes cared not a whit about their sleeping arrangements, and their bedroom was far enough away that only the noise of a small thermonuclear device would disturb them. No, that wasn't it.

It wasn't because he'd promised Maggie a platonic trip. He felt sure she wouldn't hold him to that vow, not after this afternoon. All evening she'd been sending him the oddest glances—a curious mixture of anticipation, heat and something resembling shyness.

Truth be told, he was scared. Scared in a way he'd never been with a woman, scared that he'd screw up something really important.

Maggie was really important. It had hit him with the force of a locomotive this afternoon. Not when they'd been rolling around in the grass getting overheated, but afterward, when they'd laughed and cuddled, giggled and kissed.

He'd realized he didn't just want the heat of the moment, Maggie's passion burning as she writhed beneath him. He wanted the afterward—the stroking, the petting, the sleeping curled tightly together, the waking up to see her face first thing in the morning.

The love. He wanted to love her, and for her to love him in return. That was why he sat here in bed, not reading the magazine he paged through.

Going to her meant taking a huge chance. He hadn't taken any risks in quite a while. Could he walk into her room, into her arms, and risk his heart?

Your heart's already gone, Colin. Your only risk is admitting it.

The realization galvanized him into action. Throwing back the covers, he strode naked across the room and flung open the door to the connecting bathroom.

Maggie's door opened simultaneously.

She stopped in the doorway, clad in some slinky, sexy little thing that left very little to his already overheated imagination.

"Uh, sorry," they said at the same time, both backing up a step. He couldn't take his eyes off her.

Her "You go ahead," overlapped his. She was staring, too, and Colin remembered his nudity.

"No, I wasn't—" This time Colin's mind registered that they spoke the same words. Had she opened her door with the same intention as he?

He took a step forward, then another. She eased back onto her trailing heel, more of a shift of her weight than an actual step backward.

He took another step. She stood her ground, her eyes a little wary, cautious.

He took a fourth step and stopped a foot away from her. A foot away from that delectable pink skin, that strap that slid so enticingly off her shoulder. Slowly he reached out a hand and caressed her cheek.

"I was coming to you."

She nodded.

His fingers stroked down her throat to rest at the pulse point, visible in the dim light.

"Were you coming to me?"

He felt her swallow under his thumb. She nodded again, gazing up at him with cornflower blue eyes that spoke eloquently of desire, of trepidation. He understood both emotions. The knowledge that she wrestled demons similar to his robbed him of all remaining hesitation.

He slipped his hand around behind her neck, rubbing, soothing, easing the tension he found there. Tilting her head back, Maggie closed her eyes and gave in to the sensual massage he offered.

It was all the invitation Colin needed.

He reached up with his other hand and nudged the remaining strap off her shoulder. Her gown slipped a little lower, revealing the tops of creamy white breasts that invited his caress.

What a sight. Maggie stood silently, her tilted head and parted, dewy lips speaking of her pleasure. There was nothing coy about this woman. She expressed her delight, although not in actual words, but in every puff of breath, every little half moan.

Colin was no longer content to merely watch her. He stopped his massage, and used both hands to lightly caress her breasts above the silk of her gown.

Maggie's eyes flew open. Her trepidation had vanished, leaving only the desire.

Despite the rush of longing Colin felt, he made no move beyond continuing his gentle caress, ignoring the effect it was having on his already overheated libido.

"So," he asked, in as close to a conversational tone as he could muster, "your place or mine?"

"Mine's closer." Very deliberately, leaving Colin no doubt as to her wishes, Maggie lifted his hands from her chest and planted a kiss on each palm. She backed up, her eyes never leaving his as they made their way across the room.

The backs of her legs found the bed and she stopped, suddenly nervous as the reality and the immediacy of the situation hit her.

Colin sensed the change immediately. "Doubts, Maggie?"

"No, not doubts, just..." She floundered for a moment before summoning the right words. "It's been a long time for me, and I want to please you. I haven't had that—"

Colin stopped the flow of words with a kiss. "We're not grading this, Professor."

At her tentative smile, he flashed a grin. "Besides, it's been a while for me, too. You have to promise to be gentle."

It would be all right, Maggie realized, surprised with the certainty of the thought. She smiled back more fully now, and tugged at Colin to join her on the bed.

With Colin naked next to her, the barrier of her thin chemise felt very cumbersome indeed. His hands ran over her, stroking, petting, exploring, yet he made no move to remove the gown.

"I like this," he murmured, stroking her breasts through the delicate silk. "Did you buy it for me?"

"Yes. I wanted something a little more exciting than a football jersey."

"Honey, believe me, you are plenty exciting in a football jersey. I did this to you last night in my mind—" he illustrated by laving the breast he'd been caressing "—and I didn't sleep a wink all night."

The feel of his mouth on her, even through the silk, was more erotic than Maggie could have imagined. She gasped, and tugged at his hair.

His head came up. "What's wrong?"

"I want to feel you next to me." Maggie tried to remove her gown, but the straps limited her movement. Seeing her frustration, Colin eased the garment over her head.

"Oh, my," he breathed. "Professor, if I'd had teachers like you, I never would have dropped out of college."

Brushing his thumbs across her taut nipples, he watched as they puckered even tighter. Maggie let out a tiny whimper, and he bent his head, eager to assuage, to arouse.

His hands continued their journey, shaping the curve of her stomach, trailing down to the tangle of curls below. His fingers insinuated themselves between her legs, seeking her warmth, her heat.

She was ready for him, hot and wet, arching against his stroking hand. She uttered tiny moans, as if his touch had driven all words from her mind. He wanted to make it good for her; he wanted to make it last. He didn't know whether he could do either.

Moving up to kiss her again, he whispered against her lips, "Maggie, I don't have any—"

She knew immediately what he was talking about. "On the table," she managed, and they fumbled together with the tiny foil package. She retrieved the contents at last, but when she touched him, Colin felt the last of his tenuous control slipping away. "I'd better do this," he said, stopping her hand. "Or there won't be a main event."

Task accomplished, he rolled over on top of her, settling between her legs. She pulled his head down and kissed him as he eased inside her.

As she drew him into her molten heat, Colin knew he wouldn't last long. He strove to hold on to some small remnant of control, but Maggie's mouth, Maggie's hands, Maggie's hot, tight sheath made that impossible. One thrust, then another, then another, and he felt himself falling, falling over the edge.

"Maggie," he moaned, as his climax overtook him.

Afterward he remained motionless on top of her, absorbing the feel of her beneath him, her soft breasts crushed under his chest, her hands idly stroking his back.

"Damn," he muttered into her neck, once he could breathe again. He'd been no better than an out-of-control teenager, all wham-bam—

"Don't." Maggie's hands continued their caress.

He lifted his head to look at her. "But you didn't—"

"No, I didn't," she agreed calmly. "But I do feel compelled to point out that you have all night to make it up to me."

Her logic was irrefutable. And now that he'd banished his schoolboy's heat and two and a half years of celibacy, he'd do just that.

"You're right, of course." Kissing her swiftly, he rose from the bed and headed out of the room.

When he returned, she had straightened the twisted sheets, retrieved the pillows that had been shoved to the floor and was now lying chastely under the covers.

"Not getting modest on me, are you?" he teased, slipping in beside her. Despite her quick denial, the pink staining her cheeks told him otherwise.

"Well, we'll have to work on that," he murmured, and set about doing so.

He took his time, making a leisurely inventory of every moan, every sign of Maggie's rapidly returning arousal. He whispered love words, sex words, words of praise and delight, encouraging the same from her.

He measured every response, cataloging every shiver, every sigh, every indication of her pleasure, knowing that he would arouse her time and again.

His mouth left a line of kisses down her stomach to the juncture of her thighs, and Maggie gasped, trying to pull him up over her. He continued his intimate assault until she surrendered, opening for his incursion. Holding her hips with gentle hands, he plundered her, tasting her sweetness, savoring her musky scent until she gasped and arched, shuddering in release.

He moved over her and entered her slowly, this time concentrating on every little move she made under him, every sigh of her fulfillment.

The tight buds of her breasts rubbed against his chest with every stroke; the hair on his belly brushed against her stomach with every movement. He felt more alive than he'd ever felt before, sensation upon sensation rippling through him, tiny electric pulses forecasting a greater storm.

Underneath him, Maggie lay, eyes closed, absorbing every thrust, her pelvis rising with every stroke to welcome him. Her breath quickened, her legs tightened around him, and Colin knew she was close to another release. He increased his tempo, and her hips responded in kind, driving in an exquisite counterpoint to his movements.

He kissed her fiercely. "Open your eyes, Maggie," he commanded, wanting, needing to see the pleasure reflected there, wanting, needing her to share his.

She cried out, the surprise of passion glazing her eyes, and she gripped him more tightly still, urging the same pleasure from him. He surrendered to it, drawing her closer as wave upon wave of elation overtook him, draining him, freeing him.

Smug, knowing smiles greeted them at the breakfast table late the following morning, accompanied by sidelong glances between their hosts.

"Sleep well?" Steve inquired mildly, but spoiled the effect by staring pointedly at the clock on the wall.

Maggie rolled her eyes heavenward. She knew Steve wouldn't ignore their late rising, but she'd hoped for a little discretion.

Colin, however, was undeterred by the innuendo. "Very well, thank you," he replied, reaching for the carafe and pouring coffee for Maggie and himself.

"I'm so glad," Steve persisted, a mischievous smile lighting his face. "You know how it can be—sleeping in strange beds and all—"

"That's enough," Devon interrupted, apparently sensing Maggie's discomfort.

"But, honey, I'm just being a good host."

"Maggie doesn't need your unique interpretation of hospitality, dear." Despite her stern words, she patted his hand, and Maggie coveted the open display of affection between them.

What she would give to be as open about her feelings for Colin. What she would give to understand her convoluted feelings for him.

She cared deeply for Colin, but did she dare call it love? Their night together had changed nothing; she was still leaving in a month, and despite his cavalier predictions, she didn't see how they could carry on a long-distance relationship for any length of time.

But their night together *had* changed everything; the physical pleasure they'd shared had its roots in something far deeper, far more meaningful, even if they'd both avoided saying the words that would articulate those sentiments.

I love you, Colin. She tried the words in her mind, and liked the way they sounded there. What would happen if she said them out loud? Was he ready to hear them from her?

"You in there, Professor?" Colin's voice interrupted her reverie. His face wore a sympathetic expression, as if he understood her preoccupation. "I was just telling these two that we're leaving this morning, that you've still got lots of work to do."

They'd agreed in the whispered hours before dawn that it would be best to explore this new phase of their relationship away from an audience, even one as supportive as Steve and Devon. Unspoken was the knowledge that with their future so uncertain, they needed time alone to talk, to touch, to be together.

Neither Steve nor Devon showed any surprise at this announcement; the look that passed between them indicated they'd expected this turn.

Chapter Eight

"Don't hurt him."

Maggie turned from the duffel bag she was packing, surprised to see who was standing in the doorway. She'd half expected Devon to offer her last-minute advice about Colin, but not Steve. Steve, who joked and teased and blustered his way through every serious moment. Steve, who played his cards far closer to his chest than did Devon.

"He's a good man."

She swallowed. "I know."

"He's been through a lot."

"I know that, too."

"I'm not sure you do." He glanced out into the hall, and stepped into her bedroom, closing the door behind him. "You have to understand, Lucy really did a number on him."

Maggie caught herself squeezing the T-shirt she held. She loosened her grip and refolded the garment, trying to take in what Steve was saying. "I gathered that from what Devon's told me. They weren't happy."

He shook his head. "It was more than that. Whatever he did wasn't good enough. The choices he'd made, the way he needed to live his life, weren't good enough for her. He felt incredibly guilty about that."

"Guilty?" What was Steve talking about? Devon had talked about two people ill suited for each other. She'd never mentioned guilt.

He nodded and crossed his arms over his chest. This wasn't easy for him, Maggie suddenly realized.

"Lucy died an unhappy woman," he continued. "For which Colin blames himself and himself alone. He has a mental laundry list of 'if onlys,' and he refuses to consider that Lucy could be at least partially responsible for the way things were between them."

"You sound as if you didn't like her very much."

Steve shook his head. "I tried, I really tried. She was Colin's wife, so I really wanted to like her. I knew I owed our friendship that much. But whatever choices he made, she thought he should have done more, or he should have done things differently."

Not satisfied with the explanation she'd received, Maggie repeated the question she'd asked Devon the day before. "I don't understand, if things were so awful between them, why did they stay married?"

"Colin is loyal to a fault, that's why. He makes a commitment, he keeps it. He tried everything—changing his writing schedule, traveling with her. He even bought a condo in San Francisco so they could try living there, at least part-time." He laughed, a short, ironic sound. "I knew that one was doomed to failure."

"Why? Colin grew up in San Francisco, and his parents are still there. I don't understand."

"Colin hates the city. It's weird, like he's a caged beast or something. I can't even pretend to understand it, but it's a part of him, like his hair color or height. I suppose that things being so bad between them only exaggerated that effect. And then they would argue about how much time they spent in the city versus at the cabin."

He was pacing around the room now, getting more and more agitated as he spoke. Maggie watched, fascinated by the transformation.

"Anyway, every time Colin would make a change for her, she'd be mollified for a little while, and then she'd start up again. Finally, I think even Colin realized she wasn't going to be happy, that she hated the fact he *worked* as a writer, instead of living off his trust fund. It was as if his books were competition, a thousand times worse than another woman." He stopped abruptly, and in a gesture Maggie found endearingly like Colin's, he shoved a hand through his hair.

"And then Lucy died, and Colin lost all perspective," he concluded sadly.

This was too much to take in all at once. "Have you tried talking to him about how you viewed his relationship with Lucy?"

He nodded. "About a year ago, Devon and I decided it was time for him to quit wallowing and get on with life. He didn't speak to us for six months. Like I said, he's loyal."

Maggie considered how much that silence must have hurt Steve. He obviously cared a great deal about Colin.

She couldn't stop herself; she hugged him, hard. "Colin's fortunate to have you for a friend."

He squeezed her back, laughing ruefully. "He didn't think so at the time. We still don't talk about it."

"What's going on here?"

Colin's voice startled them both, causing them to jump apart. Had he overheard their conversation? Maggie couldn't be sure until he affectionately cuffed Steve on the arm.

"Jeez, Thorne, I can't leave you alone with my woman for five minutes without you putting the make on her."

Steve made a joke, and the moment passed. If they hadn't had their revealing conversation, she never would have believed Steve was more than Colin's easygoing pal.

They departed much like their arrival—in a flurry of hugs and kisses. This time Maggie felt like a member of their charmed circle, and promised fervently to keep in touch.

"They're wonderful people, Colin," she said when they were on the road.

"I'm lucky," Colin agreed. "They tolerate a lot from me."

Remembering her talk with Steve, Maggie silently concurred.

The drive back home was fairly quiet. Maggie was trying to come to terms with all that Steve had told her, to make it fit with Colin's behavior. He was equally lost in thought. As though sensing their mood, even Seally remained quiet in the back seat.

Abruptly, Colin pulled the car into a roadside turnoff, and gave Maggie a hard, demanding kiss. "This isn't just a summer fling. I care about you, dammit."

And what an interesting way in which to express it. Maggie was too stunned by his actions and words to think any further for a moment.

Colin pulled back onto the road and drove on, his hands clutching the wheel so tightly that his knuckles turned white. Every now and then he cast sidelong glances in Maggie's direction, silently urging a response.

After several miles had elapsed, she found her voice. "I never said that we were having a summer fling, Colin."

"You didn't have to," he shot back. "You were thinking it, weren't you?"

Defensive, wasn't he? She trod cautiously. "*Fling* is not exactly the term I'd use to describe what's between us, Colin."

"What, then? Affair? *Relationship?*" He said the latter as if it were a dirty word.

"Stop it, Colin. You make it sound sordid, and it's not, even if we call it a relationship."

"What would you call it, then?" he persisted.

"Why are you so determined to label what we have and put it into a little box? Why can't we go on like we are?"

"Because that puts it into the summer-fling category, Maggie, and I won't settle for that."

Oh, he wouldn't, would he? "So what are you planning, Colin? Do you want to come back to Boston with me?" Damn, she hadn't meant to suggest that, not yet, not until she knew more about Colin, more about what Steve had revealed to her.

An inelegant snort was his only reply.

Courage, Maggie. You started this, you might as well see where it takes you. "I mean it, Colin. My apartment isn't huge, but it's big enough for you and me. And Seally, of course," she added as an afterthought.

Her suggestion seemed to have taken the wind out of his sails. When he spoke, at last, the vexation had vanished from his voice. "I'm not a city person, Maggie. A day or two, and I start feeling closed in."

In for a penny... "But if you really tried it—"

"I did try it!" he burst out. "When Lucy—" He stopped and took a steadying breath. "Lucy wanted to live in a city—any city—so we bought a place in San Francisco. Even coming back to the cabin a couple days a week wasn't enough—I felt as if my furlough had ended and I was being sent back to prison."

Anger at herself for raising such hurtful memories, anger at Colin for rejecting her suggestion so out of hand, anger that Colin was comparing her to Lucy in any way, made Maggie speak without thinking. "Well, that's just wonderful, Colin. I'm supposed to give up my life, my family and my career to move out here, based on the call of the wide-open spaces and a fabulous night in bed!"

Colin had already opened his mouth to answer when the last of Maggie's protest registered. His mouth spread into a wide, delighted grin. "It was fabulous, wasn't it?" he said softly.

Yes, it was. Before she could agree or disagree out loud, Colin continued. "But that's not the main issue here. I don't recall suggesting you abandon anything. I'm just letting you know, up front, that I can't live in a city."

No, he hadn't suggested—or demanded—anything, Maggie recalled. There she went, projecting again, when she'd promised herself only the month they had left.

"Not that I wouldn't be thrilled if you did move out here," he continued. He took her hand and rested it on his thigh, stroking it lightly with his thumb. The hard muscles underneath his jeans shifted with his movements, and Maggie had trouble keeping her mind on his words, recalling just how those muscles had felt under her fingers the night before.

"I'm also not saying I won't visit you in Boston. I have to be able to know I'm coming back here, that's all."

They came around a curve, and the expanse of the Washoe Valley spread before them, dominated by the blue expanse of its eponymous lake.

"There's something about this land, Maggie." His voice was worshipful, reverent. "I'm a throwback to my great-great-grandfather, I think. His journals describe his reaction to this place, his sense of arrival, an instinctive knowledge that he was home. I feel the same ties, the same peace, the same sense of homecoming, of belonging. I tried giving it up once, and that effort made me extremely unhappy."

In an abstract way, she actually understood what he was saying. She, too, had felt some small sense of belonging when she'd reached Nevada, a feeling that if things were different, if her life was different, she could be very happy here. The thought did not cheer her.

He patted her hand again before returning his to the wheel. "We don't have to make any major decisions right now, Professor. We've still got a month."

A month. Four weeks. Thirty days. One lousy month.

Colin insisted on carrying her duffel into her apartment when they reached Reno. Gazing around the living room, he shoved his hands into his pockets and asked, "Rent's paid on this place, huh?"

"Yes."

He wandered around a little, adjusting the picture frames on bookshelves, straightening the stack of books on her desk.

"So, what's next? More research?"

What was he getting at? "No, I'm pretty much researched out at the moment. I have to make a trip to the Bancroft Library in Berkeley, and I may have to hit the Nevada State Library again, but other than that, I'll be writing from now on."

He nodded once, and paced about the room again. "I was thinking—I mean, it's just a suggestion—but what would you think about moving up to my place until you leave?''

He'd phrased it so casually that she almost missed his meaning, yet Maggie could feel the palpitating tension underlying his words.

"Um," she started, stalling for time. She couldn't make such a major decision instantly.

He continued as if she hadn't uttered a sound. "I figure we'll probably be spending a lot of time together anyway, and this way we wouldn't be driving up and down the mountain all the time. I could run to the library for you if you needed something, and you know I'm a great cook. It would make your life much simpler."

And far more complex. "Oh, Colin—"

"Well, it was just an idea." He shrugged and headed toward the door, whistling for Seally. "Why don't you think about it and let me know. I'll see you lat—"

"Colin, wait. Let's talk about this." Maggie would have laughed at his uncharacteristic diffidence if she hadn't been so touched by his show of uncertainty. The man could tell her he cared about her, but was afraid to wait for an answer to his altogether tempting invitation.

She moved closer, looping her arms around his neck and pressing her body against his.

"You'll cook?"

He nodded. "Yep."

He'd make a great cowboy, with that laconic charm. "And you'll go to the library for me?"

He nodded again. "Uh-huh."

God, it was tempting. Her heart fluttered, her mind whirled at the notion of spending her remaining month with him. "And you'll understand when I turn into a raving loony who wants to be left alone?"

"I didn't promise that," he objected, but his grin belied his words. "Are you really a raving loony, or just a little grouchy sometimes?"

Maggie cocked her head to one side, pretending to consider. "All in the eye of the beholder, I suppose."

He slapped her bottom playfully. "Grouchy I can deal with. So what do you say, Professor? Care to spend the next month in writer's heaven? Did I tell you I'm a great editor?"

Oh, something she hadn't considered—Colin reading her work, Colin critiquing her prose with his writer's eye. Still, the idea of spending all her time with Colin was inviting. Waking up in his arms every day, like she had today...

The rent was paid here. If it didn't work out, she could always come back, she reasoned. And Colin's place was gorgeous. If she didn't spend all her time in bed, or staring out the window, she could get a lot accomplished....

"You've got a deal," she said before her mind could inventory the disadvantages of the arrangement. For once in her life she would step off her carefully laid path, and see what lay beyond.

"Do you want to go to Berkeley with me? I was planning on an overnight trip, so we'd have to do something with Seally if you came along."

Colin looked up from the book he was reading. Maggie was ever so much more fascinating than late nineteenth-century law enforcement in Montana, even when her eyes were glued to her computer screen, instead of on him.

"Seally's no problem—the Johnsons down the road will watch her." Her absent nod inspired him to tease. "You just want the opportunity to stay in a sleazy motel with me—admit it."

That suggestion caught her attention, as he knew it would. She turned and smiled fully at him. "Now, why would I want to stay in a sleazy motel when I've got Bachelor Heaven, complete with waterbed and hot tub, right here?"

In the two weeks since she'd moved up here, Maggie hadn't stopped ribbing him about his creature comforts. The heated towel racks, the satellite dish and the stair-climbing machine were all sources of great amusement for her. You'd think no one on the East Coast had an espresso machine, for Pete's sake!

Still, her presence here was a blessing, a grand diversion—in short, heaven.

They'd settled into a rhythm almost immediately. Maggie slept late while he ran, then joined him for cappuccino and homemade muffins on the deck. She spent her days immersed in her writing, taking breaks to talk, walk, nap and make love as the mood struck. In the evenings, a glass of wine waiting beside the hot tub signaled the end of the workday.

And the nights. Ah, the nights. Sleeping with Maggie—or more frequently *not* sleeping—was even more satisfying than he'd imagined it would be. She was a loving, creative, giving woman, and every day he fell more in love with her.

Unfortunately, every day also meant a day closer to her departure. He'd made a conscious effort not to dwell on that, but with little success. The mental calendar in the back of his mind was half-filled with black *X*s marking the elapsed days, and he dreaded the day it would be full. His vow to enjoy what they had while it lasted was getting harder to keep as the days progressed.

"Colin. Berkeley?"

He shook off his dark thoughts. "Of course. I want to show you the sights in San Francisco, too, so plan your schedule accordingly."

A tiny frown creased her forehead. "I thought you don't like San Francisco. Why would you want to play tour guide for me?"

"Nonsense. I never said that I didn't like it. I love visiting San Francisco, I just can't live there." There was a big difference between the two, he reminded himself.

Her frown remained. "Can we do it all in a day or so? I don't think I can spare more time than that."

Although not surprised by her request, he heaved a dramatic sigh. "If we have to." Actually, the San Francisco itinerary was still a little vague in his mind; he'd been toying with the idea of taking her to meet his parents.

Would they start dreaming of grandchildren? Worse yet, would Maggie feel an obligation to a commitment she wasn't ready to make? So far, he'd done his best to avoid placing expectations on her; he knew what a trap other people's expectations could be, and she had enough of them from her family.

He'd even avoided telling her he loved her. Talk about placing expectations on a person. He didn't want her to feel trapped, or pressured, or that she had to reciprocate. It was enough that she was here until the end of summer. It had to be enough.

Maggie curled up next to him on the sofa, handing him a sheaf of papers. "Want to read what I wrote today?"

"Of course." Another change. At first Maggie had been incredibly shy about letting him read her work, delaying him with caveats about scholarly versus popular styles and footnotes to be ignored.

He'd known her work would be well researched, he'd been a little surprised to discover that she was a truly fine

writer, as well. She avoided getting bogged down in lugu-
brious academic prose; her style was fresh, alive.

When he'd suggested she try for a more commercially
oriented style, she'd demurred at first, but was considering the idea. He'd pointed out possible advantages: increased name recognition, more money and the outside
chance to sell her story to another market.

"I think the Grosh story could make a great movie,
Maggie. Think of how many people you'd reach."

That had been the ultimate lure. Maggie loved the idea
of the whole world knowing the brothers' tragic tale.

As Colin read through her day's output—a discussion
of Allen and Hosea's difficult passage across the Isthmus
of Panama—he marveled once again at the depth of Maggie's work, not only her writing, but the deft manner in
which she integrated her research. She'd spent a lot of
hours in the library, but the information she'd gleaned in
those hours was delicately woven into the fabric of her text.

Which reminded him... "What are we doing at the
Bancroft Library? Are we still stalking the elusive Hoover
manuscript?"

Maggie rested her head on his shoulder. "Of course, although I'm beginning to suspect it's a lost cause. Still,
Charles Shinn's papers are there, and since he's the one
who cited the manuscript, maybe I can get a lead if I slog
through enough material."

"And who said writing wasn't glamorous?"

"You did," she retorted. "But I stray. The big prize this
trip are the letters written by the Reverend A. B. Grosh to
Richard Bucke. They maintained a lifelong correspon-
dence after the brothers died, so I'm hoping there will be
information not mentioned in Bucke's articles."

"The Reverend was the brothers' father?"

"Yes, and a pretty interesting fellow in his own right, which is why a lot of his papers survived. I want you to know I spent a fascinating weekend at the Moravian Archives in Bethlehem, Pennsylvania, researching the family."

"Sounds like a wild time." Colin's dry tone made Maggie laugh, a frequent sound these days. The house had never held as much laughter as it had the past two weeks. Colin wished he could bottle it for the time when she was gone.

Two days later they walked across the sunny University of California campus, making their way toward the Bancroft Library and its rare-book collection. Try as she might, Maggie was hard-pressed to keep her mind on the task ahead; her surroundings distracted her too much, fulfilling every fantasy of radical chic she'd ever entertained.

They had strolled up Telegraph Avenue, weaving past vendors selling tie-dye, incense, homemade jewelry and other relics of sixties culture. She'd heard that era was back in style, though it seemed as if it had never gone out of fashion here, she decided.

On the campus itself, walls were plastered with posters advocating revolution, the overthrow of oppressive regimes and the power of the people.

Colin noticed her wide eyes. "You think this is something, you should have been here when I was a student. Those were amazing times."

"I was accepted for grad school here, but my parents absolutely refused to allow me to come. They swore they'd disown me if I even considered attending such a radical school."

"Would they have?"

She considered. "I'm not sure, but I had no desire to find out whether I was 'going beyond the beyonds,' as my pop would say."

"My folks weren't thrilled with my choosing Cal, but they figured I was old enough to make up my mind."

Was that a slam at her parents? Just because they cared about her decisions? Maybe he called it "being old enough," but the way she saw it, his parents didn't really seem all that concerned about his life.

In the two weeks she'd been at Colin's, he hadn't spoken to his parents once, so far as she knew. She, on the other hand, had conversed with every member of her immediate family, several times over.

"Maggie," Brendan had said. "Ma says you're shacking up with some guy. What's the story?"

Rory had been more direct. "Maggie, what the hell are you doin' out there? Ma and Pop are having fits."

Sean's call had come to the crux of the matter. "Maggie, you're not going to give up all the family's worked for to support some has-been writer, are you?"

She'd been laughing too hard at the notion of her supporting the exceedingly well-to-do Colin to take umbrage with his characterization of the man, or to point out that most of the hard work had been *hers*.

Still, she felt a grin spread over her face at the memory. Colin caught it.

"What's so funny?"

"Oh, I was just thinking of Sean's phone call. The portrait of you as fortune hunter was pretty funny." She, of course, hadn't mentioned the rest of his comment.

"Yeah, I can't wait to meet the guy. Is your family always so...protective?"

Maggie felt herself bristle once again at the underlying censure she heard in his voice. "Look, they love me, okay?"

Colin held up a restraining hand. "Hey, I'm not criticizing, I just asked a simple question."

"Are they always so...*protective?*" she mimicked, drawing out the pause between the last two words.

Colin seemed oblivious to her sarcasm. "I think it's a legitimate question, Maggie. We come from two very different families."

"And yours is better, right?" Why was she doing this?

"Now, that's not fair. I've never said any such thing."

"You didn't have to. I could tell."

"Nonsense," he replied, refusing to be drawn into battle. "I just wanted to know whether I should expect those three behemoths to appear on my doorstep to defend your honor one of these days."

Maggie responded to his attempt at humor with what she hoped was a withering glare. The man simply had no understanding of normal familial interactions.

"Ah, saved by the bell," he quipped, as the carillon chimed the hour. "They should be unlocking the doors right about now."

As usual, he was correct, Maggie conceded reluctantly as he led her to the check-in area. She couldn't decide whether she loved or hated his ability to shift moods so quickly, while she traditionally stewed for hours when she got angry.

As a first-time researcher, her registration took a few minutes of filling out forms and producing the requisite identification. Colin simply gave his name, and the clerk pulled his card from a large file drawer.

"Is the information still current, Mr. McCallum?" she asked, scanning the card. She stopped abruptly. "Oh, goodness, you're C. J. McCall. I can't believe it. I've read every one of your books.''

"Thanks," Colin said softly, glancing around. "There are people wait—"

"Are you working on something new?" she persisted.

"No, I'm just helping a friend." He grabbed Maggie's briefcase. "I'll put this in the locker for you, and meet you inside."

Maggie watched him hurry off. Poor Colin, she thought, realizing for the first time what it must be like to have one's life on public display. It was one thing to have friends and colleagues in Reno ask the questions, quite another to hear them from a perfect stranger.

"Come on, you can tell me," the librarian whispered conspiratorially. "What's he working on? Does he have a new book deal? Has he gotten over his dead wife yet?"

She couldn't believe the crassness of the woman's question. Outraged, Maggie drew herself up to her full height so she towered above the seated woman. "I think Mr. McCallum answered your question more than adequately," she said in her stiffest professorial voice, the one she used when a student was trying to explain just why the fraternity ski trip was more important than his midterm exam. It usually worked.

It did this time. The woman finished her work in silence.

When Colin joined her in the reading room, she couldn't wait to complain. "The nerve of that woman! How dare she ask you—I have half a mind to report—"

Colin dropped a quick kiss on her open mouth. "Don't get upset about it, Professor. You can't change human nature. My life is considered public property, so I'm fair game."

"But it's not right."

"No," he agreed with a rueful smile, "it's not, but there's nothing I can do to control it except keep myself out of the public eye as much as possible, which I generally do. Now, let's get to work."

And he'd come with her in spite of the risk to his privacy. Oddly touched by his actions, Maggie set about her work. While Colin went to look up references to Hoover, she filled out call slips for the materials she'd already found.

When the files and books she'd called for arrived, she assigned Colin the task of examining Charles Shinn's papers for any mention of the Hoover manuscript. "Pay particular attention to the auction catalogs. When they sold off his library in the 1920s, it's possible that the manuscript was among the items up for bid."

"Yes, ma'am," Colin replied with a cocky salute, before opening his first folder and digging in.

Maggie sat with her own volume in front of her, staring down at the black binding. Inside, she knew, were typewritten transcriptions of letters spanning a twenty-four-year period following the deaths of the Grosh brothers.

She loved this part of her research. Letters told a person so much more about a subject than any published history could; one not only got the facts, but the feelings, as well. Carefully, she opened the book.

"Oh. Oh, my."

Maggie's soft, awed whisper drew Colin's attention from the papers in front of him. She was staring at her book, her eyes wide. "Oh my," she repeated.

"Maggie?" he whispered across the table.

No response. She sat motionless, eyes still locked on the page in front of her.

"Maggie," he whispered, a little louder, drawing a frown from the woman next to him, but no response from the one who mattered.

"Maggie," he repeated, and this time his voice penetrated. She looked up, and Colin saw that her blue eyes shone with tears.

"Colin, you won't believe this. Listen—

'Blind Ravine, Middle American River, December 12, 1857

Dear Governor and friends, We were snowed in in crossing the Sierra Nevada and escaped only with our lives.'

"Colin, it's from Allen to his father, a week before he died!"

Rising and circling the table, Colin leaned over her shoulder and read the rest of the letter along with her.

"Oh, Colin, it's so sad. He was so full of hope, and then he died."

The tears brimming in her eyes overflowed, and Colin decided fresh air was in order.

He hustled her outside and they walked around the plaza, his arm around her, silent but for Maggie's occasional sniff.

"I'm sorry," she said at last, and Colin gave her shoulders an affectionate squeeze.

"Don't worry about it."

"No, really. I don't know why it hit me so hard—I'm not usually this emotional."

Colin stopped and turned her to face him, wiping the tears from her cheeks with his thumbs. "It hit you so hard because you're a loving, caring woman, so stop beating yourself up." He kissed her then, a long, slow, gentle kiss that he hoped said all the words he was determined not to say.

"You've been working on Allen long enough to have developed a bond with him, and finding his letter brought him very much alive. Right?"

She looked up at him, her eyes impossibly blue under the sheen of tears. "I'm so glad you understand."

"Me, too." Colin knew all too well the concept of immersion. And while his finished product was different, much of the process was the same. You got attached to the people you wrote about, you became friends, and it was tough letting go of them when they'd served their purpose.

"No one else understands the way you do. I'm very lucky to have you."

Even as his heart sped up at her words, he thought she was going to start crying again, and gave her a wicked grin to forestall her tears. "Yes, you are," he agreed.

She smiled then, her eyes still a little misty. "Can we go back in now? I want to get back to the letters."

"Sure." Hugging her tightly, Colin tried to banish the memories of writing that his mind had summoned, but the thoughts wouldn't go away so quickly this time.

Chapter Nine

"No, Colin, absolutely not. If you'll recall, you promised me sleazy."

"I lied," he said blithely. "I enjoy my creature comforts, remember?"

The red-coated valet held Maggie's car door open, but if he was amused by their argument, he gave no indication. She ignored him to focus on the man next to her in the car. "Colin, for goodness' sake, we don't need to stay in a fancy place like this."

"I do," he replied. "Humor me, Maggie. I want to do San Francisco right."

A look into his pleading gray eyes, and Maggie forgot her embarrassment over arriving at one of San Francisco's finest small hotels in shorts and a Lake Tahoe Is For Lovers T-shirt. Forgot her only luggage was a duffel bag already ancient when she'd taken it away to college. Forgot everything but that Colin was asking her for something that would make him happy. Colin, who gave and gave and made a point of not asking for anything from her.

"All right, it's your credit card," she conceded, swinging her legs out of the T-bird.

He caught up with her at the hotel door. "Besides, if you're good," he promised, "I'll take you to North Beach and you can see all the sleaze you want."

"That's my guy. He certainly knows how to show a girl a good time." She patted his butt behind the bellhop's back, eliciting a delighted grin in response.

My guy. The words had slipped out without her even thinking about it, but they fit the man in front of her. While Colin registered, Maggie took the time to absorb his good looks once again, to appreciate anew the handsome man he was.

She'd seen the looks he got from other women, the approving stares that followed him, even here in this refined space. The looks of envy that followed her, the unspoken "What's she got?" that echoed after them.

"Now what do you find so amusing?" Colin took her arm and led her to the elevator.

"All of this." She gestured around the spacious, antique-furnished lobby, but her thoughts extended to her entire sojourn. "If anyone had told me in June that by September I would be receiving the royal tour of San Francisco with the man of my dreams, I would have said they were crazy."

Colin's face sobered. "Ah, but, Maggie, am I the man of your dreams?"

For an instant, Maggie considered a flip answer. No, she was here, and for two days she'd allow herself to live for the moment, to say what she felt, to revel in the time she had left with Colin.

Ignoring the waiting bellman, the open doors of the elevator, the impatient frowns of other guests, she put her hands on his shoulders and stood on tiptoe to bestow a tender, loving kiss. "Yes, Colin, you are," she whispered.

All at once, Colin seemed unable to wait to get to their room. He clasped her tightly against his side, his foot tapping impatiently with every stop between the lobby and their floor. "Come on, come on," he muttered when one older woman took forever to leave the car.

When they arrived at their suite, he cut the bellhop's show of amenities short with a "Yeah, right," and shoved a twenty-dollar bill into the astonished man's hand before practically throwing him out the door.

He turned and stalked back across the room, dragging Maggie down onto the king-size bed with a fluid, urgent grace she'd never witnessed before.

Always, Colin had been a tender, considerate, almost reverent lover, taking care to arouse her, bringing her leisurely to passion's fulfillment.

Tonight he demanded. Clothing flew heedlessly across the room as they rolled across the bedspread, eager to touch, to please, to capture each other's essence. His hands were everywhere, as was his mouth—tasting, possessing, whispering hot dark words of promise, of pleasure.

He drew her response, encouraging her participation. She stroked as eagerly, touched as avidly, promised pleasure as fervently.

She pushed him onto his back and placed a chain of hot kisses down his torso, not stopping until she reached her goal. Overwhelmed by the need to possess him—all of him—she tasted, offering him the ultimate pleasure she could give.

Colin groaned aloud when the heat of her mouth engulfed him. He felt her clever hands move lower, and for one mad moment, he thought he would explode with the intensity of it all.

He tugged at her, pulling her on top of him, positioning her above him. Maggie understood immediately, and bracing one hand against his chest, slowly guided him inside her, taking him slowly, inch by inch, until he filled her completely.

He could feel the tiny muscular contractions ripple through her, tiny convulsions portending a greater storm. She shut her eyes and tipped her head back, moving slowly, to the pace controlled by his hands on her hips.

Colin knew he would never forget this moment, Maggie astride him, pure pleasure evident in her every sensual move, in the flush of her skin, in the sway of her hair.

She opened her eyes and looked down at him, smiling, a smile of such womanly satisfaction, a smile that told him her pleasure, her joy at pleasing him.

Control vanished. He grasped her hips more firmly and increased his tempo. She rode him, moving instinctively in an age-old counterpoint. Her eyes closed again. He felt goose bumps rise on her skin, then she tensed before waves of release washed over her, freeing Colin to join her in exhilaration.

She collapsed on top of him, and Colin held her tightly against him, her sweat mingling with his, her heart beating at the same ragged tempo as his. For a few minutes, the only sound in the room was that of hearts pounding, and lungs gasping for air.

He felt her lift her head, and reluctantly loosened his grasp. She didn't move any further. Cracking one eye, he looked at her. She gazed back solemnly. Would she question what had just transpired between them? Would she be embarrassed about her sensual abandon? Would she tell him that she loved him?

An amused smile flitted across her kiss-swollen lips. "Nice room," she offered at last, and dropping her head back onto his shoulder, dissolved into giggles.

That comment set the tone for the evening. They had no need for weighty commentary; a look, a touch, a smile brought back every emotion, every feeling they'd shared.

Colin took Maggie on a tour of the San Francisco he knew and loved best—the narrow side streets of Chinatown, the funky shops of Haight Street. They dined at an intimate Italian café on Greene Street, above the noisy crowds flocking to Columbus Avenue. From there they walked to the waterfront, and Colin insisted no trip to San Francisco was complete without Irish coffee at the Buena Vista Café. "It was invented here, you know," he offered by way of justification.

"All right, you convinced me. Just as long as I can sit." Colin, as usual, had set a foot-swelling pace.

"Tired, are we?" He was scanning the crowded restaurant for a free table, and thus missed Maggie's tongue stuck out at his back.

The gesture made her feel much better.

Spotting a couple making movements to leave, Colin grabbed Maggie's hand and headed toward the soon-to-be-empty table, signaling to a waitress for a pair of coffees.

"Thank God," Maggie said fervently, throwing herself into a chair. "To answer your question, Colin, it is now—" she consulted her watch "—eleven-thirty. With the exception of a short dinner break, we have been walking since seven o'clock. Of course I'm tired."

"But you sat all day," he pointed out logically. "I thought you'd want the exercise, and San Francisco is definitely a walking city."

"I'm not complaining," she hastened to amend. After all, she'd been with him. Why would she complain? "Am I not allowed to say I'm tired?"

"We could have stayed at the hotel. I offered."

Indeed, he had, Maggie acknowledged with a grin. After their tempestuous lovemaking, after they had showered and made plans to go out, he had slyly suggested room service and a movie. Maggie had been altogether too tempted to forgo seeing the city, but in the end she'd insisted on the grand tour.

"We would have gotten even less rest if we'd stayed in."

"True enough," Colin agreed with a grin. "Cheers."

Maggie lifted her mug. "Cheers," she echoed. A thought struck her. "We don't have to walk back to the hotel, do we?"

"There's a cable car with our name on it right outside the door. We'll ride back in style."

She sipped at her coffee, enjoying the intimacy she felt with Colin. They could have been entirely alone, rather than in the midst of a crowded restaurant, for all that the world intruded. Every move he made was magnified, lengthened, exaggerated, from the tiniest crinkle of his eyes when he smiled to the warm brush of his hand against hers.

You'd have thought earlier would have been enough to hold us for a while. But no, she wanted more. And he knew it; she could tell by his gaze on her.

"So, what's the agenda for tomorrow?" she asked brightly. It wouldn't do to attack the man right here, not in a public place.

"Whatever you want." His look suggested his agenda.

They could have stayed home on the mountain if they were just going to stay in bed. "I meant, what else are we going to see?"

"Depends on whether we sleep late, I suppose."

He wasn't helping at all. His twitching lips reminded Maggie of the way they had felt, brushing her inner thigh. The sense memory of it lingered, making her shift in her seat.

All at once, Colin stood, tossing some money on the table and pulling her to her feet. "We'll take a cab."

They slept late.

As he strolled beside Maggie on the sunny Sausalito street, Colin smiled at the memory. Maggie squeezing herself against the door of the cab, as if the mere act of touching him would set off an uncontrollable conflagration. Maggie, once-shy Maggie, launching herself against him as they entered their suite.

He could have wondered at her evolution, but he had more immediate worries. Like how to tell Maggie they were dining with his parents in—he looked at his watch—four hours.

Maggie caught his movement. "Are we late for something?"

Ah, an opening. "No, but we ought to think about catching a ferry back to the city. We've got eight o'clock reservations at Postrio."

"Really? I heard you had to wait days to get a table there. How did you manage it, and on a Friday night, no less?"

Uh-oh. Here was where it got dicey. "I, um, didn't. My folks took care of it."

"Oh." A puzzled expression crossed her face, but she didn't say anything else. He waited for her to make the obvious connection, and when she didn't, he was forced to make it for her.

"As a matter of fact, they'll be joining us. They're really looking forward to meeting you."

"Excuse me?" Maggie stopped in the middle of the sidewalk and stared at him.

She obviously wasn't going to take this well. "Now, Maggie—" he started, but she cut him off.

"We're having dinner with your parents in—" she looked at her watch "—four hours, and you're just *now* seeing fit to tell me?"

"Now, Maggie," he repeated. "It's not like that at all. I didn't want you to get all wound up over it and not have fun today."

That didn't mollify her at all. "How long have you had this planned?"

"Since last night," he mumbled.

"I beg your pardon?"

Passersby were beginning to stare. "Maggie, come on, we're blocking the sidewalk." He took her arm to propel her forward.

She shook him off, holding her ground. "Colin, I'm really trying to be reasonable here, but I think you've got some explaining to do."

If this was reasonable, he couldn't wait to see her do irrational sometime. "I talked to them last night, while you were in the shower. I wanted to stop by and see them, but when they suggested dinner, I thought . . ." He shrugged helplessly. He couldn't refuse his parents, could he?

Her face softened, albeit an almost imperceptible amount. "Did it ever occur to you that I might not have brought appropriate clothes for a fancy dinner?"

Oh, that's what this was all about. He waved a dismissive hand. "If that's all you're worried about—"

"No, that's not *all* I'm worried about, but it's an excellent start."

"Fine. We'll go shopping." He grabbed her hand and headed toward the ferry. This would be much easier than he'd anticipated....

Three hours later he wasn't so sure. She'd dragged him through what seemed like every clothing department at Macy's, I. Magnin and the Emporium, and still hadn't found what she wanted. Colin was beginning to fear for his life and her sanity. Then it hit him.

"Come on," he ordered, and steered her down Post Street to the store his mother swore by. Taking the elevator up, he found a department full of the type of clothes they'd been looking at all afternoon.

"Sit." He pointed to a chair. "I'll be right back."

He returned with a blond sales associate named Jennifer in tow, explaining their predicament. "So, she's meeting my parents for the first time tonight. We're having dinner at Postrio, so we need—"

"Something casually dressy, classic, I think," Jennifer finished. "Size eight?" At Maggie's mute nod, she smiled. "I'll be right back. Don't worry."

True to her word, she returned with an armload of garments. As she held them up one by one, Maggie's dazed expression was gradually replaced by interest, and finally delight at one outfit.

"Stop," Colin barked. "That's it. Go try it on, and you—" he pointed to Jennifer "—find her some shoes."

"Size seven," Maggie called over her shoulder, heading for the dressing room.

When she emerged, Colin knew they'd made the right choice. The rose-colored jumpsuit had been designed with Maggie in mind, highlighting the contrast between her dark hair and delicately pink skin. While classically styled, its dolman sleeves and padded shoulders gave it a trendy air, and the softly draped silk suited Maggie's figure to a T.

"It's perfect," he breathed.

"By all rights I should take it, after all the aggravation you've caused, but it's too—"

"Don't say it." He stopped her words with a kiss. "I said, it's perfect."

Jennifer returned with a stack of shoe boxes, and the process started over again. To Colin's delight, Maggie chose a pair of high-heeled pewter snakeskin pumps that made her look even more statuesque.

"I know it's a male chauvinist kind of reaction, but you look great in them."

Jennifer had thought to bring a selection of matching handbags, as well, and after Maggie had chosen one, suggested a trip to the makeup counter for the final polish.

"I'll just bag up the clothes you were wearing while you're doing that, and you'll be right on time for dinner."

Mission accomplished, they headed out the door. Maggie stopped curbside. "A cab if you please," she commanded.

"It's only a few blocks—"

"Here's where you pay for that chauvinism. If you think I'm walking anywhere but to the curb in these suckers, you're crazy."

"Ah, the price we pay," Colin said with a sigh, raising his arm.

At the hotel they ordered the cab to wait while they raced upstairs. While Colin pulled on a sport coat, Maggie fussed with her hair in the full-length mirror.

The transformation in her appearance amazed her. She felt like Cinderella, all dressed up for the ball. The jumpsuit was incredibly flattering—its cut took off about ten pounds—and the shoes added three inches. She looked . . .

chic. The look was about as far from a Beaton University classroom as Maggie could imagine.

The woman at the makeup counter had done her face with a light hand, accenting her features rather than plastering over them. Her eyes, outlined with a dark lavender pencil, looked huge, her highlighted cheeks looked sculpted.

As if reading her thoughts, Colin came to stand behind her. "You sure do clean up purty, ma'am," he told her reflection.

"Why, thank you, sir," she responded, caught up in his game.

He squeezed her shoulders. "But if we don't quit admirin' you in that lookin' glass, the stagecoach is gonna leave without us, and we ain't never gonna get no grub."

"And Ma and Pa'll be sorely disappointed," she countered, then sobered. "You're right, we'd better go." It wouldn't do to keep two of San Francisco's finest waiting.

Colin took her arm as they headed for the door. "Don't worry. They'll love you."

He'd done it again. "Are you a mind reader, or what?"

"No, merely a student of human nature. I imagine I'll feel the same way when I meet your parents."

When. Not if, but when. The word gave Maggie a warm glow that lasted all the way to the restaurant.

The dinner had gone very well, Maggie thought. Lying in Colin's arms late that night, listening to the even breathing that signaled his sleep, she was able to look back and make that conclusion.

Over the course of the evening, she'd been at first too nervous, then too charmed, to analyze the meeting. Colin's parents had turned out to be everything, yet nothing, like she'd expected.

Upon their arrival at the restaurant they'd been whisked to an intimate banquette overlooking the entire restaurant, obviously one of the best tables in the house. Joseph and Alice had been seated already, but leapt up to greet them, Alice giving Colin an enthusiastic hug, Joseph offering his son a hearty handshake that turned into a back-patting embrace.

They'd been entirely gracious to Maggie, as well. At no time during the evening had she felt under a microscope. Although they had asked her a multitude of questions about her life and her work, the questions came from genuine interest, rather than scrutiny.

Joseph obviously doted on Alice; Maggie had gotten the impression that Alice in turn kept him from taking life too seriously. And they both adored Colin.

The relationship was hard to categorize. She knew the three of them only got together every couple of months, and that they didn't converse frequently on the phone. They had divergent interests: the senior McCallums were extremely tied up with the San Francisco art and social communities, both areas Colin ignored completely.

Yet the bond between them was visible, tangible. They accepted Colin for who and what he was, and he did the same with them. Maybe they had once wished he'd be more like them, but no more. Whatever expectations they now held for him, those expectations weren't voiced.

So very different from her interactions with her own family. Before tonight she had assumed a lack of love or interest on the senior McCallums' part, or on Colin's, but now she found herself reevaluating.

It wasn't disinterest that fueled their separation, but a different style of relating to one another. It was refreshing, in a way. No lectures, no grandchildren hints, no recriminations. And not just because Maggie was there.

They obviously accepted his choices, and wished nothing more for him than happiness.

Maggie knew this was why they'd been so thrilled to meet her. Colin's happiness was a living, perceptible thing, and they'd felt it, as well, and accepted her as its source.

And that, in turn, was why she was lying in bed, wide-awake, listening to Colin's even breathing beside her. Colin might well be deliriously happy now, but what would happen when she left? Despite his confidence about their future situation, her departure loomed like a dark wall ahead, with no way to see what lay beyond. Maggie couldn't begin to envision how a long-distance relationship would work, given her career's imminent demands and his attitude about city life.

She sighed and snuggled closer to the warm body next to her, running her hand through the curly hair on his chest.

"Can't sleep?" His voice, roughened from slumber, rumbled in her ear.

He didn't need to hear any of her doubts, not right now. "Too much excitement," she said instead.

"They liked you, you know."

Maggie let a chuckle escape. "I know, Colin, and I'm glad. You don't need to reassure me."

"Then go to sleep."

"Then go to sleep," she mimicked in a singsong voice.

He grabbed her hand and slid it down his stomach. "Or wake me up."

As Maggie turned in his arms, she let herself forget her worries for the moment. Worries could wait for another day; tonight she wanted to leave them behind and enjoy what little time she had remaining with Colin.

Chapter Ten

Gazing at the blinking light of her answering machine, Maggie was reminded once again that her worries couldn't be left behind entirely, no matter how hard she wished them to be.

She and Colin had come to her apartment this afternoon to pick up the last of her possessions, items she hadn't moved up the mountain with her when they'd returned from Lake Tahoe a month ago. Now, she wanted all of her belongings together at his place to simplify packing her car.

The answering machine was one of the items she'd left behind. Not wanting to call everyone she knew in Boston to let them know of her move, she'd left the machine plugged in, and checked for messages by way of her remote every few days. Now, while Colin boxed the last of her books across the room, she was faced with pressing the button and listening to a reminder of her real life, her past and future.

Somehow she doubted the message was from an insurance salesman.

Sure enough, when she pushed the playback button, she heard, "Maggie, this is Edmund. I wish you would return my calls. While I realize you are quite busy with your research, don't you think a month without calling is a bit much?"

Edmund. Maggie squeezed her eyes shut for an instant, as if the action would erase the message.

She'd known she would have to deal with this. Edmund had called twice before, two calls she hadn't returned. The idea of calling him from Colin's just felt a little too strange, and she hadn't really known what to say to him, anyway.

"Guess what, Edmund, I've met this great guy." Or maybe, "Sorry I haven't been in touch, but my life has been perfect for the past month, and I didn't want to let reality intrude." Or even, "Edmund, I could never in my wildest dreams feel for you as I feel for Colin, so let's just be friends."

All of them true. All of them appropriate enough. All of them things she didn't want to have to say.

"Guess the boyfriend's a little peeved."

Of course Colin couldn't have ignored the message. Maggie opened her eyes and looked across the room to where Colin stood, bouncing a book between his hands. "He's not my boyfriend." That much she could say with relative assurance.

"Oh, I don't know. He sounded pretty possessive there."

Colin wasn't going to make this easy. "Actually, I thought he sounded more annoyed than possessive," she replied, fighting to keep her voice calm. They were too close to her departure; she didn't want an argument, not now.

"Have you been ignoring his calls, Maggie? Is that why he's annoyed?" Colin's casual tone didn't hide the fact that *he* was the one who was irritated.

She shrugged, stalling. "He's called a couple of times, and I haven't called him back. I didn't think it was important, or he would have said so."

"Does he know about me?"

Well, now he was getting right to the heart of the matter. "No, he doesn't."

Colin dropped the book he'd been playing with into the waiting box and glared at her. "And why doesn't he, Maggie? Are you thinking about picking up with him where you left off?"

Maggie's stomach clenched at his words. "That's beneath you, Colin," she managed at last.

It was his turn to shrug. "You're not denying it."

"Do I have to? Do you honestly believe that I would do something like that?"

Colin had the grace to flush at her question. "Of course not, sweetheart." He strode across the room to clasp her shoulders, gazing down at her. "I guess I'm just a little stressed about your leaving. After all, we're not counting weeks anymore, we're counting days."

Five days, to be precise. She was leaving in five days, and they hadn't settled a thing. They hadn't even talked about the future. She took a deep breath, reaching for the words that would reassure him, even as she offered him the physical reassurance of sliding her arms around his waist, hugging him tightly.

When his arms moved around her shoulders into a loose embrace, she felt comfortable enough to explain, "I never had the kind of relationship with Edmund that I have with you, Colin. I considered us friends, even though I know Edmund wanted more.''

''So why not tell him about me?''

He made the question sound eminently reasonable, which in turn made Maggie rush to defend herself. ''I plan to, when I get home. I didn't want to do it over the phone.''

''Do you think that's fair?''

Tipping her head back, Maggie tried to read his face. It didn't do any good; he wore an inscrutable mask. ''What do you mean?'' she was forced to ask.

''He thinks you're coming back and that the two of you will pick up whatever kind of relationship you had. Don't you think he deserves some warning?''

''I kind of thought not returning his calls was sort of a clue.''

Her joke fell flat. Colin didn't even crack a smile.

''Seriously, Colin, I haven't felt like there's been a good opportunity to call him.''

Now it was his turn to ask, ''What do you mean?''

How to put this tactfully? ''I mean, you and I are together all the time, and you've made your displeasure over Edmund's existence obvious. I suppose I didn't want to stir things up by calling him.''

Colin released her abruptly, and moved back across the room. ''I guess that's fair.'' Picking a book off the shelf, he hefted it in one hand before setting it down again. ''Tell you what. I'm going to take Sealy for a walk. You do what you need to do.''

He was gone before she could utter another word.

Maggie stared out the screen door after him, instinctively recognizing the truth in his words.

She wasn't going back to Boston to resume her relationship with Edmund. That much had changed, even if nothing else in her life had altered. She knew now she could never settle for the kind of lukewarm relationship a future with Edmund promised, a relationship based on professional similarities rather than personal desires, a relationship grounded in intellectual reserve instead of emotional heat. Now she just had to break the news to Edmund.

She considered her options.

She could call Edmund now, or she could wait until she got home.

On many levels, it would be far easier to do it later. She probably owed Edmund the courtesy of a face-to-face confrontation. Perhaps by the time she returned to Boston, she would have summoned the appropriate words. And procrastination was always easier than immediate action.

But procrastination wouldn't ease Colin's mind. And easing Colin's mind was paramount right now. If he needed an unmistakable reassurance that she wasn't going back to Boston pretending that nothing had happened this summer, then she would give him that reassurance.

Oh, how simple things had seemed in June. She'd driven into Reno with empty notebooks and big plans, plans that hadn't included falling in love. Now she needed to reconcile those old dreams and the new ones, needed to figure out how to make the two parts of her life fit together into one whole.

She was doing good work. The book, as it was progressing, looked as if it was going to be something worthwhile, something that would serve her goals. But those goals meant she'd need to be in Boston, at least for the next couple of years.

Could she and Colin maintain a long-distance relationship for that long? She just didn't know, and she couldn't picture any other solution, not at this moment.

But she could solve one small problem right now. Maggie took a calming breath, picked up the phone and punched out the area code for Boston.

One bridge burned. Maggie almost laughed out loud as the absurd thought popped into her head. She cradled the receiver, replaying the short conversation in her mind. Edmund had been very cool, very civil, and if she wasn't mistaken, not very surprised. Perhaps not returning his calls for a month had given a hint as to her intentions.

Still, he'd agreed when she'd said she hoped they would remain friends. Perhaps the bridge was only singed.

When Colin returned from his walk, he immediately resumed packing books as if nothing had happened, as if they hadn't had words before he'd walked out the door. Maggie waited for him to say something, and when it became obvious that he wasn't going to, she crossed the room to stand in front of him. "I called Edmund. Do you feel better?"

He frowned slightly, his gaze focused on a weighty history of Nevada that was too big for the box in front of him. "Did you do it to make me feel better?"

Men. Honestly, why did women put up with this stuff? Maggie took the book from his hand and laid it aside, taking his hands in hers, and waited until he looked at her. She offered him a comforting smile. "I did it because it needed to be done. I did it *now* to make you feel better."

The corners of his mouth tipped up at her words, and he squeezed her hands. "Thank you, sweetheart. Yes, I do feel better."

Well, that was something, at least. She didn't have a clue about what she was doing with the rest of her life, but at least Colin felt better.

Perhaps that was all she could wish for, in her immediate future. She tried to ignore the little voice inside her head that told her she deserved more.

Shoving the last box of books into the trunk, Colin slammed the lid and brushed off his hands. There, it was done. She was packed. All that was left were her toiletries and clean clothes for the morning.

The morning he was dreading. Bright and early tomorrow, Maggie was leaving. He could envision her route. East to Chicago, then north to Detroit. Through the tunnel to Windsor, then east to London, Ontario, where she had one final library stop. After she did her research at the university there, she'd continue east and head straight to Boston. Simple, direct and each mile taking her farther away from him.

They'd had a difficult few days. For whatever reason, Maggie's writing wasn't going well—she'd alternated between staring at a blank screen and furiously deleting whole blocks of text she'd just entered.

When she wasn't writing, she was on the phone, trying to prepare for her classes long-distance. Since she'd put off her departure for as long as possible, she'd had to fax her syllabus to her department at Beaton, call the college bookstore about her textbooks and attend to a host of other details that would have been far simpler to handle in person. But she had insisted on staying in Nevada for as long as she could.

Colin had occupied his time obsessing over her car. It was six years old, it had a few miles on it; would the subcompact make it across the continent? He'd done his best to ensure it would, changing all the fluids, tinkering with the tuning, even buying her a new set of tires because the ones she had only held another ten thousand miles of tread.

He hadn't mentioned that. He'd recalled her embarrassment at the amount of money he'd spent in San Francisco, and given her current state of mind, he figured the new tires were better left unmentioned.

He shook himself and went inside to fix dinner. He'd planned Maggie's favorite Caesar salad and broiled swordfish for their last meal together. She wouldn't eat that well again until she returned in December.

If she did return in December. Savagely ripping the romaine into bite-size pieces, Colin had to admit that she'd never actually said she was coming back. When she'd first mentioned her sabbatical, the issue hadn't mattered, and later, after she'd moved up here, he'd sort of... assumed. She'd never said no, but she'd never said yes, either, and that worried him. What if she got back to Boston and found family or faculty ties too powerful to loosen?

Slim arms slipped around his waist and tightened, hugging him briefly. "Hi," she said, hopping up to sit on the counter next to him. "Can I do anything?"

"Nope. I've got it under control." Colin pushed his dark thoughts away. "Did you have a nice walk?"

She nodded. "Yep." She then snagged a piece of lettuce and chewed vigorously. "Thanks for packing the car for me. You did a great job."

When she'd said she wanted to take a walk, by herself, Colin had worried. She'd looked nervous, almost. Now she seemed calmer, more serene, as if she'd come to some important conclusion and was content with her decision.

After dinner, when Colin suggested a glass of wine in the hot tub, Maggie was quick to agree. The twinkle in her eye indicated she knew exactly where that would lead, but she merely winked and disappeared downstairs, tossing a jaunty "See you there" over her shoulder.

By the time Colin poured the wine and made his way down to the deck, she was already undressed and in the bubbling water. She accepted her wine with a smile of thanks and watched him strip.

"Enjoying the show?"

"You bet." When he joined her in the tub, she continued, "I'm going to miss this, you know."

"What, watching me undress?"

"Well, that, too. Seriously, all of this." She made a sweeping gesture encompassing the twinkling lights of the Washoe Valley below, the twinkling stars above.

It was on the tip of his tongue to ask her to stay, but he knew he couldn't. She had a teaching contract to honor, if nothing else. More importantly, the decision to stay had to come from her, not from him. When he'd proposed to Lucy, she hadn't understood fully the life he led, so she'd made a bad choice, a choice that had made both of them miserable. He wasn't about to do that to Maggie.

They sat side by side for a time, sipping their wine, enjoying the view, soaking up each other's presence. Gradually they shifted closer, until their shoulders touched.

Maggie rolled her head against the rim of the tub to gaze solemnly at him. "Did you lure me out here to ply me with wine and bubbles and view?"

He nodded. "The thought had crossed my mind."

She took another sip. "You men are such beasts."

"Animals," he agreed.

"What's a liberated, forward-thinking nineties woman to do?"

"Give in?"

Carefully she set her glass down, then took his and placed it next to hers, out of harm's way.

"Of course," she murmured, straddling him, "there is another option."

"And what's that?" Colin could barely force the words out.

"*I* could take advantage of *you.*" Puffs of air tickled his face, punctuating every word.

"Feel free," he managed, just before she lowered her mouth.

Maggie brushed her lips against his, tasting wine and garlic and the unique scent that was Colin.

She took her time kissing him—long, slow, wet, leisurely kisses to store for cold, lonely Boston nights. Kisses to help her remember all that was good and loving and wonderful about Colin. Kisses to block the rising certainty that this was the last night she'd ever spend with him.

She trailed wet fingers against wet skin, savoring, memorizing every curve of sinew, every hard plane of muscle. She wanted to remember forever every line of his body, from the sculpted hollow of his collarbone where water now pooled, to the graceful bulk of his runner's calves.

Still they kissed. Intoxicating, drugging kisses that fused their mouths, forbidding even the tiniest space to come between them. Her tongue danced with his, entwining, battling, stroking, challenging, begging.

His hands explored her as avidly as hers did him—caressing, kneading, knowing. He cupped her breasts, his thumbs stroking their tips to pebble hardness, then taunting them anew, until their ache was echoed low in her belly.

Still they kissed. Mouths grew slippery, movements more frantic, desire more fervid, and still they clung together.

Maggie felt Colin grasp her hips, lifting her until she rested just above his hard, arching erection. She moved to settle onto him, but he held her back, teasing her, tantalizing her with just the tip. She fought his grip, eager, wild with the need to feel him inside her. At last he relented, lowering her inch by agonizing inch until she embraced him fully.

Still they kissed. She sighed into his mouth, sated for an instant, until he moved beneath her and the madness started all over again.

They rocked together slowly, letting the rhythm of the water determine their movements, decide their pace. Maggie felt a part of Colin as she'd never felt before, as if the water and the heat had fused them together into one loving, sensing being. The water made her graceful above him; she slid up and down, her tempo increasing apace with his, their fervor increasing apace, their pleasure increasing until they could stand no more, and they shuddered together into release.

Still they kissed.

Later, snuggled in robes and lying against the mountain of pillows on Colin's bed, she asked him the question that would decide their future together.

She'd debated long and hard with herself, knowing that his answer would cast their relationship into stone or tear it wide open. Knowing that, she still had to ask, because she couldn't take the uncertainty of an open-ended parting. Because she couldn't stand the notion of a future where she'd always be the one making sacrifices. Because she wasn't sure Colin was ready for a future with her, and this was the only way she could see to find out.

"Will you come back to Boston with me?"

Colin stiffened, then relaxed. "Aw, Maggie, you know better than that." He planted a kiss on the top of her head. "I wish I could, you know."

Here goes. Maggie took a deep breath. "No, Colin, I don't know. You could come back with me—you don't have any commitments holding you here."

He sat up a little straighter, pulling away just a little. "Come on, Maggie. This isn't funny. Don't spoil our last night together, even joking about something like this."

She hated this. She didn't want to do it. She forced herself to do it anyway. "I'm not joking, Colin. I think you should come back with me. I think it could be a positive change for you."

"Maggie, drop it." His voice was a little sharper now. "We've discussed this. I thought you understood my feelings on the subject."

Adjusting the pillows behind her, Maggie shifted and looked more fully at the man she loved. "I do understand, Colin. That's the problem."

"What are you talking about?"

She couldn't stop now. Maggie shut her eyes for an instant before she spoke, praying that he would listen, that he would hear her. "I understand that you're hiding up here."

Colin stood up abruptly, and strode to the foot of the bed, where he glared at her. "That's absurd."

She continued her speech in a calm voice as if he hadn't reacted. "I understand you're letting life pass you by because of some misguided belief that—"

"Pass me by?" he echoed. "Are you nuts?"

"—that you're responsible for Lucy's unhappiness—"

He clasped the brass frame, leaning over it to eye Maggie fiercely. "Stop it, Maggie. I'm warning you."

"—and because you think you don't deserve to be happy."

That shut him up. He stared at her, hands shoved into robe pockets, before he paced across the room and stared out the window.

When he spoke again, his voice was controlled, curious even. "Why are you doing this, Maggie?"

In an odd way, his calm, rational tone was more difficult to respond to than his anger. Maggie found she had to force the words out around the lump in her throat. "Because I don't want you to waste your life up here on this mountain."

"I'm not wasting it," he argued. "I have friends—"

"Who you don't see very often."

"I have family."

"Who you see even less frequently."

"I have you."

"And I'm leaving in the morning."

"But you'll be back," he insisted.

Maggie shook her head sadly. "Not necessarily. I have a life there, Colin. I have a family—"

"Who stifle you."

"I have a job."

"Which may not last."

Clever of him to turn her technique around. But she didn't want to get off the subject. "True enough. There's no guarantee where I'll be teaching. I could wind up an academic gypsy, taking two-year posts here and there. Am I supposed to hop up here for a visit between stints? Would you really be happy with that kind of arrangement?"

"It wouldn't necessarily be like that. Maybe by then—"

"By when, Colin? You can't solve a problem until you admit it's there, and so far you haven't even done that."

Colin turned to face her, his face taut. "Okay, Maggie. Tell me, what's my problem?"

"You're afraid of screwing up again."

"And why shouldn't I be?"

Because you haven't done anything wrong. "What exactly did you screw up?"

She saw him swallow before he answered. "My marriage."

Maggie shook her head. "You can't take all the responsibility for the problems in your marriage. Lucy was at least partially to blame."

He shrugged. "She's dead, I'm not."

"So that means it's your fault? Don't be ridiculous."

"What's ridiculous is that you're trying to psychoanalyze me," he countered.

"Colin," Maggie said, desperate to reach him, "I'm saying this because I love you."

He laughed then, a hollow sound. "You have a funny way of showing it."

His sarcastic dismissal of her words hit her like a body blow. She forged ahead, ignoring the pain. "You talk a good game, and say you'll visit, and that we'll manage a long-distance relationship, but as far as I can tell, you have no intention of leaving the safe little nest you've made for yourself here. If you did you'd have to end your penance, and you're not willing to do that."

"So maybe I don't want to screw up your life."

Maggie sat up straighter, willing him to hear the truth in her words. "I'm the only one who can screw up my life, Colin. You can't do it. If going back to Boston is a mistake for me, then it's a mistake I have to make. Hiding out here in Virginia City is not going to solve any of my problems."

"So you admit you have them."

"Of course I do," she exclaimed, throwing up her hands. "My future at Beaton is uncertain, at best. I don't know if I'll get tenure."

She took a deep breath and rushed on. "I teach Western history at a school where the field is not especially respected, but I'm afraid to move somewhere else because I don't want to start the whole struggle all over again. So I'm sticking it out because it will be easier to land a tenured position somewhere else if I already have tenure."

He snorted. "And you call me afraid. You won't even admit what your real problem is."

"What are you talking about?"

Colin stopped pacing and glared at her from across the room. "You're hiding behind your family."

"Excuse me?" She couldn't believe what she was hearing. "Just because I'm close to them doesn't mean I'm hiding."

"You don't want tenure," he continued, as if she hadn't spoken. "You want to write, you love to write, but you're blindly following this career path, just because your family expects it of you, because it's safer than stepping out and taking a chance with your life."

"Safer? Tenure is no sure thing, Colin."

"No. But right now it looks like a surer bet than moving out here. What if our relationship doesn't work out? What if this book sells, and the next one doesn't? Academia is safer, even if it's not what you want to do."

No, he had it wrong. "That's not true. I've always known I would pursue an academic career—"

"Because everyone has told you that you should. What about you? Have you ever thought about what *you* expect from life?"

She gritted her teeth. This conversation wasn't supposed to be about her, it was supposed to be about him. "I'm doing what I expected," she maintained.

"And it's not making you happy. Maybe you need to look at your expectations," he concluded, leaning his shoulder against the doorjamb, arms and legs casually crossed, a triumphant smile on his face.

This conversation had gotten entirely out of hand. Maggie decided to move it back on track. "My expectations are fine. It's yours we're talking about, remember?"

"No, you're talking about them. I think I'm doing just fine."

"Only because you refuse to admit anything is wrong. You hide behind excuses such as being unable to live in a city." She stood and wrapped her robe's sash more tightly around her waist, and began pacing the room, avoiding the doorway where he leaned.

"You don't hate the city. You've hated being there when things have gone wrong, like when you wanted to drop out of Cal and go work on a cattle ranch, or when you and Lucy were having problems. It's human nature to say, 'If only I were someplace else,' but you've raised it from human nature to an art form."

"You don't know what you're talking about. You saw how I was in San Francisco."

"Yes, I did. You loved showing me the city, from a grand hotel to a tiny dim sum parlor. You even took me shopping. That was when I first realized that maybe you were protesting too much. When we drove into the mountains, I didn't see a heavy load lift off of you—we were just going to another place."

Colin crossed his arms over his chest. "Gee, Maggie, you seem to have got me all figured out. Why don't you cure my writer's block?"

Wincing at the vicious sarcasm in his tone, Maggie wished she could do anything else but tell him the truth. "Fine. One sentence. You and your writing are not responsible for Lucy's death."

He stared at her for a long moment, his tan face turning a pasty white. "This is bull—I don't have to take this," he muttered, and stomped out of the room.

Maggie listened to the sound of his footsteps recede and climbed back into the bed they had so lovingly shared. She closed her eyes and leaned back against the pillows, willing herself not to cry, replaying the scene in her head, trying to make it come out differently.

If only they hadn't gotten sidetracked with that garbage about her and tenure and her family. Maybe if they could have stayed focused, she could have made him understand her, made him see how he was limiting himself.

She hadn't even gotten to the part about suggesting they find a place outside of Boston, someplace close enough for her to commute, but far enough out that he wouldn't feel closed in. No, she hadn't even gotten to mention that idea.

Damn. She hadn't reached him.

She'd known it was a gamble, that she might not make him see, but she hadn't expected him to hold himself so apart from their argument. He'd been annoyed, then sardonic, and when she'd gotten too close to the truth, he'd walked out. Maybe she should go upstairs after him and try...

No. She wasn't going to reach him, not now. At this point, no words would convince him she was right. She'd lost.

Despite her efforts, she felt tears slipping out from under her eyelids, running down her face, but she made no move to wipe them away. Perhaps enough of them would wash away her pain.

* * *

Colin strode around upstairs, still furious after minutes of pacing. What the hell did she know about his life? She had no idea what he'd been through, what Lucy's death had done to him. No, he wasn't responsible for it—her car had hit a patch of ice and sailed off the road. Nobody could have foreseen that. True, if they hadn't had that last argument, maybe she wouldn't have driven off like she always did when they fought....

At least Maggie wasn't a quitter. Every time they'd had words she'd stood toe-to-toe with him, having her say. Of course, they'd never fought like they had tonight. It had taken every ounce of his concentration to hold back, to make sure he didn't say something that would send her running out the door.

Stop thinking about it, he ordered himself. He wasn't going to change anything. Useless "what ifs" did no good. Lucy was dead, Maggie was leaving, and he'd be here, alone, just like before. He'd be fine. Life would go back to normal. He could go back to what he'd been doing before Maggie.

Why, he could go back to cataloging the boxes of manuscripts he'd bought at the beginning of the summer at that estate sale. He hadn't even looked at them since... since walking into Columbo's that night and seeing Maggie eating dinner.

Hell, he could do that right now. It wasn't as though he was going to get any sleep anytime soon, and at least he could be thinking about something else besides Maggie's pleading face. That much decided, he went into his office and switched on his computer, pulling the box of journals out of the closet where he'd shoved them when Maggie had started occupying his days.

The data-base program he'd set up was great. Author, title, type of work, subjects, locations, dates, a memo field for some description. If he started writing again—he winced as Maggie's "you think you don't deserve..." echoed in his mind—*when* he started writing again, he could pull up primary sources on any subject, right here.

He moved slowly through the stack, fingers tapping the keys, entering the information. Toward the bottom of the pile, as he finished one diary, he came upon a stack of loose papers, and he pulled them out, smoothing their creases.

Beautiful penmanship, he noted absently. Excellent example of the flowing nineteenth-century style. Then the title penetrated. "A True History of the Discovery of Silver in Washoe, then Utah, now the State of Nevada. September 9, 1863, by Francis J. Hoover."

He began to read.

An hour later, he tipped his head back against the leather headrest of his chair and chuckled.

"Oh, Maggie. You've been searching the whole damn summer for this thing, and it's been in a box in my closet the entire time."

Ah, the irony. The Hoover manuscript, over the course of Maggie's search, had evolved into far more than merely another source. It had become a talisman, a good luck piece. If she found it, she could incorporate its material into her book, and she would surely get tenure. If she didn't find it, somehow she might just miss the mark.

And he had it. He'd bought this box, contents uninspected, from the estate of the granddaughter of a Comstock miner. It had probably been in that woman's attic since she'd inherited it herself.

So now he had it. And could do whatever he wanted with it. And Colin realized, to his chagrin, that his first impulse was to put the damn thing back into the stack, the stack back into the box and the box back into his closet. She need never know.

No, he couldn't play God, wouldn't be responsible for someone else's life again.

"I'm the only one who can screw up my life, Colin."

Colin's head jerked up. As loudly as he'd heard the words, he could have sworn Maggie was in the room.

"You're not responsible, you didn't cause..." Maggie's words replayed in his mind as he stared at the papers he clutched.

Finally he loosened his grip, letting the papers fall back onto the desk. She was right, dammit. Yeah, he'd messed up his own life some, made some poor choices and yes, some of those choices had affected other people, like Lucy. But he wasn't responsible for the choices she'd made, like driving down the mountain in her little sports car because she was mad at him, like choosing to stay married to him because she was afraid of the alternative.

A great sense of relief washed over him. Gathering the manuscript, he took it into the kitchen to wrap it in brown paper and string. That done, he returned to the office, closed the data base file, and opened the one for word processing.

Maggie would go back to Boston, and he would stay here. That was the way it should, no, had to be. She needed to write her book and make her decisions; meanwhile, he had some catching up to do. His fingers moved slowly, hesitantly over the keys, picking up speed as he went along.

Probably, if she hadn't cried herself to sleep, Maggie wouldn't have overslept, and would have been on the road by the time Colin appeared the following morning, instead of still trying to squeeze the last of her belongings into the back seat of her car.

Probably, if she'd gotten enough sleep, Maggie would have stepped away from the car before straightening when Colin uttered her name, and would have avoided knocking her head on the doorjamb.

Probably, if she hadn't had tears in her eyes from hitting her head, he wouldn't have looked so damn good, despite the fact that he obviously hadn't gotten much sleep himself.

"Good morning," she said, still rubbing the spot where her skull had met the car.

"Are you all right?" He moved toward her, but she waved him back.

"No, no, I'm fine."

He stood helplessly for a moment, then shrugged, toying with the white baseball cap in his hands. "Whatever." He glared at her suddenly. "Did you plan on leaving without saying goodbye to me?"

"Yes. No. I don't know. Look, I don't have much time, Colin—"

"This won't take long," he interrupted. "I didn't want to leave things the way we did last night."

Maggie inhaled slowly, willing her heart not to race. After their bitter words, was there anything left to say? Anything that could mend hearts bruised and torn?

Colin rubbed his face. God, he was too old to stay up all night anymore. After she left, he'd collapse on sheets that smelled like her, and sleep the sleep of the dead.

"So this is it," she said, not quite meeting his eyes.

"I guess it is." He dropped an arm across her shoulders and walked her to her car door. He looked down at her, resting his hands on her shoulders, trying to summon the words to erase every harsh sentiment voiced the previous evening.

"I'm sorry about last night, Maggie. Believe me, I have never wanted anything but the best for you, even if I expressed it badly sometimes. But in the long run, like you said, the only thing that matters is that you have what you want."

He pulled her close, inhaling the sweet fragrance of her hair, imprinting the feel of her against him.

"So go after that, Maggie. Go home, and write the best damn book you can, and be the best damn history professor Beaton University has ever seen."

For an instant, he tightened his embrace, before he let her go, slapped the baseball cap onto her head and stood back to watch her settle into her car.

He leaned down, brushed her warm cheek with a kiss, whispered, "Drive carefully, Professor," and straightened.

Maggie started the car and shifted into gear, not daring to look again at the man standing there. As she drove off, she glanced only once into the rearview mirror, memorizing his form before returning her attention to the road.

She was halfway to Salt Lake City before she spotted the package on the passenger seat next to her.

Chapter Eleven

Seally padded across the room to where Colin sat at his desk, the click of her toenails on the oak floor a neat counterpoint to the click of his computer keys. With a whine, she dropped her head onto Colin's knee.

"I know, girl, I miss her, too." Colin interrupted his typing to give the dog a reassuring pat. He stopped to read his last sentence, then shook his head in disgust and pushed the backspace key.

Had writing always been this hard for him? It seemed as though, in the past, the words had always just come to him. He couldn't remember agonizing over every phrase as he was now, writing and rewriting whole blocks of text, whole pages of his story, trying to make every word perfect.

Maybe it was just that he wasn't sharing the process with anyone this time, wasn't talking out his plotting problems or his questions about motivation. No one knew he was writing this book. Not his parents, not Devon and Steve, not even Sam Bradshaw, his agent.

And not Maggie. Especially not Maggie. When he'd watched her drive down his gravel road, he'd sworn he'd stay away until he had something to show her, something that said he wasn't hiding on his mountain, something to prove he wasn't the man she'd left thinking he was.

The mission had turned out to be harder than he'd thought it would be. This book, unlike every other one of his, was not writing itself. It was demanding every ounce of his sorry concentration, it was requiring that every word be dragged, kicking and screaming, from his psyche.

Not that he didn't love his story. Indeed, on his good days he thought it was probably the best thing he'd ever come up with. Of course, on his bad days, he couldn't believe he'd ever finish it, much less that anyone might possibly be interested in buying the damn thing. Which was absurd. After his hiatus, anything by C. J. McCall would sell like hotcakes on the curiosity factor alone.

But he didn't want this book merely to herald his long-awaited comeback. The story he'd concocted—lovers from different walks of life who had to learn to compromise to live together, who had to surrender old dreams for new ones—came too close to paralleling his life with Maggie. He wouldn't, couldn't turn in anything less than the very best work he could possibly create.

It always came back to Maggie.

She'd spoiled the cabin for him. Heck, she'd spoiled Washoe and Storey counties, to boot. He couldn't go anywhere in the area without picturing her there, without remembering their summer together.

It wasn't just the picture of her at the Silver City cemetery which rested on his dresser, or the one of her in Sausalito which sat beside his computer. Her presence filled his home, making him remember the time they had shared.

He'd found her football jersey at the bottom of his laundry basket, and he'd slept with it until her lingering scent had vanished, replaced by his own over time. He hadn't used his hot tub since she'd gone—the very memory of their last night together made him hard, made him ache for her. Even preparing meals had become a chore, remembering her sitting on his countertop, snatching bites and kisses while he cooked.

One night, just to get out, he'd decided to go to Columbo's. It had started out just like the last time he was there—Scotty offering him a beer and asking what he'd been up to—but this time no brunette sat in the dining room unwittingly waiting for him to pay her check and step into her life. He'd managed two sips before he'd had to leave.

So now he stayed home. As much torture as the cabin offered, it was a torture of loving memories, and the torment of an uncertain promise for the future.

He really ought to call Sam, he reminded himself once again. His agent might be interested to know another book was in the pipeline, that maybe Colin hadn't lost everything almost three years ago, just misplaced it for a little while.

He typed a few more words, paused, backspaced and started over again. Tomorrow, for sure. Definitely, he'd call Sam tomorrow.

Maggie stared at the telephone on her desk, trying to summon the courage to pick up the receiver and make her call. Outside Marbury Hall, the leaves had turned at last, nature's ultimate hurrah before winter set in.

Autumn had finally come to Boston. An abnormally warm October had delayed its arrival, but now, mid-November, the season was everywhere. In the last of the brilliant gold and copper decorating the trees and sidewalks, in the crisp air that made her students don extra layers, in the quickened pace of undergraduates no longer anxious to linger outside lecture halls before classes started.

Mid-November meant eight weeks since she'd seen Colin. She marked every day off on a mental calendar, every day away from him, every day that she hadn't given in to the almost overwhelming urge to call him, every day she hadn't heard from him.

Not that she'd really expected to. No, his farewell and the surprising gift of the Hoover manuscript told her he was letting her go, to write her book and decide her own future. Without any influence from him.

As if that were possible. She'd meant it when she told him she loved him, and his unselfish gift had only reinforced that sentiment. Knowing that he was alone in his solitary home in Nevada, waiting for her to come to a decision, only made her wish she could rush the outcome.

But she couldn't. She wasn't going back out to Nevada until she resolved her life, she knew that much. It wasn't fair to Colin, it wasn't fair to herself.

If she decided to stay at Beaton and pursue tenure, then she would go to Colin and tell him that. Then he'd have to decide whether he wanted her enough to work out some sort of a compromise.

They couldn't let their relationship slide along as they had at the end of this past summer, pretending that everything would work out somehow, that she would come back in December and that things would be the same. If they did that, at the end of her sabbatical they would wind up stuck in the same limbo in which they were currently mired, both wondering what the future held, both wishing things were different. She needed something, anything more definite than that, but she wouldn't have any answers until she determined her own future.

A lot of that future hinged on the book she was writing, and the way in which it was shaping up. The Hoover manuscript gave her valuable insights into the Groshes and their struggles, indeed adding a whole other layer to her story. She was more convinced than ever that they truly had discovered the Comstock Lode. Hoover's recollections, combined with his quotes from Allen's letters, gave her more specific information about the Grosh discoveries than any other source she'd found.

She spent every free moment writing. Between classes, evenings, weekends, her computer called to her, luring her to its electronic glow. The results were worth the effort. What she had written so far surpassed any of her wildest expectations. The passion she couldn't expend on Colin was going into her book, making it a darn fine read, if she did say so herself.

And that was why she was currently staring at the telephone, trying to summon the nerve to dial. At last she lifted the receiver, and punched in the area code and number.

"Carruthers Literary Agency," came the smooth, cultured voice at the other end of the connection. She took a deep breath and gripped the receiver a little tighter before she spoke. "Edwina Carruthers, please."

"You look like hell."

Colin closed his eyes, wishing for an instant that the couple standing on his front steps would magically disappear.

Nope. When he opened his eyes, they were still there, unmistakably anxious, worried even. He tried to ignore the stab of guilt that flashed through him at the sight.

"Thank you, Steve. It's lovely to see you, too. Now, go away." He started to close the door, eager to get back to his computer, to Ethan and Sarah's struggles.

Steve's foot stopped the door. "Not so fast. We didn't drive all the way up here to have you slam the door in our faces."

"Next time, try calling," he growled.

"We did," Devon said softly. "We've been calling since September, and you haven't answered, you haven't returned any of our calls."

Aw, hell. She had him there. Gazing down into the faces of his very old, very dear, very concerned friends, Colin knew he was letting them come in. Still, he couldn't help making one last stab at making them understand. "I'm working."

"Yeah, Colin, I'm sure you are. Now let us in, it's too cold for Devon and the baby out here."

Automatically, he stepped back, more than a little annoyed that Steve had brushed off his momentous announcement. "Steve, I'm *working*."

Steve, preoccupied with helping Devon out of her down jacket, once again missed the import of his words. "Yeah, right. Did you hit another auction? Buy some more journals?"

"No, Steve. Dammit, I'm *working*," he repeated one more time.

The significance of his words penetrated the Thornes' consciousness simultaneously. Four wide eyes stared at him. "You're working? Like, *writing* working?"

Colin nodded, almost reveling in the novelty of telling another person for the first time just what he'd been doing since mid-September. "Writing working," he echoed.

Steve handed Devon her coat. "Sorry, pal, we didn't realize. We'll get out of your way. Call us when you've got some time and we'll—"

"Wait!" Suddenly, now that his secret was out, he found himself eager to share it with someone, anyone, even if it wasn't quite the right someone. "I was just about to break for lunch," he lied. "Stay, please."

Devon looked him up and down critically. "Looks like you haven't been breaking for lunch very often. You've lost weight."

He couldn't help it, he swept her into an enveloping hug. "Physics in action," he teased. "Matter stays constant, so as you've gained weight, someone's had to lose it, and I offered."

Their combined laughter made him realize how quiet his house had been over the past two months, how little happiness its walls held since Maggie left. The only emotions allowed were those channeled into his manuscript; all other feelings were ruthlessly shoved aside. He had to, or he'd never finish the book, and never prove what he needed to prove.

He just hoped there was something, anything in the refrigerator. Takeout pizza was always stone-cold by the time it got to the top of his mountain.

They made their way to the kitchen, where Colin ordered his visitors to sit while he studied his larder and began preparing lunch. Frozen pesto, flour in the pantry—pizza it would be, but homemade.

Steve and Devon were still uneasy, he realized as he mixed the ingredients for a quick dough. Devon was talking too fast, offering him a moment-by-moment account of her pregnancy, from the joys of ultrasound to the kicks she'd felt in the car that morning. Steve watched him silently, obviously trying to figure out what was going on, but too wary to ask.

Colin wasn't sure which reaction bothered him more, but it hurt more than he wanted to admit that two of his best friends felt such anxiety around him.

"I'm sorry I've been such a lousy friend," he said abruptly, cutting Devon off in the middle of her painting-the-nursery saga. "You both deserve better than that from me."

Devon, true-blue Devon, leapt in to reassure him. "Colin, that's not true. You've been going through some—" She stopped, and made a helpless little gesture before she continued. "Okay, we don't know what you've been going through."

Colin sat down across the table from them, steeling himself for their inquisition. He owed them. They deserved answers to their questions, a chance to yell at him, whatever.

They did neither, of course. Devon reached over and took his hand, squeezing it tightly. "We've missed you, Colin. When you and Maggie came to see us during the summer, we thought we had the old Colin back. Now we don't know."

No, the old Colin was gone, forever, he hoped. The old Colin couldn't ever hope to claim a woman like Maggie as his own; she deserved something far better than that. The old Colin would have told Devon that nothing was wrong, made excuses about being busy, preoccupied or distracted, and promised that it was business as usual for C. J. McCall. The new Colin would tell her of his struggles, of what he'd learned about himself since Maggie had left....

"There you have it," he concluded sometime later. "This book is taking an enormous amount out of me, even as it's giving me my life back. I know that I've cut myself off, but it seemed like the only way I could make this work."

"And now we've screwed up the process," Steve said quietly. "Colin, that was never our intention. We shouldn't come up here without—"

"Don't apologize," Colin ordered. "It's great to have you two here, and I'm really grateful you forced the issue by showing up. I hadn't realized quite how much I'd missed you both."

Devon's blue eyes sparkled with unshed tears. Colin fixed her with a stern look. "And don't you start crying on me, young lady. We can't have my godchild getting upset."

She made a sound somewhere between a sob and a chuckle, and swiped at her eyes before she spoke. When she did, her tone was light, teasing again. "You are, I trust, going to provide this child with a godmother?"

Ah, Maggie. The one issue he hadn't addressed in his soul baring. Colin rose abruptly from the table and began assembling the pizza, suddenly needing to do something with his hands.

"I don't know. That one's not entirely up to me." He rolled out the dough, taking pains to make a perfect circle. Behind him, the silence stretched. Neither of his guests was going to ask him to elaborate, it appeared.

"Maggie's wishes come into play here, too, you know." He spooned pesto onto the crust and spread it evenly with a spatula.

"She's deciding what she wants to do with her life, and where I fit into that." Chopped sun dried tomatoes next, then frozen bay shrimp that he'd thawed under hot water.

Steve finally asked a question. "You're going to leave it up to her? What she decides determines what you do?"

Colin scowled at his masterpiece before he slid it into the oven. "No, I didn't say that. But I can't go after her until I finish this book."

"Why not?"

Damn, he wished Steve hadn't asked that question. How did he explain something that's a feeling, a sense rather than a rational thought?

Stalling for time, for the right words, Colin wiped down the cutting board and counter, and gathered plates and cutlery for lunch. He could feel Devon and Steve watching him, waiting for his answer.

"I guess," he said slowly, "I guess I need to finish this book so I have something tangible to show Maggie, something to prove I've changed."

He stared out the window and across the valley, hoping his answer would be enough.

Footsteps sounded on the oak flooring, and Steve's hand came to rest on his shoulder—warm, heavy, comforting. Together, they studied the first patches of snow dusting the Sierra Nevada mountains.

"You know, Colin, you don't have to prove a damn thing to Maggie."

He knew that. In his heart of hearts he knew that. Believing it was a different matter, however. "Maybe—" He stopped, suddenly reaching an understanding of what drove him, what force fueled his work. "Maybe I have to prove it to myself."

When the warm, rich voice said, "Good morning," Maggie almost dropped the phone. She'd timed her Thanksgiving phone call with the certainty that Colin would be anyplace but home on that day. She'd planned on talking to an answering machine, not to a real, live, breathing Colin.

"Hi," she started, only to have the single syllable stop somewhere around her tonsils. She cleared her throat and tried again. "Colin, it's Maggie. I called to wish you a happy Thanksgiving."

Silence hummed across the lines.

She waited, wiggling her foot nervously against the table leg, twisting the phone cord around tension-filled fingers. Just when she was about to give up, he spoke. "I'm surprised to hear from you."

She sensed caution, and more than a little restraint in his voice. A nervous laugh escaped her. "I'm amazed I called, to tell you the truth."

Again, an awkward silence stretched between them.

"So, how are you?" he said at last.

"Fine. Busy." Why hadn't she at least considered the possibility of speaking to him? Could she ask him to hang up and let her speak to his machine? "How about you?"

"I'm working."

Her heart plunged at those words. She'd heard him say those very words too often over the summer. They meant he was still hiding among his manuscripts and journals, still waiting for that elusive story to come to him. He would have told her if he was writing.

"That's good to hear," she said finally. Casting about for another topic of conversation, she said the first thing to come to her. "What are you doing at home today? I expected you to be in San Francisco with your parents."

"Why?"

"It's Thanksgiving, Colin. Families usually get together." Surely he knew that much.

"Oh. No, Mom and Dad went to Hawaii for a few days. I'm driving over to Tahoe for dinner with Devon and Steve."

At last, a safe topic. "How are they?"

"Fine. Devon's getting huge."

Oh, the baby. For an instant Maggie envied the other woman. How she would love to be settled enough with Colin to even dream of a child. "Well, give them my best, please."

"Of course."

There didn't seem to be much else to say. Maggie was trying to figure out a way to end the conversation gracefully when Colin asked, "So you'll be with your family?"

"Of course." If there had been a note of censure in his voice, she wasn't going to acknowledge it. "The whole clan is gathering at Ma and Pop's."

"Sounds hectic."

"It is. But it's a wonderful hectic. I love my family, Colin." Whatever they resolved at whatever future date, he had to understand that, period.

"I know that, Maggie," he said with a sigh, and she instantly regretted pressing the issue. "Look, I should get on the road. It's a long drive to Tahoe, and there will probably be some traffic."

"Of course." Disappointment fought relief at his words. She had so much to say to him, but at the same time, so little. She couldn't make any promises, all she could do was let him know she was still thinking of him. "Take care of yourself."

"You too, Maggie." Then, almost as an afterthought, "I'm glad you called."

His parting words warmed her as she hung up the phone.

Colin cradled the receiver, resisting the urge to pick it up again and call Maggie back. They didn't have anything to say to each other, not right now. She obviously hadn't made a decision that would bring her back to him, or she would have said so.

And as for him, well, he didn't want to tell her about his changes, he wanted to show her. And he couldn't do that until he was done with the damn book.

He glanced at his watch. Maybe he could squeeze in another hour before he absolutely had to hit the road for Tahoe.

When the phone rang, he was amazed to realize three hours had passed. He knew who was calling even before he picked up the receiver. "Hi, Steve, I'm sorry."

"It's Devon, and you'd better be. My turkey is getting dried out waiting for you." Despite her words, she sounded more worried than annoyed.

"I'm sorry," he repeated. "I sat down at the computer for an hour, and lost track of time. If I head out now—"

"Colin, it's okay. Steve and I know how important this book is to you. If you want to stay home and work, we'll understand, really."

He didn't deserve such good friends, Colin thought for the thousandth time, swallowing the lump in his throat. "How about if I drive over tomorrow for leftover turkey sandwiches?"

Devon agreed to his suggestion, and they ended the call. As he returned to his computer, Colin pondered his good fortune.

A man wasn't always lucky enough to have friends willing to understand his struggles. Now, if he could just be that lucky with Maggie.

She wasn't going to scream. It was undignified, unprofessional even, and just might deafen the woman on the other end of the phone. And she most definitely did not want to deafen the woman who had just sold her book proposal.

As she listened to Edwina outline the deal, she fought hard to hang on to the woman's words while her mind raced. She wanted to dance, but the phone cord tethered her to the desk. She wanted to sing, but she settled for doing a jig in place while Edwina spoke.

They finished the call, and Maggie rushed out into the hallway, eager to find a colleague, any colleague. She found the chairman of the history department, Ralph Burns.

"Ralph, I've just heard the most wonderful news. My agent just called, and she sold my book! She's already trying to shop it to Hollywood, which I don't think will happen, but—'' She stopped, realizing that she was babbling. The avuncular Professor Burns seemed to understand, despite her dithering.

"That's wonderful news, Maggie. You do realize what this means, don't you?"

Not entirely, she realized. Oh, she had an inkling, but the shock of the news still had her mind reeling. She cited the one thing that had hit her so far. "It means I can afford my sabbatical."

He smiled, the same gentle, tolerant benediction he bestowed on students who gave incorrect answers in class. "Besides that," he reproved. "You know you'll get tenure now. A well-positioned book will bring you and the college a good deal of favorable publicity."

A little air went out of Maggie's bubble. She hadn't even thought about tenure, not since sending the book to Edwina Carruthers. She'd wanted the sale for other, bigger reasons. Like Colin.

Ralph continued, oblivious to her wayward thoughts. "And your coup of digging up an important manuscript last seen by another historian one hundred years ago, well I don't need to tell you—"

Colin's coup. He'd given her the manuscript, he'd suggested writing a commercially oriented work.

"I need to make some calls, Ralph," she interrupted. "You understand, of course."

"Of course, my dear." He patted her shoulder. "Think about when we should begin the tenure review process. Perhaps we can meet after the New Year to discuss it."

Tenure. That word again. It didn't seem like such a shiny dream, not right now. Maggie excused herself and fled back into her office.

Cut it out, Sullivan. You're just a little overemotional right now, that's all. When you calm down you'll realize this is exactly what you want.

Straightening from where she'd sagged back against the door, Maggie marched across the room and picked up the telephone to call—who?

She couldn't call Colin, not yet. He'd want to know what she was going to do with the rest of her life, as if one phone call could decide that issue.

She couldn't call Edmund, not anymore. Despite the agreement they'd made in that phone call in September, that agreement to remain friends, they weren't. She didn't know whether he'd truly been crushed by her defection, or if she no longer fit into the appointed slot of his life plan. Whatever the reason, she knew he wouldn't be especially gratified by her call.

She couldn't call her mother. Maggie knew that if her mother mentioned the word *tenure* to her one more time, she might actually break down and scream.

So she did the only thing possible. She put on her coat and scarf and headed for the Public Gardens to watch the ice skaters and think.

"I have an announcement to make."

Maggie gazed around the dining room table at the faces of her family, waiting for her words to register. The whole family was there—Ma and Pop, the boys and their wives: Rory and Lisa, Brendan and Ellen, Sean and Grace.

The kids were at the kitchen table, and she could hear "Did so," "Did not," through the closed door. Typical Sullivan family dinner.

She'd waited until Sunday dinner at her parents' to share her news because she wanted to say the words once, to everyone together.

Not quite. In truth, she'd waited until Sunday because Ralph's words about tenure on Friday and her reaction to them had forced her to stop and think. Now that the reality of a book contract and its promise of a decent advance were sinking in, she'd realized she was free to do whatever she chose to do. Or, more precisely, she was as free as she wanted to be.

"I have an announcement to make," she repeated. This time her words reached a few ears, and after some nudging and a "Shh!" eight expectant faces turned toward her.

"Yes, Maggie?"

Ma. Maggie focused on her mother's face and cleared her throat. "I, um, sold my book."

Bedlam erupted. Sheer, utter bedlam. All eight leapt from the table to hug her at once, the commotion drawing the children from the next room to add their squeals, even if some of them didn't quite understand what the excitement was all about.

"Atta girl."

"I knew you could do it."

"Like *Beauty and the Beast?*"

"No, dummy, a grown-up book. You know, boring."

"Conor, don't call your cousin dummy."

"But she said—"

"Now you'll be sure to get tenure, Maggie."

Trust Ma to cut to the chase. At her words, everyone quieted down and turned to look at Maggie, waiting for her to agree with her mother's pronouncement.

This was not how she'd wanted to approach this part of the conversation. She'd planned on the excitement of her announcement carrying everyone through dessert at least, and then she would sort of slide into the subject of her future.

Oh, well. In for a penny... Taking a deep breath, she sat up straighter in her chair. "I may not go for tenure, Ma."

"What?"

"You've got to be kidding."

"Are you nuts? After all our work?"

"It's that man, isn't it?"

Her mother was too perceptive by half. Maggie knew that her mother had been watching her since her return in September, waiting for some discussion of her summer sojourn. Maggie hadn't offered to start one. Now she glanced around at the sea of faces surrounding her, unwilling to put her heart on the line over the roast beef and potatoes. "Maybe we should discuss this after dinner—"

"We will discuss it now."

"But the kids—"

"The children will go back to the kitchen and finish their dinner."

The children filed out of the room reluctantly, the older ones knowing they were missing something dramatic, the younger ones sensing they were missing something.

With the door firmly closed behind them, Brigid Sullivan turned to her daughter. "Now, Mary Margaret, suppose you tell us what you're talking about."

Funny how her mother could make her feel six all over again. But she wasn't six. She was an adult, and she could make a clear, logical case for herself.

"I'm not sure I want to continue teaching."

"And why would that be?"

Her mother spoke as if she already knew the answer to her question, and that the answer was "that man." Could she make her mother see that these were her doubts, her dreams? Maggie tried to put her all into the words she chose. "I've come to realize that I get a great deal of joy from writing, more than I ever have from teaching. Now that I have the opportunity to pursue that, as a career, I think—"

"It's that man, isn't it?" her mother repeated. One look at her mother's face told Maggie that Brigid Sullivan hadn't believed one word she'd said.

"I had doubts before I met Colin." *But he helped me see them clearly.*

"Maggie, people don't up and change careers in the middle of their lives." That came from Rory, who'd known all his life he would follow in his father's footsteps.

"Sure they do. The average adult will change careers three times over his or her working life."

Brendan snorted, "Statistics. You can prove anything you want with statistics."

"So is that it, Maggie? You've suddenly developed an urge to be average?" Sean goaded.

Yes, maybe I would. Maybe I'd like to be an average woman in love with a man for a little while, instead of Professor Sullivan, pride of the Sullivans. Let someone else carry the banner for a while.

Maggie didn't dare voice that thought. She said instead, "I don't know why you're all so upset about this. I'm getting paid good money for this book, more than I make as a lowly assistant professor, in fact. It's not as if I'm planning on living on the streets or something."

"After all our hard work—" Sean started.

Maggie interrupted. "No, Sean, you've all been very supportive, but I'm the one who worked hard."

"But we sacrificed—"

"Sacrificed what? My education was paid for by a combination of scholarships and student loans, which *I* am repaying, not you."

"But we—"

"Have all been very supportive of my endeavors, for which I am forever grateful. Now I'm asking you to be supportive of whatever decision I make, and I must emphasize that I have not made one yet." Could she have been any clearer?

"But we don't know this man." Her mother again. Maggie felt her stiff backbone softening at the concern in her mother's voice. "Ma, if—and that's a big *if*—Colin and I wind up together, you'll meet him, of course."

"But to move to the back of beyond."

"Reno has an international airport, Ma. It's not the end of the earth."

"Why isn't he here with you? Why are you the one sacrificing your life?"

This was funny, coming from a woman who had dedicated her entire existence to the comfort of her husband and sons. "Ma, he hasn't asked—"

"Have you even spoken to him since you came home? You're throwing away everything and you don't even know if the man wants you anymore, do you?"

Maggie counted to ten before she spoke, but she could hear the tremor in her voice anyway. She didn't care. "Ma, for the last time, I haven't made any final decisions, and when I do, they will be based on *my* goals for my life, not Colin's goals. If those goals happen to include Colin, well, I'll cross that bridge at that time."

"You're a fool, Mary Margaret, throwing your life away on a man like that."

"I had a hell of a time finding this place, you know. Had to ask some little chippy who wasn't wearing nearly enough clothing for this weather."

Maggie almost tipped her desk chair over in her haste to turn and rise. "Pop! What are you doing here?" Come to plead the family's case, no doubt. He'd been the only one not to throw his two cents into the conversation during the previous evening's contretemps.

Patrick Sullivan frowned as he gazed around the tiny, bookcase-lined room. "You know, this isn't really a very nice office for a professor and all. You'd think they'd give you newer furniture, at least."

"Budget cuts, Pop. We all have to make do," she answered, barely reining in her impatience. Not that he wasn't right about the furnishings, but that obviously wasn't why her father was making his first-ever visit to her office. Despite numerous invitations, he'd always avoided Beaton, saying he wasn't the kind of person to be walking around a college.

She watched him move around the confined space, picking up a volume lying on her table, stroking the glass paperweight on her desk. He lifted the framed photograph of Seally and Colin that sat next to her computer, and examined it closely.

"I listened to what all of you had to say last night," he said, still studying the photograph. "Your mother and brothers had some pretty compelling arguments. You'd be a fool not to listen to them."

Until that moment, Maggie hadn't known that a heart could actually, physically sink. Hers now rested like a cold lump in the pit of her stomach, beating out a slow "Not him, too." She'd known she could never count on her father to take her side over the rest of the family's, but she'd thought he wouldn't take theirs, either.

And that knowledge, of at least one person who wouldn't actively oppose her, had given her the courage to finally admit to herself what she'd known in her heart for months—that she was going back to Nevada. To stay.

Why it had taken her four months to admit that simple truth to herself still confounded her. Somewhere, in the early hours this morning, she'd sat up in her rumpled bed and finally said the words out loud.

And now her father was taking the support she'd imagined away from her. Not that it mattered. She was still going. The Sullivans would have to learn to live with it.

Before she could open her mouth to tell him that, he spoke again.

"But you'd be a bigger fool not to listen to your heart," he said, setting the picture frame back in its place and looking directly at Maggie for the first time since he'd arrived. "No matter what your mother thinks, it's your career, your life, and only you can make the decision to stay or go. You've always been sensible. You'll make the right decision."

Maggie tried to speak, but couldn't get beyond the lump in her throat. Her father gazed around the tiny room once again, as if trying to take in every detail. "I'm glad I got to see this before you left. Even if it's not much, it is the first office a Sullivan's had to herself."

His acceptance, his understanding, brought tears to Maggie's eyes. She blinked them back, willing them not to spill over onto her cheeks. Sullivans didn't cry.

He grabbed her in a bear hug, and Maggie pressed her face against his broad shoulder. "Don't worry about your ma," he whispered in her ear. "I'll tell her I've been dyin' to see Virginia City ever since the first time I saw 'Bonanza.'"

Chapter Twelve

Breathing a sigh of relief, Maggie pulled the rental car to a stop in Colin's snow-covered driveway. Driving up Geiger Grade in a howling blizzard gave her an entirely new appreciation for the travails her miners had experienced while crossing the Sierras—she couldn't even fathom attempting such a journey with a recalcitrant mule, let alone on foot.

The normal half-hour drive had taken her two hours. Two hours of creeping along in virtual whiteout conditions, clutching the steering wheel so tightly, her fingers still trembled, hunching her shoulders and straining to see through the blowing snow. Only the thought of Colin at the end of the road had pushed her on, had kept her from giving up and taking a motel room in Reno.

And ironically, now that she was here, a part of her wanted to turn around and go right back down the hill, to plunge back into that storm, ignoring the inviting lights of the cabin in front of her.

It had been over three months since she'd left Colin, a month since their Thanksgiving phone conversation. Would he want to see her? Or had he finally written off their relationship as that summer fling?

She only had that one frustrating, inconclusive call to go on, and she still couldn't tell what to make of that. His reticence during the conversation had equaled hers, but at least she knew and understood her reasons. His were a mystery to her, and she would have imagined the worst were it not for the gift of the manuscript.

After all, if he could give her that valuable work, didn't that mean he still cared about her, that their quarrel and harsh words hadn't destroyed forever what they'd shared and the potential for what they could share in the future?

That was what she was gambling on, now that the academic quarter had ended. She was free. Her sabbatical meant she didn't have to go back to Boston, but could stay here if she so desired.

If Colin so desired.

She was getting colder by the minute sitting in the car worrying. No point in putting off the inevitable. She wasn't going back down that mountain tonight.

Grabbing the package next to her on the front seat, she stepped from the car into the storm. The wind whirled around her, forcing her to half stumble, half run to the front door. She pounded hard, praying that he'd be quick. The wind tugged her cap off, whipping her hair around her face. When the door opened, she fell inside, into his arms.

"What the—Maggie!" he cried, recognizing her. He pulled her into the living room, toward the brightly burning fire. Tugging a hassock onto the hearth, he ordered, "Sit," pushing on her shoulders to punctuate his command.

Seally came bounding up the stairs and across the room, eager to lick Maggie's face. She'd gotten off not more than a single swipe before Colin pulled her away. She dropped at the side of the hassock, resting her head on Maggie's snow-dusted leg.

Kneeling in front of her, Colin brushed her hair from her face, and began assessing the cold's damage, as if she'd been out in it for any length of time. He began talking, quietly at first, his mutterings growing louder as he methodically pulled off her boots and chafed her feet. "What in hell do you think you were doing, running around in a storm like that? Don't you know you could have frozen to death out there if something had happened to your car? These roads are treacherous, and I'll bet you didn't even have the sense to rent something with four-wheel drive, did you?"

He didn't wait for an answer, but unbuttoned her coat, pulling off her gloves and offering her hands the same treatment he'd given her feet. "This isn't Boston, you know. How could you be so stupid? God, if you'd lost the road..."

Maggie could only sit passively and allow him to do his work, let his words wash over her while she absently stroked Seally's head. He was probably right. She could have run off the road, or gotten stranded. But she'd made it. She was here, and she wasn't leaving.

He'd stopped talking now, and Maggie stared at the fire, afraid to look at him, afraid of what she might see, or not see, in his eyes.

"Maggie?" Colin's voice softened, concerned. She finally turned her head.

"Hi," she said quietly.

"Hi," he echoed. Then he smiled, a glorious grin that lit up his face, and Maggie began to suspect everything would work out. She threw her arms around him and held on tightly, reveling in the iron bands of his answering embrace.

They rocked back and forth, holding each other, while minutes passed. Maggie buried her face against his neck, inhaling the familiar masculine scent she'd missed so much. When Colin echoed her gesture, his lips tickled the sensitive skin beneath her ear.

Maggie pulled back to gaze at him. "Your hair's longer."

"Yep."

She reached a cautious finger out to stroke the silky mass. "I like it. You look more like your book jacket again."

He nodded. "Yep, C. J. McCall is back."

She wasn't quite sure what he meant by that, but she figured she'd play it by ear for now. "And how do you feel about that?" she asked cautiously.

"Good." He paused, and the grin that lit his face told Maggie he meant it. "Really good. It's on my terms this time, not anyone else's. I know what I'm doing this time around."

Dangerous territory. There was an awkward pause before Colin spoke again. "In fact, I'll prove it." He tossed the words over his shoulder as he disappeared down the stairs.

When he returned and handed her a gift-wrapped box remarkably like the one Maggie had carried across the country with her, she knew what it had to be, but didn't want to believe it. He'd written something, something that he wanted to share with her.

She ripped the ribbon off, and tore at the paper. Fumbling with the lid, she finally opened it and found a title page reading *The Cowboy and the Lady.*

"It's the story of a Boston schoolmarm who comes out West and meets a disreputable cowhand. Turn the page, Maggie."

She obliged, and read his dedication. "To Maggie, for putting the words back into my heart.

"Oh, my," she said softly. She recalled her long-ago fantasy of Colin dedicating a book to her. Reality was far sweeter.

"So, what do you think?"

"I think it's wonderful." Maggie struggled not to cry.

"I should warn you, my agent will be announcing the return of C. J. McCall after the first of the year, so I suppose we'll be hearing from the tabloids again."

His light words gave Maggie time to compose herself. She riffled the pages in her lap, dying to curl up and absorb the whole thing, but that could wait. It looked as if they were going to be snowed in for a few days.

Still, she had one question. "How does it end?"

"He sees the light, and follows her to Boston, where they live happily ever after."

"Hmm. Won't do at all. You'll have to change it."

She set the manuscript down and looped her arms around Colin's neck. "You see," she explained solemnly, "a more believable ending would be that she goes back to Boston, and sees her life in an entirely different light. She realizes there may be a whole lot more than the options they've considered, so she comes back to him. *Then* they live happily ever after."

"Are you sure?" Colin understood what she was saying, that she was talking about far more than the book.

"Positive. Your ending doesn't work, mine does."

"I'll work on the rewrite tomorrow."

Maggie struggled to equal his flip tone. "Well, as long as we're exchanging Christmas presents, I brought one for you, as well."

She looked around, and spotted the box she'd dropped at the front door. Colin's eyes followed her gaze. "You sit, I'll get it."

She watched him move across the room, her eyes hungrily taking in the sight. He still moved with the rangy grace she loved, his shoulders appearing broader than ever under the bulk of a heavy sweater, his hips seemingly narrower in his worn jeans.

"Like what you see?" He'd caught her staring again. Oh, she'd missed him!

"You bet." She shifted so he could sit beside her on the hassock, and he joined her, eyeing the package in his hands suspiciously.

"Open it," she prompted.

He shook his head. "It's only the twenty-third. I never, ever open presents early."

"Look, buddy, I carried this thing not only across the country, but up the mountain in a blizzard. You'd better open it."

Colin laughed, and Maggie welcomed the sound. It had been too long since she'd heard it.

He was the kind of person who opened a package carefully, removing the ribbon and coiling it neatly, slipping a finger under the tape so as not to tear the paper.

Maggie couldn't stand the wait. "Just rip it, Colin, please."

He shook his head. "Good things come to those who wait. I love anticipation." At last, he slid the wrapping paper off, folding and setting it aside before lifting the lid. Maggie held her breath, and let it out with a whoosh when he smiled.

"*Silver Dreams*. That's nice. Sounds like one of my titles."

Maggie laughed nervously. "Yes, it just sort of came to me. This is only the rough draft, and it still has a long way to go before publication, but I wanted you to have it now. Go on to the next page," she urged.

"To Colin, for teaching me that the story really does write itself," he read aloud. "Thank you, Maggie, I'm honored." His simple words filled Maggie's heart.

He gazed down at the book, not turning the page, not saying anything else. Maggie found she couldn't stand the silence. "It's going to be published. I sold it. I mean, I got a New York agent and she sold it. I still can't quite believe it—I mean, me, an author...." Her voice trailed off, and she shrugged helplessly.

Colin shook his head. "I can believe it. You're a wonderful writer, and I know this book deserves to be read. I'm very proud of you." He hugged her again, then pulled away.

Standing, he swept her into his arms. "Come on, woman, you need to be warmed up."

"Yes, sir." It was awfully tough to be prim and obedient when the man you loved was sweeping you off your feet—literally. She resisted the urge to kiss him; she hadn't fought a mountain to break her neck on a flight of stairs.

When they reached the bedroom, she saw a pair of suitcases out of the corner of her eye. She'd have to ask him about those, later, much later.

He undressed her as if she were another Christmas present, slowly, patiently, peeling layer by layer off until she stood naked before him.

"Oh, I've missed you," he whispered, cupping her breasts gently, watching her nipples pucker.

He had too many clothes on. Maggie tugged at his sweater, finally jerking it over his head. The jeans were quick to follow, and she and Colin tumbled onto the bed.

It was as if they'd been away from each other forever. The hunger, the need they shared raged, begging to be assuaged.

At the same time, it was as if they'd never been apart. Maggie knew every line, every hollow, every sinew of Colin's body intimately.

"I can't wait," he whispered, and rolled her over onto her back. Maggie opened herself to him, and when he entered her, let out a joyous cry.

She urged him on, wrapping her legs around him, pulling him closer, absorbing him into her. He arched his head back, pure pleasure written on his face as he slid in and out of her welcoming heat.

She was with him, stroke for stroke, movement for movement, in a communion of the senses that lasted forever, and ended too soon. She was with him as his pace quickened. Greedy, she clasped his hips, driving him on, urging him faster and faster, until together they reached their pinnacle, and absorbed each other's shudders and cries of joy.

At last able to move, Colin rolled over onto his back, pulling Maggie against him. She raised herself onto her elbows, studying his features closely, seeing changes in the three months they'd been apart.

His face was thinner. His cheekbones were more prominent, their fine contours adding a new definition to his face. He'd lost weight. His stomach had gone from flat to almost concave; he'd gone from lean to rangy. The added definition looked good on him, but Maggie wasn't sure she liked it.

"We need to fatten you up," she said absently, frowning down at him.

Colin smiled at Maggie's worried expression. God, he'd missed the way her every emotion played itself out on her face. She'd be a lousy liar, thank goodness. He'd always know where he stood.

They lay together, stroking, touching in the aftermath of their passion. "What made you decide?" he asked at last, when it looked as if she wasn't going to speak.

After a long pause, Maggie answered. "Not one thing, really. I've known since I left that I was coming back, but I didn't know whether it would be to stay or to deliver an ultimatum. But as the term progressed, I found myself getting more joy from writing and less joy from teaching."

She stopped again, and Colin murmured softly, urging her on.

"Anyway, the situation came to a head when I sold the book. When my colleagues spoke of tenure, I realized the book was a valuable accomplishment in itself, and not a means of increasing my academic worth, and I wanted it recognized as such. It made me reevaluate."

She stopped again, gathering her thoughts. "When I tried to explain that to my family, suggesting that I might not pursue tenure, Ma and the boys were incensed that I could consider doing anything other than teaching."

"And that reaction tipped the scales?" His stubborn Maggie. He could see her taking umbrage if someone, anyone, told her what to do. Hints about expectations were fine, ultimatums were not.

"Not exactly. I think deep down someplace I already knew, but their reaction forced me to think it through and admit to myself that their dreams weren't my dreams, and that I didn't want to spend the rest of my life basing my actions on what they expected of me. What made telling them easier was when my pop encouraged me to make my own decision, much to my surprise."

"Why surprise?"

"You'd have to know Pop. Ma is a true matriarch, and he has always deferred to her on family decisions, so for him to stick his neck out—"

"Shows just how much he loves you."

Her tone softened. "Yeah, I guess it does." She ran her fingers through the hair on his chest, tugging lightly. "He's looking forward to meeting you, you know."

Yeah, right. "With a shotgun, I suppose."

"No, that would be Sean." Her laughter told him he didn't have any real worries.

Now he had to tell her what he had decided. "If being a continent away is going to be too hard on you and your family, we don't have to stay in Nevada, you know. I'm not sure I could handle living right in the middle of Boston, but maybe we could find someplace just outside the city."

Maggie rolled over and rested her arms on his chest, raising herself so she could see his face. "Now it's my turn. What brought about that change?"

Here it was, confession time. Colin decided that it didn't feel too bad, all things considered. "A lot of what you said in September was true. I was doing penance by hiding out here. Writing the book became a way to prove I'd done my time, that I was ready to move on."

Maggie shook her head, frowning slightly. "You didn't need to prove a thing to me, you know."

Tugging her back down beside him so he could hold her, Colin nodded. "Steve was kind enough to point that out to me. I realized I was proving to myself that I was ready, that I was doing this for all the right reasons. When I typed 'The End' I wanted to catch the first plane to Boston."

"What stopped you?"

"Logistical stuff. I went to see my folks, I got in touch with my agent, I called Beaton to see when finals ended."

"What?" Her head came up from his chest.

"I figured if I showed up on your doorstep while you were buried hip deep in blue books, you might not be quite so happy to see me, and I wanted the best odds possible."

He felt her whole body shake with her chuckles. "You amaze me, you know."

"And I'm about to amaze you further."

Sliding from her embrace, he rose from the bed and padded over to the suitcases. He felt Maggie watching as he rooted around for a moment before returning to the bed with two small velvet boxes in his hand.

He set one on the bedside table before settling back down beside her, and tipping her face up so she met his eyes. "As you may have guessed by the suitcases, I was coming to Boston. I may be a little slow, but I'm not stupid enough to let the best thing that's ever happened to me slip away." He slipped the box into her hand. "Maggie, will you marry me?"

"Are you sure this is what you want?" Maggie heard herself ask, almost not recognizing the voice as her own, it had gone so shaky.

"Absolutely. I can live anywhere, but I can't live without you. The past three months have been the most exhilarating and frustrating in my life, learning to create again, but not having you with me to share the process. I won't go through that again."

Maggie felt tears gather, but she willed them away. The look on Colin's face was so fearful, so apprehensive, that she needed to reassure him.

"Like I said, I've known since I left that I was coming back. I didn't know when, I didn't know how, but I knew that you and I weren't done. When I started really writing the book, it became something entirely different from my original concept, and I knew it was because of you. I knew you added something so vital to my life that a part of me would be forever missing if I stayed in Boston without you."

"But I told you, we can live in—"

She put her fingers over his lips to silence him. "I know that. It's me that's changed, or maybe just listened to myself instead of to other people. I don't need to live in Boston. I want to write more, teach less. I've got a proposal in at the University of Nevada, Reno, and I meet with them after the first of the year. If not there, someplace else," she concluded.

"But will you marry me?" Colin persisted.

"Yes, Colin, I'll marry you."

They held each other for a moment, treasuring the closeness.

"You gonna open that box?"

Maggie had all but forgotten that she still held it. She sat up, wiped her eyes and stroked the velvet lid before pulling it open. A brilliant diamond sparkled against its black velvet bed. She stared. "It's huge," she managed at last.

"Two carats." He took the box from her suddenly limp hand and slid the ring onto her finger. "I wanted you to be dazzled, just as I am by you."

"Dazzled," she echoed. She was going to cry, absolutely start bawling any second now.

"But I also wanted you to be surprised," he continued, picking up the other box. "I like to keep you on your toes."

Tears forgotten, Maggie looked down at the box he'd pressed into her hand. He couldn't be giving her another ring, could he? Dazzled was one thing, this kind of extravagance was ridiculous. She popped open the lid and when she saw what was inside, laughed out loud, immediately understanding the meaning of the silver key on a black leather fob.

"Red, I assume, and a convertible?" Only Colin would punctuate a marriage proposal with the key to a 1966 Mustang.

Colin nodded. "Absolutely cherry. I bought it off a collector who'd restored it and put it on blocks for the last ten years, so it's perfect. I'd let you see it, but you'd have to get out of bed, and I can't see that happening for days."

She sent him a misty smile. "So this is my engagement car?"

"Something like that." He rolled over on top of her and pinned her back against the sheets. "I want to make all your dreams come true."

"Colin, that's corny."

"Maggie, I hate to break it to you now, when you've already promised to marry me, but I'm a corny kind of guy."

Epilogue

$C.$ $J.$ *McCall was back in the saddle again.*

The silly thought popped into Maggie's mind as she gazed about the crowded restaurant. She couldn't restrain her amazement at the sight of a veritable *Who's Who* of the New York publishing world milling about the room, their ranks interrupted by a sprinkling of the Hollywood types Colin had worked with over the years. Yep, C. J. McCall was back in the saddle again, and people were only too happy to celebrate that fact.

Across the room, her father chatted with the grizzled character actor who had played the miner in the television adaption of *Claim Jumper.* Her brother Rory was leading Lisa toward movie director Kurt Michaels, who had directed *Winchester Justice.* Rory had always been a big fan of his. It was great to have her family here, enjoying themselves as if they'd been born to slick parties, caviar and champagne.

Even Colin's parents had come, thrilled to see their son happy and productive again.

She thought back over the past nine months, a whirlwind of simple days at the cabin interspersed with such activities, beginning with the small wedding she'd insisted upon having. Colin would have been perfectly content to run down to the courthouse in Reno on December 26, but Maggie knew her family would never forgive her if she eloped, so they'd braved the tabloids and had been married in January at the same Boston church where three generations of Sullivans had been baptized.

She'd resigned from her position at Beaton University, and now lectured part-time at the University of Nevada in Reno. Her book would be released in a few months, although, she acknowledged wryly, not to nearly as much fanfare as Colin's.

"Having fun?" the object of her thoughts interrupted.

She turned to smile at her husband. *Husband.* Even after eight months of marriage, the term made her smile.

And tonight she was going to give him something to smile about in return.

She concentrated on his question. "Of course I'm having fun. Somebody knows how to throw a great party."

Colin reached over and snagged two glasses of champagne from a passing waiter. "Yes, indeed, someone does." He handed her a bubble-filled flute. "To us."

"To us," she echoed. After clinking her glass against his, Maggie raised it to her lips, then lowered it without taking a sip. It wouldn't do, not now. "How soon can we get out of here?" she couldn't help asking.

"I was just thinking about that. Since I'm the guest of honor, I should probably wait until after the speeches." He tried to keep a straight face, but his twitching mustache gave his amusement away.

His mustache. Somewhere along the way Colin had decided to regrow his mustache, completing his journey back to C. J. McCall. Maggie liked it; she liked the way it looked, loved the way it tickled when he kissed her, loved the way it moved when he smiled. Now she couldn't help answering his smile with one of her own.

The two of them did that a lot. Some days, Maggie's cheeks hurt from smiling so much, and until this morning, she wouldn't have believed she could be any happier. Now she knew differently, and couldn't wait to share that happiness with her husband.

After the party. She could probably wait that long. If she had to.

"Colin? Could you come up here?" Harrison James, Colin's avuncular publisher, was motioning him to the front of the room, summoning him to the microphone set up there.

"It's show time," Colin muttered, sliding an arm around Maggie's waist to usher her forward.

When they reached him, Harrison positioned them beside him. He spoke into the microphone again. "Does everyone have a glass? Good. I'll keep this short and sweet, but I'd like to propose a toast to Colin. It's good to have you back."

Maggie could see that the older man's simple, sincere words had moved Colin deeply. He swallowed once, twice, before touching his glass to hers and Harrison's and taking a sip.

Then he stepped up to the microphone, still holding on to Maggie. He slid his hand from her waist to clasp her hand, and gave her a quick squeeze before he began speaking. "Harrison, thank you. It's good to be back. It is, quite frankly, a thrill to be here with all of you, friends and family alike, celebrating this project, a project that never would have happened had it not been for the inspiration of one woman—my wife, Maggie.''

Oh, gosh, now he was going to embarrass her. Maggie tried to pull her hand away as the crowd applauded, but Colin held tight. "I have to tell you all, her coming into my life was a perfect surprise, but one that I wouldn't trade for anything in the world. This book is hers.''

He stepped back from the microphone as the room burst into applause. For good measure, he leaned over and kissed Maggie, the kind of kiss that had made the crowd at their wedding applaud, the kind of kiss that still made her go weak in the knees, the kind of kiss that made her want to drag him right out the door.

"There," he murmured. "That'll give *The Tattler* something to talk about.''

She looked up into his laughing eyes. Oh, *The Tattler*, was it? If he wanted to give that rag something to write about, she could handle that. She could even top a sizzling kiss in front of the New York publishing world.

As he kissed her again, she thought about her surprise. What better place and time to tell him? Here, surrounded by people who loved them, among the family he was so proud to claim, this was the perfect moment to tell him his family was soon to grow a little larger.

She stepped up to the microphone before she could talk herself out of it. "Thank you, Colin," she started, as the applause abated. "I wish I could take the credit here, but I know the work was all yours, in this case." She glanced back at him and held out her hand to tug him closer. "However, with our next project, I'll be doing all the work for the next seven or eight months, even if you were right there for the project's, um, conception.''

The room was silent for an instant before her meaning was understood. Colin got it first, and with a whoop pulled her into his arms. "A baby? We're going to have a baby?''

he whispered into her ear as he held her against him. "A baby?"

Maggie couldn't do more than nod, he was squeezing her so tightly.

He set her away from him, grasping both her shoulders. "A baby," he repeated once more, his words nearly drowned out by the noise of the crowd around them.

He seemed to become aware of where he was. "Come on," he said abruptly, grabbing her wrist and dragging her through the crowd to the nearest door, oblivious to the people trying to congratulate them.

Maggie followed as he led her down a hall, farther away from the reception room. When he entered the brightly lit kitchen, a white-clad chef, with Frederich stitched above his breast pocket, tried to stop them. "Sir—" he started, only to have Colin cut him off.

"We'll only be a minute."

Maggie was aware of how odd they must look, a tuxedo-clad man dragging a woman in a black cocktail dress along as if they were being chased by the entire New York Police Department. Colin looked around, and spotted a door to one side. He pointed. "In there."

Frederich tried to intrude again. "Sir, you can't—"

"Look, my wife's going to have a baby."

Maggie laughed out loud when the chef's confused gaze went automatically to her as-yet-flat stomach. She jumped into the fray. "We just want to be alone for a minute. Is there someplace...?" Her softly spoken plea worked where Colin's curt orders hadn't.

"My office, of course," Frederich said, gesturing to the door Colin had noticed before.

As they entered the tiny room, Colin turned back to Frederich once more. "You haven't seen us."

"Seen who?" Frederich quipped, pulling the door shut behind them.

Maggie leaned against the wall, laughing and trying to catch her breath all at once. Colin leaned over her, bracketing her head with his hands. She felt the first shivers of doubt when she saw his serious expression.

"How long have you known?"

Uh-oh. Perhaps she'd miscalculated. She'd wanted to shout her news from the rooftops, but maybe she shouldn't have usurped Colin's evening.

She swallowed. "I've suspected for a couple of weeks, so I did a home pregnancy test this morning while you had breakfast with your editor."

He stared down at her. "So why didn't you tell me?"

Oh, she really had blown it. She twisted her hands together before laying them on his chest, pressing herself closer to him. "I wanted to wait until after the party, but all of a sudden it just seemed like the right moment."

"Didn't you think I'd want to know first?"

Maggie felt the hint of tears threatening her carefully applied makeup. Oh, heck, she'd heard pregnant women got emotional, but she thought she'd have a little time to get used to her condition before *that* started.

"Why'd you do it, Maggie?"

She couldn't look at him, or she really would start crying. "Oh, Colin," she said on an unsteady breath. "You talked about me being such a wonderful surprise in your life, and I just wanted to give you another one."

Through the door came a muffled "Out! Out of my kitchen. I allow no one in here. *No one.*"

"Thank you, Frederich," Colin murmured, and Maggie heard the laughter in his voice. She looked up through her welling tears and saw him trying valiantly to contain a smile.

"Oh, you—I thought you were mad!" She punched him in his broad chest, a feeble effort, but one that made her feel immensely better.

"Sweetheart, how could I be angry about such wonderful news?" He swept her into his arms and held her close. She felt the pounding of his heart, his uneven breath, and knew he spoke the truth.

"We should get back to your party," she said at last, not at all anxious to leave his warm embrace, but knowing that not one person was leaving that room until they reappeared.

"Mmm," he agreed. "All three of us."

Maggie shut her eyes and took another breath, trying to control her racing emotions. "So," she managed at last, "do you want a boy or a girl?"

She hadn't thought it was possible for Colin to hold her any closer. "Why don't we let that be our next perfect surprise?"

* * * * *

Silhouette®

SPECIAL EDITION®

COMING NEXT MONTH

#961 RILEY'S SLEEPING BEAUTY—Sherryl Woods
That Special Woman!
Abby Dennison's last adventure before settling down had landed
her in trouble that was seemingly inescapable. Only Riley Walker
could call her back from a terrible fate—but would his love be
enough to save her?

#962 A FATHER'S WISH—Christine Flynn
Man, Woman and Child
When she had Alexander Burke's baby, Kelly Shaw gave it
up for adoption, thinking he didn't want her or the child. Now
she was back in his life, and old flames had begun to ignite
once again....

#963 BROODING ANGEL—Marie Ferrarella
Blue blood had met blue collar when Mary Elizabeth Clancy and
"Mitch" Mitchell loved and lost years ago. Now a tragic twist of
fate had brought them together, and only Mitch's determination
could prevent them from losing each other again.

#964 CHILD OF HER HEART—Arlene James
Gail Terry had finally found the daughter she'd thought lost to
her. She never expected to fall for the child's guardian, rancher
Rand Hartesite, whose sexy charm—and dad potential—were
hard to resist.

#965 THE GIRL NEXT DOOR—Trisha Alexander
Simon Christopher was Jenny Randall's best pal—but her secret
feelings for him had long ago gone beyond friendship. Now
opportunity knocked at Jenny's door—along with Simon, who
suddenly realized that just being friends could never be enough!

#966 A FAMILY FOR RONNIE—Julie Caille
Forced to share guardianship of her nephew with old flame
Luke Garrick didn't make things easier for Alicia Brant.
Especially when both wanted sole custody—and both still
desperately felt the love they'd once had....

Take 4 bestselling love stories FREE

Plus get a FREE surprise gift!

Announcing
the New **Pages & Privileges**™ Program
from Harlequin® and Silhouette®

Get All This FREE
With Just One Proof-of-Purchase!

- **FREE Travel Service** with the guaranteed lowest available airfares plus 5% cash back on every ticket

- **FREE Hotel Discounts** of up to 60% off at leading hotels in the U.S., Canada and Europe

- **FREE Petite Parfumerie** collection (a $50 Retail value)

- **FREE $25 Travel Voucher** to use on any ticket on any airline booked through our Travel Service

- **FREE Insider Tips Letter** full of fascinating information and hot sneak previews of upcoming books

- **FREE Mystery Gift** (if you enroll before May 31/95)

And there are more great gifts and benefits to come!
Enroll today and become Privileged!

(see insert for details)

PROOF-OF-PURCHASE

Offer expires October 31, 1996   SSE-PP1